No Fallen Angel

Sadie Winters

2016

Bella Books, Inc.
P.O. Box 10543
Tallahassee, FL 32302

This is a work of fiction. Names, characters, businesses, places, events and incidents are either the products of the author's imagination or used in a fictitious manner. Any resemblance to actual persons, living or dead, or actual events is purely coincidental. The publisher does not have any control over and does not assume any responsibility for author or third-party websites or their content.

Printed in the United States of America on acid-free paper.

First Bella Books Edition 2016

Editor: Cath Walker
Cover Designer: Linda Callaghan

ISBN: 978-1-59493-476-6

About the Author

Sadie Winters lives by the sea in a village on the southwestern tip of England. She is a poet and freelance writer who loves combing the beaches and watching the waves, rummaging around at flea markets, and working in her garden.

For Barb

CHAPTER ONE

Nothing got her spirit soaring like perfect choreography, a thumping beat felt deep in the pit of the stomach and, of course, good tips. But for Angel Khoury, ready to dance her next set at the Cheeky Monkey Gentleman's Club, the only thing soaring was her temper. Even though tips were in short supply on a slow Tuesday night and the loser DJ had cued up the wrong music, things had gone bad long before that. Like really bad. Like finding your girlfriend in the throes of passion with one of the waitresses bad. Still, the show had to go on.

"Here she comes: Bountiful Nebibi, Queen of the Nile. Give her a hand and let's watch that booty burn down the house." Reg, the club owner at the Cheeky Monkey, was filling in as Angel approached the stage. Wearily she sucked in her stomach and turned to face the music, literally, a smile firmly in place. A short, middle-aged man with steely eyes and a complexion like moldy cheese, Reg with a microphone was like a kindergartner in a classroom using his outside voice. The motley assortment of regulars gathered around the bar laughed and cheered Angel's entrance, their fingers in their ears.

Nebibi, shortened to Bibi, was an Egyptian name meaning panther, thought up by Reg who liked all the girls to have stripper names and props in keeping with the club's exotic theme and his own warped fantasies. Angel parodied a sexy, albeit rather tacky Cleopatra, complete with masses of gold jewelry that caught the lights in dazzling bursts. She was actually Lebanese on her father's side, but as far as Reg was concerned, it was all the same. With her olive skin and black hair, Angel knew she certainly looked the part. She also knew if she played the exotic maiden and rewarded the customers with a belly dance or two, Reg would be happy. When Reg was happy, everyone was happy.

As Angel sashayed toward the stage in sync with the thudding beat and neon beams that bounced off the walls in arcs of light, something caught her eye. That something was the shining round globe of a perfect ass attached to long brown legs bouncing up the steps. Yvonne. At the sight of her girlfriend—well ex-girlfriend really—Angel's heart skipped a beat. Even as she tried to push aside the sorrow of this latest affair with the waitress, Angel couldn't help wondering, as she had so many times over the past few weeks, if the pain came from Yvonne's betrayal or from knowing the last three years together had been a lie. *How could I have been so stupid? Not seen the writing on the wall?* She had already forgiven her twice before, but this time Yvonne had struck out.

"Come on Bibi, give us a treat," hooted a patron, wobbling on his bar stool and raising a beer glass in mock salute.

Angel pantomimed a curtsey and tried to pull herself together. *Damn Yvonne.* But the betrayal was raw and the humiliation cut deep. This latest liaison had been going on for some time and with a woman, just a girl really, over a decade younger than either of them. Those nights when she was 'hanging out with the waitresses' was Yvonne doing just what Yvonne did best, charming the pants off everyone in her life. Screwing the waitress in the dancers' lounge right there under Angel's nose, most likely. But anger was good. Way better than eating a whole package of cookies and feeling sorry for yourself, like last night.

As she climbed the steps to the stage, Angel slowed to tease a patron who had tipped generously during the first set. A forty-something, smartly-dressed man with the beginnings of a comb-over, he settled back in his chair, skinny legs spread and crotch pointed at her, before digging into his pocket and placing a damp bill in her cleavage. Maybe anger and good tips would get her through.

The light show pulsed, beams darting across the room and climaxing into strands of blazing brilliance. She strutted provocatively from one end of the small stage to the other, her hair a halo in the stage lights, and slowly wound herself into a back walkover, releasing the straps on her top. A roar went up from the assortment of regulars dotted around the club, culminating in a group moan as she fondled her breasts with one hand and inserted the other through the waistband of her shorts, all the time gyrating her hips, low and slow. The regulars cheered their delight and the glass containing her tips started to fill.

As the last strains of the song died away, Angel grabbed the glass, and headed for the dancers' lounge. The bartender gave her a wave and pushed a drink in her direction, gesturing with a nod to the guy who'd tipped her earlier. The drink was a coke and she knew the money for the real drink was on a tab at the bar. As she came alongside him, the man beckoned her to join him. "Thanks hon," said Angel, ignoring the request and giving a quick wave over her shoulder. She tottered off to the lounge and shot through the door.

"You're on fire tonight," said Sylvie, a tiny dynamo of a woman with wide-set blue eyes, a turned-up nose and voluminous masses of blond curls, who was sitting at a dressing table squinting into the mirror.

"Not really," said Angel, forcing a smile, "I feel like crap." She staggered over to Sylvie, put her drink on the table and flopped down into a chair. "Maybe I should switch teams. Men are so much less complicated."

"Oh, right, in your dreams," murmured Sylvie sarcastically. Having survived her share of bad relationships with men, Sylvie's take on this was somewhat warped. "Look love, I'm sorry," she added after a pause. "I know it's hard the way that bitch treated you. You of all people: the sweetest love I know who wouldn't hurt a fly. Want anything?"

"Thanks. I'll be okay," said Angel wearily. She headed for the lockers and pulled an outfit off its hanger.

"Nice," said Sylvie. "That new?"

"Nah," sighed Angel, maneuvering her breasts into a tiny, heavily-sequined black bikini top with a plunging neckline. She sat down heavily and then flipped her hair over, spraying it wildly, head between her knees. She finger-teased stray locks into place and blasted some cologne at her thighs. "God, I just wish I could lose some weight," she said with disgust, kneading the skin at her waistline and trying not to think about last night's cookies.

Sylvie started to cough and waved away the lingering scent. "Don't be ridiculous," she said. "You look great. Everyone thinks so," she added.

"Exactly. Since when did a bunch of sad old guys set the standard?"

As Sylvie raised her eyebrows, shaking her head resignedly, the lounge door opened and a statuesque golden body blocked the glare from the club lights. "Here we go," murmured Sylvie, turning her back on Yvonne and making a point of rummaging for something in the drawer.

"Hey, what's up?" Tall and lean with skin like burnished copper, Yvonne strode into the room and threw herself on the sofa. She was mostly naked except for a sliver of a G-string and an elaborate silver necklace wound around her neck. Her beautiful head was shaved and her eyes, darkly lined, were shaded by impressive eyelashes that always reminded Angel of humming birds when Yvonne blinked. Angel averted her eyes and tried to keep her focus on Sylvie, now applying makeup.

"Hi," repeated Yvonne, glancing first at Sylvie, but letting her gaze rest on Angel.

No one answered. Angel concentrated on Sylvie lining the contours of her mouth with dark crimson. She tried not to think about that woman's wide, generous mouth and full lips on her own.

"Come on, is no one talking to me?" cooed Yvonne. "We can get through this."

Angel concentrated on Sylvie applying a coat of mascara and watched her do a final clamp with the eyelash curler. Interesting how her eyes now leapt into prominence.

"I was hoping we could talk. All be friends again like old times," Yvonne pleaded.

"Oh, please, don't pretend there's anything left between us. You made that very clear when you fucked that waitress—"

"Good Lord, Yvonne, you'll catch your death," interrupted Sylvie, stopping the avalanche about to break loose. She threw Yvonne a towel that narrowly missed a shelf piled high with cosmetics. Grudgingly Yvonne wrapped the towel around her lean body as Angel marched out of the lounge, slamming the door behind her.

It was Angel's last set and she was working the pole. Music thudded a steady rhythm timed with the lights, green, red and purple, flashing across the dingy walls of the club. She strutted to the pole, grabbed it with both hands and pressed her crotch against it. Then she spun round, hoisting her leg up around the pole to support her body as she stretched taut. Her hair flew as she felt the rush of cool air on her back. Someone had opened the side door and it felt good. All her insecurities slipped away and for a moment she felt beautiful, alive and free. She remembered for an instant why she'd once liked this work.

The energy in the club shifted as the crowd increased. Tables were starting to fill and a noisy group hanging out by the bar hooted their approval as Angel executed a perfect split. She teased with a sexy wave and then turned away, swinging around in a circle with the pole jutting upward between her widely spread thighs. The crowd applauded and stomped with the beat, pleading for Angel to go all the way. One firm leg straddling the pole for balance, she tantalized by lifting the tiny triangle of fabric and moaning a parody of pleasure that ended on cue as the music climaxed. After the finale, as Angel draped a glittery shawl around her body, she noticed the smartly-dressed guy with the comb-over trying to book a private booth. The Monkey was known for its booths where patrons got their own private dances.

The hostess hesitated and caught Angel's eye, simultaneously glancing at the clock hanging above the bar. "Sorry love, her shift's over," said the hostess to Angel's admirer. Fran was a hefty woman who also doubled as manager and had worked at the Monkey forever. "She's on this weekend if you're still around, though." Fran smiled politely up at him, her body impassive and her look resolute.

"No, I need to talk to her…" Sylvie's music had just begun, drowning out the rest of his plea. As Angel watched, a bouncer appeared out of nowhere and steered the guy back toward the bar. He had seemed harmless enough but was starting to give her the creeps. She thought about the stalker last year who had scared some of the dancers, herself included. After that Yvonne was always telling her to toughen up, put on a mask and never look into customers' eyes. You Americans, Yvonne would say affectionately, are so naive and way too friendly. These weirdoes like it when you tempt and don't give a damn, she'd insist. But Angel did give a damn and usually found herself hoping they had some nice little woman at home waiting for them. It probably made her ill-suited for what she did night after night, but there you had it. A marshmallow at heart. This job was really beginning to lose its appeal.

As Angel approached the bar, the man looked at her imploringly. "Just talk to me," he said. "I'd like to make an appointment. It's a business proposition." He held out his card.

"Of course it is, love," replied Fran patiently, stepping in beside the bouncer to block access to Angel. "It's *always* a business proposition."

"But you don't understand; I'm an agent—"

"And I'm Mickey Mouse," said the bouncer, moving the irate guy out of earshot just as Yvonne appeared in thigh-high boots, a tight tiger-print bikini top and a pair of matching short shorts, stripes gleaming fluorescent white in the strobe.

"See, look who's here now," said Fran reassuringly.

"You want to play?" Yvonne turned and coyly wagged a finger at him over her shoulder.

"Thanks," said Angel grudgingly, glad to be off the hook. She glanced away quickly to avoid those eyes she knew so well.

The guy gazed at Yvonne's bottom for several seconds and then mumbled something to Fran, throwing a handful of bills on the bar to cover his tab. As he turned to leave, he tripped over a server, scattering her tray in an impressive sequence caught up in the slow motion of the strobe. Hoots from the assortment of regulars drinking at the counter pierced the air as fries flew and red ketchup spread slowly on the dingy carpet. The man spun around and gave Angel a startled look before he was gone.

* * *

An hour later, Angel was barreling home in her old Volkswagen, blasting the radio to keep herself awake. As she pulled into her street in the north London suburb, darkened now at this late hour, she started the tedious search for a parking space. *Hallelujah*! There was an almost-too-small spot along the curb across the street from the laundromat by her building. She eased into the space, pleased with herself for accomplishing the left-side parallel-parking job that used to confuse and frustrate her to no end when she first moved to London. Angel then saw a small Mini Cooper parked with its lights on. It didn't register until she walked by and caught a flash of movement out of the corner of her eye that there was someone in the car and he was looking straight at her. Her heart flew into her throat as she realized it was the skinny guy from the bar.

Angel's first thought was not to panic, but memories of last-year's stalker flooded back. Trying to quell rising anxiety, she walked briskly toward her building.

A car door slammed. "Hey, wait," he shouted. "I want to…" The rest of his words were lost as Angel started to run.

"Leave me alone! You know the rules. No touch. No talk." Almost at the door now. Hands shaking, she fumbled with the keys, looking over her shoulder to see him gaining on her, arms gesturing and shouting something she couldn't hear. *Where did these guys get the nerve?* She slid through and heard the heavy door close behind her. *Phew.*

Once inside with the flat bathed in light, Angel turned on the television and felt her pulse return to normal. What a sad perv. She was really sick of this job.

Sleep came easily after a soak in the tub, what she liked to think of as her ritual "club cleanse" that washed away the grime and tension of the job.

Woken in the pink blush of dawn as garbage trucks thumped outside emptying dumpsters on the corner, she snuggled back down into her cozy nest, pulling the quilt over her ears. When her phone buzzed sometime later, Angel was hunkered down in the same position, trying to ignore the thin grey light seeping through the tiny gap in the curtains. She was just drifting back to sleep when her phone started up again. Reaching over, she saw it was Kate. Her sister. Best get it over with.

"Did I wake you?" said Kate, an edge to her voice. "Late night?" Accusation hung in the question.

"It's called work, Kate. It's what I do for a living." Angel staggered to the kitchen and made coffee with one hand, the other holding the phone at arm's length from her left ear. Anyone would think she spent hours in dingy old bars entertaining perverts for fun. She let Kate rattle on about her new yoga class and the conference she was attending at the weekend. Kate was a lecturer and taught English literature. Drinking and getting laid was at the top of her students' to-do lists, but Kate liked to think it was Shakespeare and Chaucer. Married to an Englishman and an attorney, Kate lived in Chelsea, a nicer part of the city than Angel's suburb of Edmonton Green.

Angel made the right noises at the right times to keep up her end of the conversation and managed to procure a half-decent cup of coffee. She looked at the pile of dishes in the sink and debated whether she could get them done before Kate finished her saga, but memories of the night and that look, a mixture of cocky arrogance and remorse, on Yvonne's face crowded in. Yvonne's departure had left a gaping hole. She grabbed the coffee and plodded back to bed, trying to ignore the faint beginnings of a headache throbbing at her temple.

"And so," Kate was saying, "I thought it might be something you'd be interested in."

"What?" Angel had tuned out the last ten minutes.

"Never mind," said Kate reproachfully. "Gotta go."

"No tell me again. Please," Angel added, back in the kitchen and smearing a piece of toast with butter. Maybe some food would help. As she munched on the toast, Kate proceeded to repeat her story about a colleague who moonlighted as a journalist for a travel magazine, which was looking for someone to work out in the field and help prepare articles about some of England's public gardens. It was short term: a couple of months max.

"And the thing is," said Kate, "and the reason why I thought of you, is they want someone with a background in horticulture." Kate was always hoping Angel might use that degree she'd almost got from the University of California before moving over to the dark side.

"What's it called?" asked Angel.

"What's what called?"

"The magazine," insisted Angel, picking up crumbs with her fingers and trying to ignore a sudden craving for a cigarette. She'd been doing so well and hadn't had one in weeks. Until now and this new drama with Yvonne.

"*Country Escapes* I think," replied Kate.

"Great name," said Angel. "I'll think about it."

"You will?" Angel could hear the surprise and excitement in Kate's voice.

"Maybe." No use getting her hopes up.

"And I was thinking I could talk with Lucas Therot. You remember him? He could help you find a place to stay if this thing works out. She said the first gig's in Cornwall."

"Who said?"

"What?" said Kate, exasperation edging her voice. "The woman at the magazine. Jeez, Angel, what's wrong with you?"

Kate paused and started again, her voice low and deliberate. "The first assignment's in Cornwall. I was saying Lucas lives there. He's divorced now, you know. Owns a property management firm near Truro."

Angel tuned back in. *Remember him?* She remembered Luscious Lucas very well. Mr. Seventeen-year-old Teenage Heartthrob who'd stayed with their family as a French exchange student all those years ago? About twenty years to be exact, that given she was thirty-three now. She knew little about his whereabouts these days except a few snippets of news gleaned over the years. But Kate kept in touch and Angel recalled her mentioning he'd studied business at university and then married at some point. Now might be the time to switch teams after all.

"Of course you remember him," laughed Kate. It wasn't that she disapproved of having a lesbian for a sister, only that she hoped it was just a phase. "What were you, fourteen at the time? Angel, you still there?"

"Thirteen," said Angel thoughtfully.

"Well, anyway, think about it and let me know, but soon. These freelance jobs go super quick."

Angel smiled to herself, inspired by memories of Lucas and the opportunity to take charge of her life again. She had been feeling uncomfortably out of control the last few months. It was making her anxious, a new development for someone who usually liked to go with the flow. She'd never used to worry about something working out or not because it usually did, and if it didn't she'd just go on to the next thing. But this problem—'problem' didn't exactly describe how she felt about Yvonne—had put her over the edge. And then there was the guy following her home last night, reminding her of their old stalker.

"It might be the best news I've heard in a while," Angel declared, downing the last of her coffee and padding over to make another piece of toast. Hell, she'd eat the whole loaf if she wanted. She was sick to death of having to eat like a bird to fit into a stupid costume. Yes, maybe a change was in the air.

CHAPTER TWO

The minute Angel saw the place, she was smitten. What better escape than this tiny cottage with its breathtaking view of the grey, grinding sea? A far cry from her noisy, cluttered flat with fumes from the laundromat downstairs, it was small, serene and symmetrical. And it reeked of promise. She'd done it. Even the new paint smelled hopeful. The worst was saying goodbye to Sylvie and trying to ignore Yvonne's excuses and rehearsed speech about dumping the waitress and picking up where they'd left off. Angel had been tempted, briefly, but knew it would just be a matter of time before she was cheated on again. Yvonne was reckless and impulsive. She always lived in the moment.

Angel liked to think of herself as a free spirit too, but her version involved carefree mornings lounging in their bathrobes and reading the paper, or strolling hand in hand through the London fog. She loved it when they got lost together in the winding streets as shadows lengthened in the fading light of winter afternoons. How they had looked forward to evenings at the club with all the camaraderie of the girls. Not this wild ride.

And the latest news that Yvonne 'borrowed' Angel's credit card and racked up more bills than they could afford was the final blow. Yes, life with Yvonne involved fabulous ups and fearsome downs and way, way too many secrets.

"You like?" Lucas' voice reverberated through the empty kitchen and roused Angel from thoughts of Yvonne seeping into her brain. He leaned his lanky body against the kitchen door and smiled sweetly into her face.

"Love it," she said, doing the hair flip thing in a gallant attempt at sophistication. The years slipped away and she was back at the dance recital from hell that Lucas attended to support Kate and her kid sister. Awkward Angela in her chubby thirteen-year-old body, sweating and anxious with unresolved passion, dancing to Petula Clark's "Downtown" in purple tights and a lime-green bowler hat. Her forgetting the routine in the final verse and Lucas with an amused look on his face. *Oh mercy!*

"Ready to do it?"

"Do it?" Angel laughed at the thought.

Lucas laughed too and then handed her a pen. "Sign here, here and here. Three months, first and last, damage deposit, all utilities included." He quoted a hefty sum and Angel thought, not for the first time, how she owed Kate big time. There was no way she could afford to live on the small stipend from the magazine without Kate's financial help, especially with her plummeting credit rating thanks to Yvonne.

Once Angel told her sister about the man from the club following her home, Kate had flown into top gear, pulling some strings with the *Country Escapes* editor. All Angel had to do was visit some public gardens, take a boatload of photographs and write up her notes into something the team could craft into snazzy articles. She knew her sister hoped this opportunity might get her out of the clubs permanently and, from Kate's perspective, keep her safe. When she learned that Angel's relationship with Yvonne was over, Kate was ecstatic. She had never approved of Yvonne, who exuded danger and who went out of her way to shock Kate at every turn.

Lucas reeled off the terms of the lease and then paused, looking for the addendum. Their eyes locked and Angel thought how easy it would be to seduce him right there in the kitchen. A sudden fleeting thought that slipped away just as quickly. "Here we go. And no pets," he said.

"No pets?" That was disappointing. She had hoped for a cat or a goldfish or something. Maybe goldfish didn't count. Yvonne hated animals—another major difference. How could a person hate animals? She paused with the pretense of organizing the pages of the lease and felt a sting of tears threaten again. *What is wrong with me?* Letting memories of Yvonne hound her soul, not to mention thinking about committing one of the worst rebound sins of all time. She hadn't been romantically involved with a man in, well, technically, ever.

Lucas interrupted these thoughts with a kind arm around her shoulder. "Let's celebrate?" he said, the question materializing as an announcement.

"You do this for all your clients?" she replied, trying to sound perkier than she felt.

"No, just the famous ones."

"Sure you don't mean infamous?"

"Ah, all the better." He gave her a sexy grin and uncorked the half bottle of champagne with a flourish. "Here, *santé.* To a few months in Cumberland Bay. Hopefully not too mundane." On the southern coast of England, it was a sleepy little fishing village where strip clubs were as foreign as the Gobi Desert.

"Cheers." Angel raised her glass and clinked it gently against his. "Mundane is okay. Even boring is appealing."

"Boring?" Lucas spluttered, pretending to choke as he pantomimed delight at seeing her bottom perched on the stool. Angel sucked in her stomach, not sure if he was making fun of her and watched him take another sip of champagne. He twirled the glass in long, elegant fingers and let his eyes rest on the pink lace at her cleavage. He did seem to like what he saw. "No place could possibly be boring with you in it," he exclaimed.

And then, seemingly coming from his trousers, the sultry strains of "*La vie en rose*" suddenly filled the tiny kitchen. Lucas clutched his pocket, smiling sheepishly. Only Luscious Lucas, no doubt inflamed with French nationalism, would have Edith Piaf as his ringtone.

"Daphne, *bonjour.*" Cradling the phone, Lucas moved into the kitchen alcove and gestured his apologies. Angel watched him speaking *en français* softly into the phone and contemplated her predicament. It was weird having a man, other than a customer of course, flirt with her and she was surprised by the hard, handsome angles of his face.

But she found herself thinking about the softness of Yvonne's body, how her nipples darkened and puckered when she was aroused and what the hell she was thinking about doing with Lucas anyway. He definitely looked cute with the late afternoon light shadowing his strong jaw. Plus this was a long time in coming. But no. The thought of Yvonne's soft, pliable flesh made her body ache. Absently she pulled her hair back into a ponytail and strained to hear the conversation. It sounded like someone named Daphne was being stood up and given a promise for tomorrow.

"*Tout va bien*? Everything okay?" asked Angel primly when Lucas returned. His surprised look almost made up for the years she'd lived in Paris thinking she would never learn the stupid language. Not to mention the fact she'd picked up words working in the clubs not used in everyday polite conversation.

"You're full of surprises *chérie*," he said, pocketing his phone.

"*Qui moi?*"

"Yes you," he laughed. "And, if I say so myself, you are *très belle*." Just to prove it he sat back down and reached to kiss her. Angel moved quickly and playfully ducked away just in time.

She tried to smile but was transported back to one of the times she'd last seen him: an evening many years ago when he'd returned to the United States for a vacation and had made an impromptu appearance at a camping trip Kate had organized. Angel was fifteen at the time and had spent restless days worrying he might show up and worrying he wouldn't. It was a difficult period, not long after their parents had died in a car accident. She remembered sitting by the campfire as moonlight slid over the mountain and lit up the lakeshore. Lucas reached to kiss her cheek then in exactly the same way as now, before leaving her to join a blond girlfriend in the little tent they erected close to hers. She ought to have put two and two together when the image of the hot girlfriend stayed with her just as long as his handsome profile.

"How 'bout we move outside?" he suggested, interrupting her reverie. "Check out the garden." On cue a slice of sunshine skittered across the kitchen floor. Following the ray's path out through the window, Angel spied cheerful splotches of daffodils waving in the sunshine. Relieved, she poured the remaining champagne into their glasses, handed him one and tottered out through the back door, swaying slightly on high heels until she reached the terrace. He followed like a lamb. As they stood side by side gazing out across the garden, out beyond where craggy moors tumbled over ancient rocks toward the sea, Angel breathed in the hyacinth-scented air and turned her face up toward the watery sun. Around them were flowerbeds dotted with bright red tulips looking hopeful against the late spring sky.

A companionable silence fell between them as they took in the sights and smells of the garden, the stunning view of the village and the steel grey churning sea beyond. Nestled in a valley, Cumberland Bay was built around a cove beyond which loomed rugged cliffs and dazzling green headlands. They looked down on the village's tiny harbor, bordered by a shingle beach close to the quay on one side and a sandy beach on the other. The village appeared to tumble down the sides of a ravine toward the bottom where a river flashed, carrying fresh water to the harbor and then out to sea. Whitewashed cottages dotted along terraced lanes clung heroically to the steep hillsides.

As they stood side by side gazing down into the valley, the river inked purple in the late afternoon light and Angel contemplated her predicament. Thoughts of Yvonne teased her. Yvonne, long-legged in her boy shorts on a Sunday morning, trying to surprise Angel with breakfast in bed but setting off the smoke alarm and waking up the neighborhood. Yvonne, naked in their bed on her day off and happy just to give Angel a backrub after a long night at the Monkey. It felt like purgatory, these memories that threatened to color all her waking hours.

She had another sudden urge for a cigarette—anything to help cope with this heartache.

"Come on," Lucas whispered, sauntering over to a gnarled old apple tree sheltered by the curve of the cliff face that promised a particularly spectacular view out beyond the headlands. "You okay *ma chérie*? What with the texts the other night." His voice interrupted her thoughts and she could see doubt clouding his eyes.

"Ah, those," said Angel, cringing as she stepped along the path. They'd had some X-rated late-night texting in negotiating the cottage. Coming as they did in the height of her despair over Yvonne, it had seemed like a teenage fantasy come true.

"And there I was so worked up I thought I might have a heart attack," he insisted, planting a chaste kiss on her cheek.

"I'm sorry. You were awesome, even from a distance," she said. It was true. He was.

He snorted, eyes now smiling into hers. "Never mind," he said kindly. "But since you're playing so hard to get, you with all your curves and me with no brakes, maybe I'll have to wine and dine you instead—"

Footsteps suddenly pierced the air. Lucas tensed and Angel grabbed a low branch to steady herself, slipping and skidding on the wet grass in the process. In an heroic attempt at chivalry Lucas ripped several buttons off her shirt trying to break her fall, but left her sitting on the wet grass with her shirt undone and eye to eye with a pair of mud-encrusted wellington boots.

The intruder coughed, looked away in embarrassment and gestured toward a dilapidated building in the corner of the garden. "Umm, rhodie bushes. Note says to leave them by the shed."

Slowly Angel raised her eyes from the boots to faded jeans hugging firm thighs and up to a threadbare plaid shirt open at the neck to reveal an expanse of tanned skin adorned only by a small gold crucifix hanging from a slender gold chain. From there Angel registered an unruly shock of short, golden blond hair tumbling over clear blue eyes almost violet in their depths. A hesitant half-smile played over the woman's wide, generous mouth and crinkled the corners of those amazing eyes. Realizing she was staring at a perfect stranger while sprawled on the ground, Angel accepted the outstretched hand and struggled to her feet.

"You all right?" she asked.

Angel felt the surprising roughness of her hands and the strength of her grip. As long, cool fingers threaded through hers, Angel registered the almost familiar way the woman's hand had closed around hers. "Thanks, I'm fine…" Angel stammered, frantically trying to fasten her shirt, eyes locked on this amazon who towered over her. With her husky voice, tight body and kiss-till-you-drop mouth, she was beautiful in the most earthy, disheveled way.

"Here, let's go," interrupted Lucas, glaring hostilely at the intruder and gently steering Angel along the narrow path toward the cottage. Although she was annoyed at Lucas's possessiveness, Angel appreciated being spared from the woman's steady gaze. Used to being half-naked in front of total strangers, Angel wasn't usually one to feel shame or the bleakness of self-betrayal. It is not what you think, was the message she wanted to tell those violet eyes.

* * *

Nell Frank watched through her rear view mirror as the woman went back into the cottage with Lucas Therot in tow. She appreciated a body with some substance and that woman certainly had more than her share of curves. So dark and gorgeous. She looked sort of plump, but strong at the same time—a perfect combination from Nell's perspective. And short. She must be barely five foot and Nell liked that too. It was wrong to eavesdrop on their conversation, but the reward of having a few minutes watching that voluptuous body undetected was worth it—even if she was straight–and being with that French twit, most likely loose. Just what kind of sordid texts were they referring to? Nell could feel herself getting hot and pushed away the thoughts, disgusted with herself.

She maneuvered the truck along the narrow lane back down into the village to deliver another order, barely noticing several passersby who waved hello. Everyone knew her, as they'd known her father too. The business relied on this kind of patronage. And most people liked her. She knew that, even if they didn't always approve her life choices. In the past she didn't care, but lately with her involvement at St. Theresa's things had changed. It was a surprise and a joy to discover—rediscover, really—her faith. Everyone there was so supportive when she needed help and quite honestly she wasn't sure how she'd have coped without them.

But now she was back on her feet and starting to be more visible at church, there was this creeping sense of disapproval. Not that anyone came right out and said you've got to stop loving women. They were too polite of course. And it was also like they were sorry for her. Yes, that was it. Their sympathy made her feel uncomfortable and vulnerable at the same time. Oh well, thought Nell as she navigated a tight turn at the edge of the village, better to be struggling for some kind of truth and sanity than be back in the void that was her life before. Still, these thoughts about the woman in the garden were unsettling, reminding Nell of the struggles in her soul, not to mention the old mantra that seemed to follow her through life: loss follows love. When she let herself love. bad things always seemed to happen.

Absently she switched on the radio and then switched it off. Same old depressing news. She fired up the iPod instead and was rewarded with the sultry strains of the Indigo Girls singing "Blood and Fire," an old favorite: "I am looking for someone, who can take as much as I give; give back as much as I need..." Immediately the woman with her gorgeous body leaning against the tree at the cottage appeared in Nell's mind. Nell bet she could give and take all right. The woman's accent had sounded American, though she looked like maybe she was Indian or Pakistani or from somewhere in the Middle East. She'd never been with someone so...so *dark*...and had to admit it rather excited her.

Stop! Nell tried to squelch her impure thoughts, worried that they might be racist and not wanting to have even more to confess to Father Joseph than usual. But Jesus she was horny. And now she'd have to confess to blasphemy as well as everything else.

A driveway approached and she swung the truck into the opening. It was adjacent to a big old house being remodeled as a bed and breakfast. Nell had contracted for the landscaping and was delivering potted azaleas to the owner. She tried to keep her mind on the job, but her head was full of the woman in her tight jeans and high heels, as well as her open shirt. Great hair, jet black and sort of wild-looking. Nell tried to remember the color of her eyes. Grey, she thought. Yes, dark greenish-grey like the color of the ocean at night. On autopilot Nell unloaded the last of the azaleas and started to back up the truck.

"Hey, you forgot to have me sign the invoice." The soon-to-be bed and breakfast owner was looking over with a smug look, enjoying catching her out with such an easy slip. Nell Frank was known as a single-minded and morally upright businesswoman who was not easily distracted.

"Oh, right," said Nell, fiddling with the invoice pad to hide her annoyance. Embarrassed to think such thoughts were affecting her work, Nell turned the conversation to what she knew best. "It's coming along nicely, Steve. You'll be opening in time for the season by the looks of it. Good choice on the azaleas. You might want to work in some iron sulfate to get that soil just right and not too much fertilizer." Steve smiled to see Nell back on form and waved as the truck pulled away.

Truth was she was having a hard time stilling her thoughts. She tried to dispel the image of that curvaceous figure as she maneuvered the truck into the nursery yard, dropped off a copy of Steve's invoice in the little sanctuary of an office that doubled as her home away from home and strode over to the nearest greenhouse to finish up the watering before they closed for the day. But the memory of those soft hands and their surprisingly firm grip crowded her thoughts and she realized it had been some time since a woman had occupied her mind like this. But oh, that hair cascading over her shoulders and those eyes that turned down at the corners and made her look a bit sad. And then there was the rest of her body, remarkably athletic looking for being so stacked. Good Lord, her breasts spilled out of that shirt like nobody's business and it seemed as if she'd been poured into those tight jeans. In those few precious minutes in the garden Nell realized she'd memorized everything about the woman.

"Penny for your thoughts?" Isabel, Nell's help, was looking at her askance. "Looks like you're done with that flat of pansies."

Deep in thought about whether her use of the Lord's name in vain was worse than her erotic fantasies, Nell startled at the sight of the flooded aisle and all the bedraggled pansies about to float away. "Bloody hell!" she cried, jumping to turn off the water. Color flooded Nell's face as Isabel gave her an amused look and retreated into the office, chuckling to herself.

Nell repotted the pansies and cleaned up the mess. She found herself feeling annoyed that Lucas Therot had already made his mark, especially after he'd hurt Maddie, Nell's very best friend in the world. As she worked, Nell caught herself once more in the midst of a fantasy starring herself and this woman, the imagined pleasure of that sublime body moving sensuously over hers and just exactly what those soft fingers could do to her hot and ready flesh. And then the image of Lucas Therot appeared. She knew it was un-Christian of her to think such things, but she wished she could just take out that French sod and be done with it.

CHAPTER THREE

Two hours later Angel was tucking into crab cakes, salad and potatoes *au gratin* at the Three Ships Inn, a hotel in the middle of the village and a five-minute walk from her the cottage. She'd decided to follow Kate's suggestion to stay the first night at the inn and tackle getting things sorted tomorrow. So good to be able to eat again, she thought, forking a hefty forkful of potatoes into her mouth. She'd gained four pounds already in the weeks since she left the Cheeky Monkey, but it couldn't be helped. She was still trying to avoid cigarettes, so a person had to eat.

Trying not to think about how many fat calories were swimming in that particular cheesy bite, Angel stared back at several locals curious about the stranger in their midst. Her accent generated interest and she was certainly the darkest person in the room. Angel had been in situations like this more times than she could possibly count. Sometimes people were friendly because they saw her as foreign and exotic. Other times it was like they were threatened and showed surprise when she opened her mouth and could actually speak English. Such racist bullshit either way. So people thought she looked Middle Eastern. Big deal. That hardly made her a terrorist, although in some people's small, warped minds, it was all the same.

As Angel contemplated getting herself a headscarf just to be provocative, a middle-aged man at the bar, already on his umpteenth screwdriver by the look of him, lowered his glasses and positively leered. However, he seemed to be more acutely focused on her breasts than any terrorist threat, unless of course he thought they doubled as weapons of mass destruction. Angel smiled at her own joke and wished she had someone to share it with. Yvonne would have got a real chuckle out of that one.

Angel looked around. It was a cozy room with about a dozen tables squeezed between the bar and entry hall that led to stairs and hotel rooms on the upper floors. A gleaming array of liquor bottles behind the bar reflected light from glass sconces along the walls and deep red crushed velvet-flocked wallpaper gave the room a Victorian feel. Several other small lamps caught the light and glittered in the mirrors lining the walls.

"Pudding Miss? Are you interested in a sweet?" The waitress, a teenager with a slight lisp confounded by an impossibly thick Cornish accent, was asking about dessert. She probably took one look at my butt, thought Angel and decided it was the question to ask. No point in disappointing, she'd already blown her calorie count for the day by lunchtime and so ordered the cheesecake.

"Hey..." This greeting, directed at the bartender, was drowned out by the noise in the bar, but the voice was distinctive. Angel lifted her eyes from the dessert menu and turned to see Lucas taking a stool next to the Screwdriver Guy. Enjoying her anonymity, she ordered and sat quietly to watch Lucas flirt with the bartender, an attractive woman about her own age with long red hair swept up in an untidy, falling-down bun that was quite lovely. Wisps of hair were starting to unravel around her face.

The bartender caught Angel's eye and winked at her, responding to the men gathered around in a good-natured, no-nonsense way. "Oh right, that'll be the day." She rolled her eyes and gave a sigh. "I really do work here every night just so I can meet men like you blokes. That's a real incentive for slave labor."

They laughed and Screwdriver Guy leaned over drunkenly and slapped Lucas on the back. As Angel listened absentmindedly to the patter, she noticed Amazon Woman herself sitting at the end of the bar. She cleaned up pretty well—faded denim shirt draped with a soft periwinkle scarf. Her short hair, the color of autumn wheat, stuck up in all directions and looked to have been styled with blunt nail scissors. She needed a good cut. Angel couldn't tell for sure, but guessed that scarf brought out the lavender-blue depths of her eyes.

Angel continued to watch her from across the room. It was interesting. She radiated aloofness, perched on the edge of the conversation, almost disapproving, but not quite. Angel took in her tousled, bed-headed attractiveness and wondered why she seemed so…what was the word? Solemn? Maybe stoic was the word. Angel smiled to herself, thinking "stick up the butt" might be the term if she'd still been in junior high (which felt about right given the encounter that afternoon with Lucas). And speaking of Lucas she realized the woman was particularly disapproving of him and sneered every time he opened his mouth, especially when it involved the bartender.

Angel continued to watch unnoticed until her dessert arrived. She took a mouthful, savoring sweetness mingled with bitter chocolate and then opened her eyes to see Amazon Woman lean in and whisper something to the bartender who smiled in reply. It looked like they had something going. Maybe they were just very good friends. Angel's "gaydar" had gone off the minute she saw her in the garden, but the bartender seemed pretty straight.

Angel was thinking these thoughts as a noisy new group of patrons tumbled in from the street. Lucas turned and caught sight of her. *Shoot, so much for anonymity*. She'd been enjoying the view. He smiled her way and then leisurely approached the table before sliding into a chair by her side. Their parting at the cottage was about a seven on the awkwardness scale, so she was glad to see him up and fully charged again.

The waitress reappeared to fill Angel's water glass and blushed when she saw Lucas. "Anything else Miss?"

"Yes, can I get you a drink, *ma chérie*?" Lucas leaned back in his chair until it balanced precariously on two legs. He let the chair fall back into place and moved so close Angel thought he'd enough nerve to kiss her right there in front of the waitress and half the bar.

"I'll have a martini, extra dirty," Angel replied naughtily, hoping, just a little bit, that the woman at the bar was listening. As the young waitress bolted, Angel imagined Amazon Woman blushing to the roots of her golden hair. "Hey, no double dipping," joked Angel. Lucas was reaching for a second bite of her cheesecake. "And you keep your hands off my pudding."

"I'd give anything to get my hands on your pudding."

Angel roared with laughter. He laughed too and then clutched at his chest. "If you weren't smiling I'd say you were having a heart attack," she said.

"You don't get rid of me that easily," he replied, extracting the phone from his suit jacket and putting on a work face. "New house on the market," he announced after a while, rubbing his hands together and smiling at her across the table. "*Ciao.* Good luck with the cottage. I'll call you." Lucas blew her a kiss, paid for her drink and then sidled out the door. Cool air from the street rushed in, disturbing the warmth of the bar.

The martini arrived as something of an anticlimax, but Angel sipped it anyway, her eyes roaming the crowded bar. When she caught sight of a shock of golden hair in her peripheral vision, Angel offered what she hoped was a saucy smile for good measure and waited for one back. None came.

But before she could register the embarrassment she felt at this slight, a burly man got up from a table in the corner, staggered menacingly toward the bartender, and slammed his fist down on the counter. Conversations faltered as he ignored the cold stares and thinly-disguised disgust of the assembled crowd. It was like the scene when the cowboy saunters into the saloon and gets called to a shoot-out along Main Street.

Before the man could raise his hand again, Angel saw Amazon Woman jump up and block the man's access to the bartender. Despite her sanctimonious manner–*yes, that was the word*–her fearlessness was impressive. Angel loved the intensity of women who looked like they worked hard and knew their strength. "I'd leave if I was you," the woman told him. She moved away from the bar to hold open the door. "Now would be a good time."

When he left, the energy of the place shifted with what seemed like a group exhalation. The bartender pushed a stray lock of red hair behind her ear and turned to take an order. Screwdriver Guy was looking around in a boozy kind of way, like he knew he'd fallen asleep and missed something important. The heroine of the moment sat back down and Angel met her eyes again. Angel refused to look away and held her gaze until the bartender took the woman's attention, putting a half pint in front of her and mouthing a "thank you" in response to her gallantry.

"Tea or coffee Miss?" Angel started and turned to look at the waitress. The dining crowd was thinning out and Angel understood this young woman hoped to call it a night. She most likely still had homework to do by the look of her.

"I'll have a coffee please," said Angel, "but I'll move and let you finish up." Trying to be inconspicuous, Angel carefully chose a seat at the far end of the bar. Although tired, she was enjoying the pleasures of being in a public place without having to be social. A fly on the wall.

And besides, it was that awkward time for a traveler—too early for bed and too late for new adventures. When she thought about it, Angel realized technically she wasn't a traveler anymore. This was to be her home for at least a couple of months. Suddenly lonely, she wrapped the cashmere shawl, which she'd brought with her to keep away the draughts, more tightly around her shoulders and let her cheek rest momentarily on the soft wool. Yvonne had given it to her for her birthday, now the last birthday they'd ever share together. She'd gone several hours without thinking about Yvonne, but now memories of that dark lanky body wound around her in their bed, the way she'd always sleep with one leg over Angel's thigh, brought tears to her eyes. She turned away hoping no one would notice and busied herself looking for a tissue in her bag.

"Here you go Miss," said the waitress arriving with her drink. It was then that Angel saw a message from Kate on her phone.

Best get this over with. Kate was probably in a twitter because she–Angel–hadn't checked in yet. Sliding out of her seat on her way to the foyer to make the call, she took a sip of her drink and tried to banish all thoughts of Yvonne. *Live in the present. Like how do the English always manage to ruin good coffee?*

By the time Angel returned, feeling better and downright virtuous that she'd responded to the call so promptly, the bar was almost empty, except for a straight couple left sitting at the counter, fawning over each other. She chose a stool at the opposite end to avoid them as the bartender looked over and raised two perfectly arched eyebrows at the amorous couple.

"Wish they'd get a room. I have too many empty ones up there aching to be used." Despite the comment on slave labor, the bartender was also the innkeeper. "Madeline Tregarrick," she said, holding out her hand to Angel. "Call me Maddie. Speaking of rooms, I think you're staying with us tonight," she added. "Welcome."

Angel loved the way she pronounced "noight" as if it had several vowels in it. "Thanks. Angela Khoury. I go by Angel. Good to meet you," she said, shaking Maddie's hand.

"American?"

"Yes. Mostly ex-pat at this point. Born and raised in Seattle, up in the northwest corner."

"Oh mountains, right? Lots of rain?"

"You got it. Why I feel so at home here."

"Well we aim to please." Maddie laughed and refilled a patron's glass before returning to visit with Angel. "I hear you're moving into Tulip Cottage," she said.

Angel was caught off-guard. She would have to get used to the small town gossip. "Yes, just signed the papers with Monsieur Hottie." That might give them something else to talk about.

Maddie poured another beer for the flirting couple. Seduction was thirsty work. She got the foamy head just right and put the glass in front of them, looking back at Angel with a smile. "He might have met his match with you."

"You think?" Angel gave a wry laugh and wondered if Maddie had overheard her silly flirtation with Lucas, searching her face in an attempt to see if she was judging her. If she was, it didn't show. She decided to order a Kahlua to go with the fresh refill on her coffee and found herself smiling into the bartender's kind green eyes. Her complexion was like porcelain, pale, almost ghostly, set off against dark red hair.

"So what brings you here?" Maddie wiped down the counter, rubbing a particularly obstinate spot.

Angel took a sip of the liqueur and chased it with a gulp of coffee, savoring the hot, sweet taste. "Got an assignment doing research for *Country Escapes*. It's a magazine. Maybe you've heard of it?" Maddie thought for a moment, nodding absently while she added the couple's drink to their tab. "They're doing a feature on Cornwall's famous public gardens."

Maddie nodded again. "Yes, we're proud of those. Really beautiful, actually. Go back centuries and full of all kinds of exotic stuff."

"So I've heard."

"Are you into gardening then? Or are you just a journalist?" Maddie loaded the dishwasher with a rack of dirty glasses and looked back and caught Angel's eye. "Sorry, I didn't mean 'just' a journalist. I'm sure it's not an easy job."

"No offense, but no I'm definitely not a journalist." If only Maddie knew her real work history. "I'm freelance." *Freelance?* Angel liked the way that sounded. It was almost as if she knew what she was doing. "I'll be taking photos and doing some research that gets sent to a team at the magazine," she explained. "They do the final writing and formatting. I just do the grunt work." Angel paused and took another sip of her drink. The coffee flavor hit the back of her tongue, rich and dense with just a hint of cinnamon. "I am a bit of a gardener though, or at least was. Past life." It delighted her to think which part of her life–the exotic dancer or the ex-horticulture major–was most likely to surprise. "Just love to get dirty," she added suggestively.

Maddie stifled a giggle. "You're kidding, right?" Angel saw her take in the dangly earrings, the red lipstick and the high heels.

"I know, I don't look like the gardening type, but honestly I have a very green thumb." Angel laughed and held up a well-manicured hand. "And I always wear gloves."

"Okay, I believe you. Especially the gloves part." Maddie grinned widely.

"Yes, unlike some amateurs I've known," Angel paused and pantomimed a sneer, waving away an imaginary audience and putting on her best fake English accent, "I'm six credits shy of a *bona fide* degree from the University of California and have lots of useless facts about plants in my head."

Maddie held up her glass of lemonade. "Let's drink to useless facts."

"Cheers," they said in unison.

When Maddie left to bid farewell to the kitchen staff, Angel swirled the last of her coffee around and thought about college and how she'd let it slip away. She'd been so close to finishing. Too much partying and sleeping late, missing class and not showing up for her fieldwork. Failing coursework had led to academic probation and then an opportunity to appeal her suspension. It hadn't seemed worth it at the time. On a lark she'd moved to Paris with her roommate when the roommate's brother had offered them floor space and an opportunity to waitress. When their work permits ran out and the roommate returned to the States, a friend she'd met got her into the clubs. It had all seemed so exotic at first and naughty. She'd enjoyed the freedom and the money. Then she'd met Yvonne and ended up at the Cheeky Monkey, hounded by perverts. It all sounded a little melodramatic, even though it was true.

Maddie left again to cash out the flirting couple's bill and returned to sit opposite Angel. "You okay living on your own in a strange place?" She reached over and refilled Angel's coffee, now switched to decaf. There was anxiety embedded in the question.

"You sound like my sister," exclaimed Angel. "Not that that's a bad thing," she added, shaking her head at the thought of Kate and her irritating ways. "She's five years older and helped raise me through some difficult teenage years. That was after our parents died, and that was hard enough. We have role confusion if you know what I mean. She thinks she's my mother."

"I'm sorry about your parents, but it sounds like she *was* your mother, or had to act like one."

"Yeh, good point," said Angel stirring her drink. "She really did her best. Especially since I was only fourteen at the time and I was just terrible. Kate would say I'm the typical problem younger child. Too used to having my own way and being spoiled rotten."

"That's harsh," laughed Maddie.

"No, not really," said Angel seriously. "She's right. I am used to having my own way. Kate worries because she sees me as a risk taker, even though I like to think of it as adventurous." Angel gave a sly grin. "She doesn't always approve of my free-spirit ways."

"Ah, I see." Maddie moved to line a shelf with sparkling clean glasses. "And coming to England. Was that part of your adventure?"

Angel hesitated, deciding what to share about her life that was acceptable and didn't guarantee an end to polite conversation. Like "I worked as a pole dancer while my girlfriend screwed waitresses right under my nose."

"Yes, England's always been an adventure," she said instead, "and easy because my mom's originally from Scotland and that's why I could get a work permit. Kate already lived here. She's a university lecturer and met her husband Robert when she was on a teaching abroad thing. I was visiting them when I met my partner…" Angel hesitated, wondering if she was blabbering too much and how much she could share even if she wasn't, but Maddie nodded and encouraged her to continue.

"There was a big party for Robert and my partner was working waiting tables." (It was almost true—dancing by night). "I don't know, I loved the accent I think." Angel paused, thinking how stupid this sounded and what a fool she'd been. "Anyway to cut a long story short we ended up living together," Angel paused and took a sip of her drink. "Then I got cheated on for the last time, tried to give up smoking *and* had my credit rating ruined all in the same month."

"I'm sorry."

"No, it's okay. It gave me an out, actually." Angel realized she was sharing much more than she usually did, but didn't care.

Maddie nodded, her eyes wide and honest.

"Yes, it was like when you think the person you love is the smart, deep-thinking type, who can do no wrong," explained Angel, "and then you realize they just don't have anything interesting to say and are a complete phony." She pursed her lips, remembering all the bad times. "And those things that used to be part of why you loved them just become downright annoying." She was desperately trying to gather together all the negative memories of her relationship with Yvonne to stem the tears threatening to break loose.

Maddie nodded again and smoothed down her apron. "I know what you mean. But it sounds like you never married and so that must have been easier at least." Angel frowned and tilted her cup so that the last of the foamy drink swished around its edges. So much left unsaid. And easier? Easier than what? Love spelled trouble enough. She'd tried it and knew it for a fact.

"How about you? Married?" Maddie seemed straight and Angel had noticed the lack of a wedding ring on her finger. She immediately regretted the overly personal question when she saw Maddie's face.

"No," Maddie stammered. She pushed a stray lock of hair back into her bun and rubbed the side of her neck. "My husband James died a few years ago."

Alarmed, Angel watched Maddie's face crumple and her eyes fill with tears. She reached out and touched Maddie's arm, hoping to console. "I'm sorry, I shouldn't have asked. That was insensitive of me." This wasn't the club where women walked around naked, talked openly and held little back.

"No, thanks, I'm okay. It's weird how these things hit you. I've been able to talk about this without crying for ages. I usually like to talk about him, actually. You'd be surprised how many people ignore it because they don't want to say the wrong thing. I can understand why, but it always makes me feel like that part of my life is insignificant, if you know what I mean."

Angel nodded. "People get embarrassed and don't know what to say. They don't want to upset you even if you want to hold onto that memory of him when it's all you have."

"Exactly." Maddie looked at her, surprised by the insight. "Did you feel that way about your parents?"

"All the time. I wanted to talk about my mom especially. How she smiled and how she smelled. I worried that if I didn't talk about her I'd forget her."

"Oh my God, that's it exactly." Maddie sniffed and attempted a weak smile. "Sad thing is our little girl, Julia, she's almost six, barely remembers him at all now. I talk about him but she's losing interest." Tears welled up in her eyes again.

"That's normal," said Angel. "I had to forget just enough to be able to function." She smiled over at Maddie, deeply moved by her pain. "At least you have your little girl," she said. "That must be a comfort."

"It is. A lot of work and worry, but the best thing that ever happened to me." Her eyes started to clear. "You ever thought about kids?"

"I've always wanted kids," said Angel honestly. "Ever since I was little I wanted to be a mom."

"Plenty of time," said Maddie encouragingly. "When you find the right person." She sat down heavily on a stool behind the bar and dabbed at her eyes with the corner of her apron. "Sorry, talking about Julia always puts me over the edge. Maybe I'm just exhausted." She wiped her eyes again and sniffed. "And then there's Bill."

"Bill?"

"He's my brother," said Maddie. "A real git. Absolute ignorant tosser." Angel laughed at the expression, but realized Maddie was deadly serious. "You saw him in all his glory in that scene he made tonight. Always been a drinker, and we have financial issues. We actually own this place together, but it's a long story." She shook her head and suddenly looked very tired. There were crinkles around her green eyes and frown lines at her forehead.

"Maybe one of your friends will sort him out." Angel was thinking about Ms. Sourpuss Amazon Woman who looked like she'd move heaven and earth for her.

"Yes, I do have good friends," said Maddie solemnly, polishing a glass and reaching up to put it on the shelf with the others. She caught Angel's eye and smiled. "Friends are everything."

"Yes, indeed," said Angel, returning the smile and hoping she'd become one of them.

CHAPTER FOUR

"That's actually not a bad idea," said Sylvie when Angel shared her new plan about trying to get a part-time job in the village to meet people and make some extra money.

"Exactly," said Angel, cradling the phone and picking up on Sylvie's enthusiasm. "I know I just got here, but was thinking if I got a second job, I'm free to pay my own way and won't have to rely on Kate so much. Try and be more self-sufficient, you know. Maybe help Maddie at the inn here. In the kitchen, perhaps."

"Right, plus you've always been such a good cook," added Sylvie.

"Jesus, give me a break," responded Angel good-naturedly, though she had to admit Sylvie had a point. She was missing Sylvie like crazy. "Anyway, the money would be nice," Angel mused, recalling two missed calls she'd received last week and messages she deleted without listening to them. All from the collection agencies going after the credit card Yvonne had taken. Hopefully they wouldn't be showing up on her doorstep any time soon, God forbid. "And I'm not getting much from the sublet," she reminded Sylvie, "not after such short notice. Or my last tips from the Monkey—"

"Don't tell me that!"

Angel immediately wished she'd kept her mouth shut. Classic, sneaky Reg, of course. "Damn him," said Sylvie. "I hate his ferret face."

Angel laughed. He did actually look a little ferret-like. "Well, it ended up okay," she explained. "Some guy came into the Monkey asking for my phone number–another of Yvonne's bad checks no doubt–but Fran refused to give it and when they complained to the ferret, he wouldn't give it up either. So all's well that ends well. I'm glad to be gone and not have to face things anymore."

"If you say so, love" said Sylvie, letting the conversation wind down. Sylvie was such a doll. Neither of them mentioned Yvonne again and from where Angel was sitting, that was just as well.

After they said their goodbyes, Angel dozed, half-heartedly listening to the quiet of the morning. She put her face against the cool damp pane and closed her eyes, craving a cigarette. No good trying to fight this when you felt lonely and depressed she reasoned, applying the useful logic of moral licensing. Plus the alternative was eating a second breakfast. She deserved a cigarette, no doubt about that. Feeling only slightly guilty, Angel swooped the blanket off the bed, wrapped herself in it, and padded across the room to extract the emergency packet from the side pocket of her suitcase. *Ah...*

She heaved against the window latch and a rush of damp air entered the room, leaving droplets on her eyelashes and cooling her cheeks as she blew out the smoke into the drizzling rain. From her perch she had a bird's eye view looking out across the harbor where boats bobbed in the waves. A couple of fishermen were talking together on the quay and one was gesturing to a third working with what looked to be crab pots.

Angel pulled the blanket tighter around her body and leaned back against the wall, thinking about her new plan. The trick was to keep it light and not fall into old patterns of self-loathing. She always seemed to get down on herself somehow. To try and rouse herself she thought about Lucas and cast around for old feelings, but they barely percolated to the surface, just a slight rumble of interest. And there was this Daphne, whoever she was. Probably some gorgeous French woman. Angel realized she might actually be more interested in this mysterious French woman than her old adolescent infatuation. It was true Lucas didn't live up to her teenage fantasies. In fact she had to admit he wasn't exactly floating her boat or tickling her pickle or whatever the term was. What a mess, she thought, not for the first time.

After checking out, the drizzling rain had moved into complete downpour mode. Fortunately, she had left most of her bags at the cottage yesterday, so as not to have to lug them back again this morning. As she stepped gingerly along the lane, trying to dodge puddles and keep her umbrella from blowing inside out, Angel could hear the waves beyond the headlands crashing ferociously on the rocks. The roar reverberated across the harbor. She turned her back to the cove and found the lane leading up to the cottage, steeling herself for the uphill trudge. It had seemed such a good plan to walk to the inn last night when the weather was nice.

She passed a B and B with a "rooms to let" sign creaking on its post, and then several other whitewashed cottages. A child's tricycle was propped against the gate of one and a load of wet washing hung dejectedly in the garden of another. Someone had forgotten to bring it in last night. She rounded the corner and there was Tulip Cottage with her old beat-up Volkswagen loaded with her stuff in the tiny gravel driveway. The cottage looked smaller than ever today as it sat heroically against the cliff braving the onslaught of weather. The rain beat sideways against the house and trees around the garden swayed in the wind.

The cottage sat above the lane, separated by a crumbling wall layered with moss and a few straggly plants that had taken up residence in the cracks. It was surrounded by terraced rock gardens flanking narrow slate steps that led up to the front door. Positioned with perfect symmetry on each side of the door were windows divided into small mullioned panes and shutters painted a fading sky blue. The front of the house was cloaked in vines that traced along the upstairs windowsills. Each upstairs window sat above its downstairs lookalike. A small rounded window, almost like a ship's porthole, was perched above the front door. Rhododendron and azalea bushes bordered the path around one side of the cottage and the small orchard, the site of yesterday's adventure, adjoined the other.

Angel edged her way around the corner of the cottage, ducking under an untidy magnolia sheltered from the weather. The weedy flower beds were overgrown, but a host of daffodils was still putting on a good show despite the rain, as were the tulips, the cottage's namesake. Around the corner she spied a kitchen garden with various sorry-looking herbs struggling amidst weeds and discarded pots.

Fumbling in her purse for keys, Angel was soon inside, shaking the umbrella out the door and leaving a small puddle of water on the slate doorstep. The place was furnished and supposedly a cleaning crew had gone through, but it still needed some lick and polish, especially since the gloomy weather made it feel drabber today. She was keen to get her stuff out of the car and organize things.

The first problem, however, was the kitchen faucet. Once she managed turn it on, no water appeared. She tilted her head to check out the problem as a weird gurgling sound filled the kitchen. "Ah!" she screamed as rusty brown water sputtered out of the tap, stopped, started and then subsided to a steady brown trickle. *Damn.* It splashed on her jeans, staining them. As she got down on her knees to check below the sink, there was a tap on the door.

Wearily Angel got to her feet and saw Lucas Therot's handsome face distorted through the fisheye lens of the peephole. The front door stuck as she tried to open it. "Shoot," she said, wrestling with the door. "Great timing."

"Glad to oblige." His smile froze when she appeared in the doorway, hands on hips. He took a step back and tripped over a dead potted plant on the step.

"There's rusty gunge coming out of the tap," she declared, "and my jeans are ruined." Angel rubbed at a brown wet patch on her left thigh and stomped back into the kitchen. He followed.

"Rusty gunge? Sounds like a punk rock band."

"Not funny," she said, smiling nonetheless. "See." On cue rusty water sputtered out of the tap.

"Oh..." Lucas pulled out his phone and tapped the screen.

"And I just paid you a huge deposit for this place—"

"Jenny, you got a minute? Yes, bit of a problem with the plumbing at Tulip Cottage. Okay love, thanks." He waited for the transfer, bestowing a sexy grin on Angel standing with her arms crossed in the middle of the kitchen. She gave him an exasperated look, but felt the annoyance slipping away as he arranged for a plumber to do a thorough inspection that afternoon. Then he called his property management firm and insisted they cover Angel's bill at the Three Ships until the plumbing was fixed. He put away the phone and turned back to face her.

"Always at your service, day or night," he said, loosening his tie. "Plus a special twenty-four hour hotline just for you, with emphasis on the 'hot' if you know what I mean. And here, Cornish pasties!" He reached for a damp, crumpled bag dropped on the hall table and held it up triumphantly.

Angel burst out laughing. "You sure you don't have some tasseled nipple patches in that bag?"

He hooted with laughter. "Ah, I didn't think about that. They'd be right down your alley."

"Up your alley," she laughed. "The phrase is up not down."

"Up, down, who cares? Just imagining you with them on those gorgeous boobies is enough for me."

"Boobies!" She slapped him playfully.

He feigned hurt and gave her a pout. "And after I stood in line for almost half an hour. Come on, try them. And I have drinks too. Fortunately," he added, "since it looks like water is a bit scarce around here right now."

He looked good standing there in his black fitted jacket and grey wool slacks. Amused, she shook her head and rooted around in the kitchen for some plates and cutlery, setting everything down on the rickety kitchen table.

"Cornish pasties! These are great!" Angel licked the flaky pastry from her fingers and took another bite of the crimped, savory treat. They're like *sambousik*, these fried Lebanese pastries we used to eat," she said, smiling at the memory. "My grandmother would make them with meat and onions and pine nuts, I think." Maybe she'd try making them sometime. There was probably a recipe online. She watched Lucas pick up a bit of pastry stuck to his thumb and felt the last of her irritation drain away. The talk turned to France, her life there and his memories of home. Angel could tell he was warmed by her familiarity with his language and knowledge of Paris. Her curiosity piqued.

"I hope you don't mind my asking," she said, preparing to fork the last morsel into her mouth. "How did you end up here in Cornwall or Cumberland Bay come to think of it?" Angel watched him swallow and hesitate. He avoided her eyes and poured cola into their glasses.

"Love of course," he said finally, handing her a glass. "I met her when I took my first business class. Love at first sight." He smiled ruefully. "A terrible match and a volatile marriage. We actually stayed together about four years. Three and a half years too long." She heard him tap his foot, almost an involuntary gesture and felt his impatience.

"But I stayed here," he said after a while. "What can I say? The business is good. I have friends here, but of course I stayed in England for the food." An old joke, especially coming from a Frenchman.

"Sort of my story too," said Angel, picking crumbs off her plate. "I left Paris and then got swept off my feet by a hot Englishwoman." She hesitated, not sure how much he knew and how much to disclose, but he seemed completely unfazed, instead inviting her to join him for dinner when he returned from a business trip to London. She agreed. Why not accept a free dinner out? It wasn't like she had other plans.

After Lucas left, Angel roamed the cottage, unable to settle, but thrilled by the Christmas-morning sense of the house as if each room was a present she could open, one at a time. Nice, but pricey. She resolved to talk with Maddie or maybe get a job in a restaurant or coffee shop if that didn't work out. The thought gave Angel an idea. There wasn't much to be done here without water and she would only be in the way when the plumber arrived. Grabbing her coat, she decided to check out the café down the road and maybe even explore some of the other shops. She could always work retail if it came to that.

The rain had abated and a watery sun edged around the clouds. An umbrella was still in order, but at least the wind had eased. Gravel crunched underfoot as she made her way toward the village green, a small rectangular plot crisscrossed with paths and benches and with a memorial to World War I as its centerpiece. It featured a bronze statue of two soldiers flanking a nurse wearing a sweeping veil with the Red Cross insignia. Someone had left a bunch of plastic flowers at its base and there were several bedraggled red fabric poppies presumably left over from Remembrance Day many months earlier.

The Jewel Café looked out over one of the intersecting paths behind the memorial where the sea was just visible, a sliver of steel grey on the horizon.

"Tea for one," said Angel, ordering a small pot that she carried to a table by the window. Tea was always safer in England. But the café seemed to be doing a good trade if the number of patrons sitting at mismatched bistro tables was anything to go by. Angel listened to the cheerful banter around her, punctuated by the singsong announcement of patrons' names when their order was up. If this were New York she'd say the barista was hoping for a career on Broadway. Angel smiled to herself and wondered if she was the only one who sometimes made up a name just to hear it called. She'd been known to call herself Magnolia and Peony just for the hell of it.

"Anastasia," sang the barista. "An-ast-as-ia," she repeated. There you go. Sounds like she wasn't the only one to try a fake name after all.

Angel gazed hypnotically at the rain and saw a sign for the Smugglers' Museum. The windows were steaming up, but if she rubbed the glass she could just see the building, which looked like it did in the brochure she'd found at the inn. Maybe she'd take a look.

After draining the last of her tea, Angel got up to gather her things. Suddenly shy about asking whether they were hiring any help, she decided to talk with Maddie first about working at the inn. Slinging her purse across her body, she reached for the umbrella and stepped back out into the rain.

"Sorry about the smell. Used to be a pilchard warehouse. Never lets us forget." The voice belonged to a now-familiar face. Still clutching her coffee, Anastasia emerged from behind the reception desk at the entryway to the museum.

"Oh hi," she said, recalling Angel. "You were just at the Jewel, right?" She was in her mid-twenties with darkly-lined eyes and hair dyed a hot pink not found in nature. Despite numerous piercings and dark Goth looks, she had a sunny disposition and was soon giving Angel a tour, pointing out the various exhibits on display. The museum was a renovated warehouse with new paint over a clapboard exterior.

"We share space with the historical society," Anastasia explained, "so we've loads of local things if you're interested." She led Angel to a side exhibit of cases of what looked like ancient brandy. "This was found in a cellar down by the harbor," she explained. "Boats came across from France at night and left brandy and tobacco and stuff like that. Locals hid it and then it was off to London."

"Quite the trade," said Angel. She flipped through a musty album with plastic-sheathed old photos of sailing ships. "Any photos of the cottages around here?"

"Oh yes. The historical society, I mean we, we're really the same, has photos of old houses in the village. They're over this way." Anastasia led Angel to several deep drawers with masses of photographs encased in more plastic pockets, neatly numbered. "Are you looking for anything in particular?"

"Tulip Cottage. Up on Borman Lane."

"Hmm," said Anastasia, rapidly typing a code into the computer. "Here we go." She wrote the call number on a post-it note and handed it to Angel. "Should be in the second drawer over there, right side."

There was a blurry photo labeled May 1901 that showed the front of the cottage with what looked to be a huge hydrangea planted next to the front door. It was no longer there, but maybe a blooming hydrangea was just what the cottage needed to bring it back to its former glory. It was a stupid idea really. It wasn't her cottage and she'd only be there a short while, but still, nice to dream and maybe she could get a discount on the rent if she did up the garden.

Back out on the street Angel thought about the history of the house. All the love and losses it had witnessed for over a hundred years. She walked slowly, pulling her jacket around her until the rain settled into a drizzle and finally stopped. Once back at the village green she took a winding road toward the ravine where more cottages and a few shops lined the steep slope. Anastasia had given her the lay of the land and mentioned there was a nursery or garden center on the top road. Maybe she'd find a cheap hydrangea which would give her bit of color in the summer. Even a wild goose chase could be written off as research. It was a garden center after all.

The lane looped around, then climbed steeply away from the coast and up toward a top road promising a gorgeous view of the river below. At the top Angel paused to catch her breath and sat for a moment on a stone wall by the intersection, picking at a scuff on her high-heeled boots. She really needed to get some sensible shoes if she was going to be hiking up these lanes. But the view really was spectacular and that almost made up for it.

Suddenly a maroon-colored pickup truck merged from a side road onto the lane and slowed down as it approached her wall. A shaggy black dog lolled out of one open window and a freckled arm leaned on the edge of the other. As the truck sidled alongside, Angel recognized the mop of unruly golden hair sprouting from under an old baseball cap. The driver must have seen her first, but gave nothing away except for a nod and a slight movement of her fingers on the steering wheel.

Angel noted the rosary hanging from the rear-view mirror and remembered the gold crucifix from their interaction the day before. The emboldened her somehow and she thought about yelling something trite like "Hi, sailor" or "We've got to stop meeting like this" just for the heck of it but smiled sweetly instead. Again no response. Except for an excited here-I-am-pat-me whine from the dog, who seemed much friendlier than the driver. Trying not to feel stupid, she watched the truck make a left turn into the entrance to a garden center. It looked like they were headed in the same direction, God forbid.

* * *

Nell parked the truck and rolled down the windows for Gruff. "I won't be too long, boy," she murmured giving him a farewell pat. She didn't usually bring him to work because he got bored and misbehaved, but today she'd felt lonesome and wanted the company on the drive over. But how quickly she'd gone from feeling miserable to getting all hot and bothered, her mind full of the woman sitting on the wall, smiling at her no less. She was all sweaty and felt her nipples hardening against the thin fabric of her t-shirt just thinking about it.

Nell guiltily banished all vulgar thoughts and tried to pull herself together. No point inviting new material at confession. Besides, Angel was straight. She'd found out her name after two minutes with their talkative postman. Worst of all, the woman was involved with Lucas Therot, and so she needed to back off and stop behaving like an idiot. Wearily Nell plodded across the car park toward her office tucked behind one of the greenhouses.

It was then that she saw her. She seemed completely absorbed walking slowly among the woody perennials, gently touching leaves and peering at tags. She moved so beautifully, so gracefully and there was innocence in her almost childish absorption and tactile focus that took Nell's breath away. She watched her weave between rows of rhododendrons, camellias and laurel, caressing the glossy leaves and gazing at a deep red camellia flower laced through her fingers. She moved between the plants, seemingly lost in thought, every now and again reaching out with a slender hand to touch a leaf. Hidden by the greenhouse partitions, Nell stood transfixed, reflecting on this woman named Angel who looked to be living up to her name.

After a couple of minutes and feeling increasingly flustered, Nell poked her head into the nearby potting shed, hoping to find Isabel, her help, and avoid having to serve Angel. "Isabel, are you there?" Where was she when you needed her? Nell crept back into her office hoping to find her there, but no luck. It looked like she'd have to face this herself.

The moment had arrived. "Do you have any hydrangeas?" said Angel boldly, her face open and trusting. It didn't seem to bother her that she'd been shamelessly flirting with you-know-who in the pub last night as well as almost getting it on in the garden at the cottage. But the look in those big grey eyes made Nell think Angel could read her mind, that she knew all along that while Nell acted like she found these behaviors sleazy, in actual fact they were a real turn-on for her.

Nell felt suddenly exposed and embarrassed by the color rising in her face. Angel stood so close that Nell sensed the rise and fall of her breasts. And when she reached out to read the tag on the oak-leaf hydrangea, Nell registered how the soft wool clung around the curve of her waist and hips. Feeling herself getting aroused, Nell pulled the jacket tighter around her body in an attempt to hide the peaks hardened against her shirt.

"I was looking for hydrangeas," Angel said again, licking lips that glistened with some sort of girly lip gloss. Nell realized a reply was expected, but stood there transfixed, staring speechlessly into that sweet oval face with its biscuit-colored skin, almond-shaped eyes and long, aquiline nose. She was so close Nell could smell her perfume, a heady, musky scent that sent Nell into a cold sweat.

Angel cocked her head with eyes narrowed, most likely wondering if Nell had lost her voice or perhaps her mind. Nell felt herself panic. "They'll get root rot in a heartbeat if they're in soggy soil," she blurted out, pointing at the hydrangea. "Can't tolerate wet feet. Don't even think of it if you can't give it good drainage." It came out as an admonishment.

Angel's eyes widened and a quick smile flittered across her lips. Then, quick as a flash she gave an indignant look, although Nell couldn't tell whether or not it was feigned, all the more confusing. "Yes, it isn't a native here," Angel was saying. "Best to stick with the *hydrangea macrophylla*, but then *hydrangea arborescens* is quite nice too, especially for a slightly harsher climate."

Nell gaped at her, mouth open. Sweating again and light-headed, she tried to run a hand through her hair and again reddened on finding she still wore the cap. The sparkle that flickered in Angel's eyes at seeing that was the worst of all.

CHAPTER FIVE

It was early and slow in the bar but Angel ordered an appetizer and prepared to wait until she saw Maddie putting on her apron and taking over from the bartender. "Hi," she said, giving her new friend, who was unloading a tray of clean glasses, a little wave. "All I do is eat." Angel laughed wryly at this unfortunate feature of her country life.

"Nothing wrong with that—eating is good," said Maddie, seemingly happy to see Angel again. "You're looking good too. Great color on you." She looked admiringly at Angel's red sweater and her chunky black rhinestone jewelry.

"And how's your day? House all right?" She filled a pint and left it on the bar for the waitress.

Angel told Maddie about her run-in with the pipes, embellishing the story with a demonstrative rendering of her lunch with Lucas the day before. Maddie looked away a little awkwardly and busily set to shining the beer taps. Interesting development, but of course Lucas had likely made it with every woman in Cumberland Bay. Angel filed away the information and changed the subject to the trip to the museum and the idea that took her to the garden center.

"Ah, but you must have met my friend Nell who owns the center," Maddie said.

"Yes, I did," said Angel, trying not to smirk. It was amazing she'd remembered the names of the hydrangeas and most likely had got them all wrong, but this Nell woman must have been too flustered to notice. Angel knew Nell was attracted to her and was annoyed not only that Nell wouldn't show it but also that she acted so standoffishly. The least she could have done that first night in the bar was return a smile, or given a wave when she passed in the truck. And then this last interaction at the garden center.

Angel swished the lemon in her sparkling mineral water and tried to feel compassion for Nell's social anxiety—if that was it—but somehow all she really felt was irritation at her rudeness. And embarrassment at being rebuked. Still, thoughts about Nell flittered through her mind as she watched Maddie work the bar. Seemingly the very opposite to Nell, Maddie had a relaxed and easy manner with the customers, open and personable but not intrusive. She also acted like she didn't know how attractive she was what with the dimples, flaming hair and that gorgeous pale skin.

"We grew up together, went to the same school," Maddie said, returning to join Angel, but concentrating on preparing several colorful-looking cocktails. "Knew her partner too. Ex-partner, that is."

Angel perked up at the "ex" part, disappointed when Maddie was interrupted once more by a patron requesting two gin and tonics. As she watched Maddie work, Angel concentrated on not appearing too interested in Nell who nonetheless seemed to be occupying much of her thoughts. When a boisterous group entered the pub and advanced on the bar, Angel realized Nell's story would have to wait. She gave Maddie a quick wave, took the last swig and left her chair to the delight of another customer hoping for a seat.

Once up in her room, Angel tried to read, happy when interrupted by her cell phone. The ringtone was Sylvie's. "Hi love. What're you up to?" Sylvie cooed.

"Oh, just reading and thinking I could get used to this hotel kind of life. I'll be here a bit longer 'cause a bunch of pipes in the cottage are corroded pretty bad—"

"Oh," interrupted Sylvie, "what're they going to do?"

"The owner's installing copper pipes and a new hot water heater so I'll be in the lap of luxury for another couple of days, maybe a week." Angel wiggled her toes. It had been ages since she'd painted her toenails.

"Well good for you. Enjoy it while it lasts. What did your Maddie friend think about your new idea?"

"Oh, that." Angel sighed disappointedly. "No go, I'm afraid. Said she can barely afford to keep the staff she has and will probably have to cut back if business doesn't pick up."

"Oh." Sylvie made the appropriate noises about maybe something else would turn up and then began a tirade about old ferret face. At some point she dropped the news that Yvonne had left the club.

"Really?" asked Angel. "Where did she go?"

"No one knows. One minute she was here and the next her locker was cleared out."

"Maybe took off with Jamie." Jamie was the teenage waitress: the object of Yvonne's affections.

"No I don't think so," replied Sylvie. "Yvonne was insistent about it being over with Jamie. True, it's hard to believe anything she says at this point but I think in this case she was being honest. Jamie's still around looking all glum…You still there, love? You're being all quiet."

"Yeh it's okay. Just thinking now it's really over."

"Oh please, Angel. Don't go there. Not after the way she treated you time after time."

"I know. What I'm trying to say is when I could imagine her at the club, she was still in my life, even in a bad way. You know what I mean? Now she's *really* gone."

"Well, yes, that's just as well. Believe me," Sylvie insisted, and then hesitated as if to gauge Angel's emotional stake in this before changing the subject. "So how's the hot French bloke? You still sworn off girls?"

"Not exactly." Angel thought of telling Sylvie about Nell. She got this close to sharing how funny she'd been, going from sanctimonious to all shy and embarrassed face to face, but it seemed too complicated and she didn't want Sylvie making it a big deal. So she talked about Lucas instead. "He's very cute, but my heart tells me it's a bad rebound move," she said before pausing and imagining Sylvie's 'I told you so.' "But I'm having dinner with him when he gets back from London," she added.

"Well take it easy. Don't do anything I wouldn't."

"All right, that leaves me with lots of options," said Angel, laughing. No sooner had they said their goodbyes than the front desk called to tell her there were some flowers downstairs to pick up. *Flowers?* When she got to the foyer, her heart skipped a beat. There on the counter by the desk stood a huge bouquet of pink roses arranged with an abundance of lavender. The delicate rose blossoms were just opening and the lavender fragrance was rich and intense, wafting through the lobby.

"For you too Miss," said the waitress, who doubled as the receptionist. Angel peered at the envelope in her hand before tucking it in her back pocket. As she buried her face in the blooms, inhaling the heady smell, she spied a tiny florist's card poking among the stems: "*Roses pour une belle femme et lavande pour tu rappeler de Provence*" said the sappy little note: "Roses for a beautiful woman and lavender to remind you of Provence."

Lucas. Her heart fell. *Damn.* Why did she think these could possibly be from Yvonne? As she read the words again her jaw set. Sadly, she picked up the flowers and headed back to her room. Once inside, she tore into the envelope.

> "Dear sweetest," the card began,
> "I had such a good time with you today and hope you like your flowers. I couldn't resist *ma petite amoureuse.* I thought they were quite beautiful—almost as beautiful as you. I don't seem to be able to get you out of my mind, not that I want to, of course. It seems like destiny

that we meet again like this. And now the bad news. I'm sorry but I have to stay in London much longer than I thought and must postpone our dinner date. Can we still get together when I return in a week or two?
Amour et câlins [love and hugs] until I see you again. I'll text you!
Lucas"

Angel reread the note, written so neatly inside a card the front of which featured a stenciled rendition of his office building and an embossed address and details of his work below. She surprised herself with an immediate feeling of relief with postponing the date and being able to hang out in her pajamas instead. Plus she sensed something between Maddie and Lucas. If her new friend had any interest in him, that would be the end of it. It was Angel's personal ethic never to get involved with someone else's girlfriend, or boyfriend (not that she'd ever had to face that one before). It was just something she would never violate, probably out of empathy given all the times she'd been cheated on. As she lay quietly admiring her flowers, wondering if Daphne should be included in this discussion of ethics, the phone on her bedside table rang again.

"Oh good you're still there. Hey, this is Maddie," the voice said. "Sorry I couldn't talk earlier. We're having Julia's party on Sunday, two o'clock and I wanted to see if you could come." Maddie's daughter was turning six. "Hang on…" Angel heard Maddie yell something about bedtime before she returned to the phone. "Sorry about that. It's a madhouse here. I was also wanting to tell you I had an idea about earning that extra money…" Children's laughter erupted again, swallowing the rest of her words. "Okay, gotta go," said Maddie. "Come over earlier on Sunday if you can, and we can talk about it before the real madness begins."

* * *

The weather was gorgeous as Angel sped along in her old car to Maddie's place. The directions were tricky. She no longer had phone reception on the coast road and barely had a working radio in her car, never mind a GPS. As a result, she had directions from the waitress at the inn. People here were very loose with such things, waving their arms and telling you it was a mile or two, or three or four, so hopefully she wouldn't get hopelessly lost. But it was a fabulous day, unseasonably warm for this time of the year apparently and even losing her way didn't seem like such a bad thing.

The sun was shining and the harbor shimmered with a profusion of new boats bobbing on the water. Angel hoped she hadn't overdressed in her sparkly t-shirt and tight black skinny jeans that didn't look all that skinny on her butt. She'd left her hair loose and it was starting to curl in the humid air. Along with the mental note to talk with Maddie about Lucas, Angel realized she also needed to talk with her about her past — the stripper part—and the present—that she dated women. *Jeez, it was complicated.*

As she rounded a corner the sloping pastures dissolved into harsh moorland landscape dotted with sheep and interspersed with craggy rocks and low-lying marshes. Angel tried to keep her eyes on the road but kept slowing down to look for the wild ponies that Maddie said roamed the moors. Eventually she came around a particularly tight bend and there stood a row of white-washed cottages with a view out over the English Channel. Maddie's was the second one, with dove-grey trim and a profusion of daffodils swaying in the breeze.

Angel was the first adult guest to arrive, met by Maddie and a little girl wearing a pink party dress. She was a little blond miniature of her mother, complete with dimples. Maddie ushered them inside the cozy front room that in the way of many historic English cottages opened directly onto the street.

"Hi. Happy birthday, Julia. I'm Angel. Are you having a fun day?"

"Yes," she replied, holding on to Maddie's skirt and shyly giving a cheeky grin. "You sound funny." She squealed and ran around the corner into the kitchen and joined two other little girls giggling by the window. They were eyeing the present Angel carried tucked under her arm.

"Sorry about that," said Maddie. "Too much excitement. I don't think she's ever heard an American speak before, except on TV and that's usually *Sesame Street*."

Angel laughed. "Then I'll do my best to talk like Cookie Monster." She put on her Muppet voice and pretended to eat the crackers laid out on Maddie's kitchen counter. The little girls shrieked with delight and ran out into the garden.

Maddie smiled and picked up a tray, grabbing a bottle of Chablis and two glasses. "Let's sit outside if it's not too cold and we can keep an eye on the girls. Can you grab the food?"

The tiny patio was bordered by weedy flower beds, but it had a gorgeous view of the headlands. Maddie wiped off a couple of deckchairs and gestured for Angel to sit, kicking off her sandals and stretching long white legs that looked like they hadn't seen the sun in some time. They sipped on the wine and nibbled on cheese and crackers.

"From the cook at work," explained Maddie, pointing to a small plate of rich chocolate truffles on the edge of the tray. "Best cook I ever hired. He always says Julia's birthday is really my day. He does this every year. Right now I think he's on a mission to turn me into a tub o' lard."

Angel enviously contemplated her new friend with her long legs and lanky frame. There was only one tub of lard around here. Yvonne always said she liked something to hold onto and compared Angel to a full-bodied wine, like a robust Cabernet or Malbec. But then why had she been having an affair with that skinny little Jamie? Didn't that prove it was a lie? Yes, when it came right down to it, Angel would prefer to be a lean Pinot Grigio or something else less rotund. Maddie could be compared to that. She was slim, but still radiated strength in the way she moved her body. Not to mention the way she talked and approached life.

As they munched, picking up crumbs with their fingers, Angel decided to come out to Maddie. They were becoming friends and it was time to forge ahead with honesty. And if she took that well, Angel was prepared to give her the rest of the scoop.

Maddie seemed unperturbed when Angel explained that her ex was a woman. "Ah," she said, a mischievous look on her face. "All the better."

"What do you mean by that?"

"Oh, just thinking. It actually fits my plan very well."

"Your plan?"

"Yes, I'll tell you later, go on—"

"Okay," said Angel warily, looking at her sideways. "I can't wait." But she barreled on, launching into her history with Lucas, warped teenage fantasies and all. "And so it's probably a bad rebound idea," she said. "Plus I think there just might be something going with you two," she added quietly.

"You might be right about the rebound idea, but me and Lucas? No way. We were an item for a while…fun at first, but got old real fast. She looked knowingly at Angel. "Really," she insisted.

"Hmm. What do you mean by 'got old real fast'? What went wrong?"

"Well he's sweet and romantic, very French and chivalrous."

"Oh yes, he's that—"

"Right, he's definitely that. And quite smooth in bed, although I was especially vulnerable. It was my first real relationship after James died." Angel felt a small stab of jealousy associated with the object of her teenage infatuation and then sudden remorse, followed by embarrassment. "Yes," continued Maddie. "I never brought him back to meet Julia, for example. He wasn't someone I'd imagine waking up with every day; someone who'd still love me when I was old with wrinkles. I guess deep down I really didn't trust him with my heart, or Julia's heart more importantly."

"That's smart of you," said Angel, looking at Maddie enviously. "Did you know then or was that something you figured out later when you became such a wise woman?"

Maddie's face fell and she kicked at a weed growing in the gravel.

"I'm sorry," said Angel, "I didn't mean...that came out as patronizing—"

"No, it's okay. I know I can be a bit pedantic."

"I'd tell you 'no you're not' if I knew what pedantic meant," said Angel, laughing at her own joke.

"How's stodgy?" suggested Maddie.

"You are definitely not stodgy. And now I know you're not pedantic either."

"Okay, I suppose I'll take that as a compliment."

"Good, because I think you're awesome," exclaimed Angel. "Actually you're intimidatingly awesome, enough to make me quite jealous."

"Don't be silly," insisted Maddie. "Everyone around here has the hots for you. Ever since you walked into the Three Ships the whole village has a crush!"

"Even those old guys with the crab pots? They just happen to like big-boned gals." That made them both explode into giggles, loud enough that Julia and her friends ran over to see if they were missing out on something. Eventually convinced that the swing set held more promise, they scampered away.

But seriously, how could Lucas be interested in her when he could have this sweet woman? And with porcelain skin, no less. Angel felt the old self-hatred bubbling up and looked away, trying to regain her composure. She willed herself to concentrate on the steely grey horizon where the sea met the sky. Maddie sensed the shift in Angel's mood and patted her arm. "Anyone would be lucky to go out with you."

Tears welled up in Angel's eyes as she registered the kindness of Maddie's touch. "Sorry, I'm such a big baby." Maddie said nothing, but smiled warmly and poured Angel another splash of wine. As the golden light shimmered over the headlands they let the conversation die and chose instead to sit companionably looking out across the sea.

"Look, I haven't told you this," said Angel, breaking the silence, "because some people don't take it well. But we're becoming friends, at least I hope we are, and so you ought to know." For some reason, Angel felt very secure in sharing details of her life with Maddie, despite their relatively brief acquaintance. Angel had been at the inn less than a week but had spent some part of almost every evening chatting with Maddie. The innkeeper invited the kind of intimate conversation usually only experienced after years of close friendship.

"We are, but why am I suddenly worried about what you're going to tell me?" Maddie laughed nervously.

"Well it's not such a big deal, but..." Angel pushed the hair from her brow and took a deep breath. She looked into Maddie's face as she spoke. "After I flunked out of college and was living in Paris I had trouble finding a job that paid well. I told you about that, right?"

Maddie nodded as Angel continued. "Well a friend of mine was working in a fancy strip club in Paris and encouraged me to try it. I ended up working there for a couple of years." She watched as Maddie's eyes grew huge. "It felt fun and sexy and the work was so easy. I could always dance and did gymnastics for years. All you had to do was twirl around and gyrate on a few tables and you could make all this money. And guys really like big girls like me."

"You're not big," insisted Maddie.

"No, I'm short, but I mean, you know, big breasts and hips and stuff."

"Wow." Maddie's green eyes widened with astonishment.

"And then I got into pole dancing—better in lots of ways—more skill and very athletic. Great tips too."

"Wow," Maddie repeated. "You're kidding?"

Angel felt suddenly panicked that this might be more than Maddie could handle. "Did you dance nude? I mean, sorry if that's too personal, but what was it really like?"

"No, that's okay. Yes occasionally, and down to a G-string that didn't cover much. Sometimes we were supposed to lift it and move it off our bodies to flash nude, but not for long. That way they could say we were nude without breaking any laws." Angel grimaced and laughed lightly. "It felt weird at first but you get used to it."

"Wow," repeated Maddie. "I am what you call gob-smacked."

"Sorry…it was just a job. And I met a lot of interesting people if you can believe that. Became some of my very best friends." She imagined Sylvie and tried not to think about Yvonne.

"Really?"

"Yes, most of the girls were great." She looked Maddie straight in the eye, "I was lucky I never did drugs and stuff though. That's when you really get into trouble."

"I bet."

"Some of the girls would do it to deaden the pain or shame if that's what they felt."

"Did you? I mean, did you feel shame?"

"No, not really. You get used to being wanted, you know, adored every night." It was true, that had helped her feel better about herself. "But a lot of the girls with problems. They'd been abused, many as children. A lot were runaways. That was sad."

"Oh that's awful."

"Yes," replied Angel, "they were the most vulnerable. But even some of them," Angel paused, thinking about Sylvie, "did okay despite everything."

Maddie nodded solemnly, intrigued by Angel's story.

"But then keeping your body just so. That was a struggle. I was hungry all the time and just wanted to eat everything in sight. But you always had to think about what if you gained a few pounds in the wrong places. Lots of the girls were bulimic…I have to admit I tried that once, but I was so disgusted with myself." She sighed and sipped her wine. "Anyway, when we moved to London and I started pole dancing, things improved. I mean this is difficult stuff and you need a ton of upper body strength to pull it off. I found I was actually pretty good." Angel looked over at Maddie's astonished face before she continued. "Then there's shaving everything," she said. "Such a hassle—especially for me, I'm so dark–and so time consuming. We did the complete wax job. Very painful. I hate it." She suddenly laughed, realizing what she'd said. "Hated it, I should say. Now I'm going to enjoy getting all hairy."

Maddie laughed. "Let's drink to that."

"To hairiness," they said in unison, laughing at the thought.

"I'm sorry, maybe you think less of me now," said Angel as their giggles subsided.

"No, it's interesting. Fascinating, actually," said Maddie. "I don't think any less of you. In fact I really admire you."

"You do?"

"Yes, I think it's very courageous. And beats some boring-arsed job that pays almost nothing. That's what so many women end up having to do, right? So why not?" Maddie reached over and gave her a hug. "But why did you stop then?"

Angel told her about Yvonne and the creepy guy that reminded her of the stalker and how everything had suddenly become old and tired. "Thanks for understanding," she said finally.

"Wow," said Maddie one more time. "I'll just need a bit of time to let all this sink in."

They sat in companionable silence watching the children play. "You didn't ever…you know, have to…"

"Be a hooker?" Maddie nodded and Angel realized she was glad she'd anticipated the question. "No, never had to go all the way. That's what we'd call it." Angel lifted her glass and spun it gently so the wine sloshed around inside. "We used that distinction," she explained, "knowing we were all on some kind of continuum when it came to selling ourselves. I'd open my legs in public to get guys off."

She saw Maddie wince and wondered if she'd said too much. But Maddie caught herself and touched her hand, encouraging her to continue. "I mean, I prostituted my body for money. I just didn't have sex with anyone. All part of the same thing really. I was lucky I suppose. Knew plenty of girls who were, who had to, you know and some who did it proudly. The oldest profession and all. But I always had support and enough cash and sense to keep me on the straight and narrow." She sighed. "Well if you can call erotic pole dancing such a thing. Not very straight and certainly not narrow."

Maddie giggled and shook her head at Angel. "Wow. I'm sorry I keep saying that, but I'm still in shock." She craned her neck to keep an eye on the girls playing on the lawn.

"Well I'm the one who's sorry," replied Angel. "I hope it won't change things."

"In some ways it's bound to," said Maddie, "but it's okay."

"I just don't want to lose you as a friend," Angel insisted. "That would be terrible."

"Not likely, love," said Maddie, reaching over and patting her hand. As they looked out over the headlands toward the sea, they let the silence of the afternoon, punctuated by the children's shrieks, envelop them again. "Look over there," said Maddie after a while. "See the house over by the bluff—great view of the coast—that's Nell Frank's place."

"Nice digs."

Maddie looked inquiringly at Angel. "You don't like her? You think she's a jerk?"

"No, I actually think she's quite fascinating. Let's say she just *acts* like a bit of a jerk. Sometimes, at least around me." Angel recalled all the rebuffs, shrugged, and picked up a truffle. "Speaking of warning labels. These look like killers." She popped one whole into her mouth and quietly faked orgasmic sounds.

"Shh, not in front of the children. Especially knowing you're an expert at this." Panicked, Angel looked at Maddie, fearing her disappointment. "No, seriously, I'm just joking." Maddie slapped her thigh for emphasis and shook her head again at Angel. "Amazing, an exotic dancer…Where was I?"

"Nell pompous Frank."

"Angel! No, you need to know she's a nice person because that's my idea for your financial future—"

"Oh no! What does she have to do with my future?"

"Listen. I'm sorry I don't have the funds to hire you. But here's my idea. So Isabel, Nell's help at the garden center, is going back to uni. She's already given notice and Nell needs someone part-time to help out. She told me the other day." Maddie looked smug. "You'd be perfect. You know more than a bit about plants, you need work, she needs help. What more is there to say?"

"Well, she's cute—"

"Right then," cried Maddie as if it was all decided.

"But she comes across as arrogant and self-righteous, not to mention she acts so weird around me—"

"Unless you had other work in mind," insisted Maddie, reassuring Angel's startled look with a smile and raised eyebrows. "At least hear her story and then decide."

"I can see on the face of it how you think this might work," Angel said, trying to placate, "but you've seen how she scowls at me, right? Remember last night when I was playing darts with those friends of yours? We were having such a fun time and all she could do was sit there and nurse her beer, looking all grumpy and sour. I don't know, maybe she scowls at everyone, but it does seem like she saves the best ones for me." She looked at Maddie, daring her to disagree. "Don't tell me you haven't noticed. Plus isn't she really religious? I seem to recall more holy statues among the lawn ornaments at the garden center than gnomes." Angel chuckled at her own joke and found herself remembering the crucifix Nell wore and the rosary hanging in her truck. "Seriously, she'd have a conniption when she heard all the God-forsaking profanities that come out of my mouth."

"No she wouldn't. She's not like that at all. You have to trust me on this. Just give her a chance—"

"I can't hear you." Angel had her fingers in her ears, chanting the words.

"Oh, come on. And," said Maddie sheepishly, "if I'm not mistaken I think she's really got the hots for you." She gathered up the empty glasses and stacked them on the tray before sitting back down and turning her face toward the sun.

"Right," replied Angel, playfully slapping Maddie's arm. "Then that's the best reason why we shouldn't work together." Now it was Angel's turn to look askance. "She likes to look, for sure," Angel continued, "but she's like those boys in elementary school who pull your hair in the playground and chase you around because they don't know how to say they like you." She reached in her bag for sunglasses and settled herself back into the lawn chair. "True, I do think she's attractive and I find her a bit intriguing—"

"See!" declared Maddie.

"Yes, but working with her would be something else entirely."

"No, Angel, really. She's great. Would I lie? Plus," said Maddie before Angel could respond, "she helped me no end when James died. We grew up together. Neighbors. I've known her forever. Comes from a big Irish Catholic family with lots of sisters. She's also an amazing cook, which you have to admit is an added bonus because I know she takes treats to work all the time. You should taste her ginger snaps. Completely melt in your mouth."

"Oh great. I'll gain another ten pounds putting up with her."

"Will you stop," yelled Maddie, feigning exasperation. "Let me finish. She was partnered with another friend of ours from the next village, childhood friends. Camille Sutherland was–I mean is–her name. We all went to the same Catholic school and got into all kinds of scrapes.

Now Angel was intrigued. "I bet you guys were a riot."

"I was a little beast and loved making Camille jealous. She was very possessive about Nell, even then."

"I bet you led that poor girl into untold dangers," said Angel, imagining the sour Nell Frank in her school uniform playing with the wild Maddie Tregarrick.

"Oh she was wild too. We all were. What do you expect? We were at a Catholic school after all!" Maddie chuckled at the thought. "Except little Camille," she added, "who was a dreamer. Always had her nose in a book. Became a teacher too, which fitted her perfectly."

"So what happened to them?" asked Angel, curious now, sensing there was something else Maddie wasn't telling her.

"It's sad. Everything seemed perfect. After university they moved back to Cumberland Bay and Nell took over the garden center from her dad. Then Camille had a son—that was the talk of the village, I can tell you—Trevor was his name and they built the house over there."

"*Was* his name?" inquired Angel, frowning. Noting the past tense.

"Yes, terrible. Little boy died when he was barely four. Sweet boy, quite the towhead. Blond hair and blue eyes like both his mothers. It was an accident when they were on holiday in Scotland fortunately, if you can say anything about the whole thing was fortunate," she added, rubbing her forehead. "He was hit by a car. But at least it wasn't around here. That would have been much worse. Like most couples when a child dies, they blamed each other, Nell and Camille, that is.

Maddie rubbed her hands together and shivered slightly. "Poor Nell."

Angel felt a pang of regret. "They split up then?" she prompted.

"Right, they split up and Nell's just trying to deal with life's challenges like all of us. And then she got really involved with the church. I thought that was good at first, you know. It gave her instant community for support and maybe an explanation for why such a horrible thing could happen in the first place." Maddie shivered as the sun went behind a cloud and breezes ruffled the showy spring flowers. "Lately I'm thinking she's become a bit fanatical about it all. It just makes her feel guilty because she's a sweet person, but not the perfect church-goer she'd like to be. It fosters her already low self-esteem and basic insecurity. That church pretends to be open-minded, but I don't think they're as accepting of gay people as they claim. You know what I mean? Thanks to the church, I think Nell is now wracked with guilt and self-loathing, which is just crazy given her past. We all love her, but she doesn't seem to love herself anymore."

"Oh, yes." Angel did know. She'd had her share of do-gooders telling her she was sinful. That she could be saved. From sex and from stripping. Still, she could understand why people might turn to religion when their whole world collapsed. It would be a burden, though, if you thought you had to live your life in a certain way to avoid damnation or some other retribution.

"So those are all the reasons you must give her a break," said Maddie, looking Angel in the eye and daring her to disagree.

"Well if you say so. But again, knowing she's some Jesus freak only makes me think we'd be terrible working together. Let's face it—in her eyes I'd be just a fallen angel, wicked through and through," said Angel, her voice a whisper for full effect. "Not to mention she most likely thinks I'm some Islamic terrorist. Ha!" Suddenly weary, Angel leaned back in her chair. Talking about her past and dealing with small-town prejudices was always so tiring.

"She's Catholic," concluded Maddie after a pause, "and hardly a Jesus freak. And you're no fallen angel either, or some kind of a terrorist, for goodness sake." Now she laughed and looked into Angel's eyes.

"Well," said Angel wearily, "some would beg to disagree, at least on the fallen angel part…But if you say so." She relaxed into her chair, closed her eyes and listened to Maddie giving elaborate descriptions of Nell Frank's house, its private beach and gorgeous views. Angel continued to listen half-heartedly until Maddie described her attempts at matchmaking, at which point Angel tuned back in to the conversation.

"I've tried to set up Nell with a couple of my friends, but no go. The one on New Year's Eve seemed perfect, but didn't go well. This thing with the church and all the "should" and "thou shalt nots" just leaves her thinking less of herself and others. Not to mention her parents screwing her up over the years. They almost disowned her at one point when she came out to them. Anyway, the woman I set her up with had a child from a previous marriage and Nell just couldn't do that again. But you know the thing is she's really good with children and Julia adores her. She's her godmother." Maddie hesitated before dropping the final bomb. "She'll be here in a minute or two, actually. So you can see for yourself."

* * *

"Look at me Auntie Nell. Look at me!" Julia twirled around, showing off her sparkly new pink shoes and grabbing her party hat. It flopped back and got caught up in her ponytail.

"Here Julia, hold on a sec." Nell disentangled the elastic from her hair and set the hat back on top of her head. Julia whirled away to join her friends as Maddie silently mouthed her thanks. Nell had thought up lots of excuses to avoid this party, but she didn't want to disappoint Julia.

Well, the truth was the only person she didn't want to disappoint was herself, having some masochistic desire to see Angel again. Now that she knew her name, she could barely say it without getting all hot and bothered and feeling stupid about having a crush on a straight woman. Complete no-no. Still, she was so infatuated she couldn't help hanging around the bar all week watching Angel chat with the locals.

And she'd learned a lot. Like Angel was just two years younger than her and that her father was Lebanese. Always the life of the party, she was quite the extroverted Yank. And bold. Some drunken bloke had the nerve to ask what harem she belonged to and she'd kept referring to him as "Lawrence of Arabia" behind his back, but so the rest of the crowd heard. Everyone thought it was hilarious and then she proceeded to make a fool of him by beating the pants off him at darts. Earned her a lot of respect in the bar and an even higher estimation in Nell's eyes.

Nell had watched all this with anger rising, ready to intervene on Angel's behalf if she needed it. It helped make Nell see how difficult it was to be different in villages like Cumberland Bay where you stood out if you weren't some straight white person. Yes, her respect for Angel had really soared afterwards. Angel could hold her own, and anyway, what did it matter if she *was* a Muslim—which let's face it, she probably was if her father was Lebanese? At least it meant she believed in something. Better than most people around here.

Now she was across the room leaning against a kitchen counter, sipping on punch and chatting with a couple of women, the mothers of Julia's friends who'd also just shown up. The shimmery t-shirt was tight enough to make out the lines of her bra through the fabric. And the trousers showed off that ample bum. Enough said. And her hair falling in a dark glossy mass over her shoulders. Incredibly sexy. Nell couldn't take her eyes off her and desperately tried to think of something to replace the image of her naked in the garden. Not that she'd actually seen her naked in the garden, which was why she couldn't stop imagining it. *What the hell is wrong with me?* Nell just wished she could get past feeling so awkward around her. She acted like a blithering fool every time Angel so much as looked at her.

"Yes and then I thought Montessori, what's the difference between that and Waldorf?" said the young mother. "And so I asked her teacher…" Nell observed Angel patiently listening and making small talk. She really had the gift of gab. Nell could tell she knew she was being watched.

"So, how's work going?" It was Maddie by Nell's side offering her a beer and looking at her sheepishly. Why did it always seem that Maddie could see right through anything she tried to hide? "I hear Isabel's going back to uni," she prompted.

"Yes, terrible timing. What with spring and new planting and all," replied Nell. Maddie had pulled up a chair and was very close. "Unless of course everyone's going to Walmart," Nell added, "and then all I'll need is a tax lawyer to file bankruptcy."

"You're not serious?" said Maddie, giving her full attention. "It's not that bad is it?"

"Not sure. Sales are down compared to last year, but too early to tell." Nell tilted her glass and watched the foamy beer spread around the edges.

"I hear Audrey and Dave just bought a new house," said Maddie in an attempt to change the subject and ease Nell's dismay.

"Yes, I'd forgotten to tell you," said Nell thankfully. "Huge place up the coast. They got a good deal because it needs some major remodeling. The property's been neglected for years. It'll be quite the job to get it sorted…They've asked me to do it. The outside stuff, that is." She paused and scratched her head, wondering how she'd got herself into this. "Big project and tricky—the lot sits on a slope. But it'll bring in some cash. But you know my sister. She wants everything perfect for a house-warming party in the summer and pleaded with me to take it on." Nell ran a hand through her hair and took another drink. "I might need to hire some help to get it done in time. To get it done at all, actually."

"Ah is that so?" Maddie paused expectantly and let the comment hang in the air. She tilted her head and gave Nell a saucy look.

"What? Why are you looking at me like that? I know that face," exclaimed Nell.

"Nothing, just thinking," said Maddie, glancing over at Angel and raising an eyebrow.

Angel felt their eyes on her. *Why were they looking at her?* "What?" she said turning to meet their stares.

"Nothing." Maddie feigned nonchalance.

"What am I missing?" Angel could tell something was going down and guessed what Maddie was about to say next.

"I was just talking to Nell here about her needing some help in the garden center," said Maddie, hiding a smile. "Especially now since she's doing the landscaping for Audrey's place."

"Audrey's place?" inquired Angel, confused.

"No Maddie," said Nell, as red as a beetroot. The poor woman was blushing right to the tips of her ears. "Maddie will you stop. Let's talk about something else," Nell muttered, trying to regain her composure by getting up and speaking too loudly.

"Yes stop," laughed Angel, realizing they agreed on something at least.

Maddie ignored their exasperated looks and continued sweetly. "You need help," she said pointing to Nell, "and you…" She waved a hand at Angel. "You know something about plants and, if you don't mind me saying, need extra money. Perfect arrangement."

Angel's first response was to grab the dishrag from the counter and throw it at Maddie. Not exactly mature, but it gave her a moment to prepare her defense. "Look, nice idea, but…" Angel hesitated and saw Nell running her hand through her hair with a look of sheer desperation.

Suddenly a little boy burst into the kitchen. Very plump with curly strawberry-blond hair, he was wearing big boy jeans cut short at the leg to fit his girth, much larger than his short height would suggest. He was trying not to cry and looked at the adults expectantly, not sure what he wanted, but obviously upset and needing something. Maddie let their conversation drop and went over to him. "What's wrong love? You okay?" The little boy's lip quivered as he looked from one adult to the other and then settled his gaze on Nell.

"Justin, come here lad. I've got something in my pickup I want you to see." Angel watched as Nell beckoned to the boy and maneuvered him out the kitchen door. They both seemed glad to have an excuse to leave by the look of them. Angel and Maddie moved to the window to see Nell and Justin sitting on the tailgate of her truck. She was showing him a small poster of a sports team. It looked like a publicity-type thing, possibly to entice people to buy tickets to the game. Whatever it was, the child was soothed and started to smile. And Nell was actually smiling too.

As Maddie gathered up the dishes she turned to give Angel another self-satisfied look. "Told you so," she said. "Give her a chance won't you? Justin's Bill's boy you know. Nell hates Bill, as you saw in the bar that night, but loves that boy like nobody's business."

Angel shook her head and shrugged. "Something tells me you're on a mission."

"No, just telling you like it is," replied Maddie, stacking dishes in the sink.

"All right, I'm listening," said Angel. She was balancing plates and squeezing between two mothers at the kitchen counter still deep in conversation about alternative education. "But don't get too excited. Here let me tidy up these things first." Angel strode back into the living room to grab the empty glasses and came face to face with Nell and Justin coming back inside to join the party. "That was really nice of you," she said, watching the little boy run off to join his friends again.

Nell looked like she'd been caught stealing from the cookie jar. "Justin's going through a rough patch," she replied gruffly. "Difficult time."

"He's chubby," said Angel. "I know what that's like. I was a very fat child. They called it 'pretty plus' in my day. All the kids at school made fun of me."

Flustered, Nell didn't know where to look. Eventually she spoke. "Yeh, I wasn't fat, but the kids found a way to humiliate me too. I got called Frank the Wank," she said eventually.

Angel put down the tray of glasses and snorted out loud. "Oh too funny," she exclaimed, laughing into Nell's eyes. "That must have been awful." She caught the look on Nell's face and chuckled again. "Sorry, but if it helps at all, my middle name is Fatima and the kids would scramble it and call me 'I'm a fatty.' Totally humiliating because of course I was one."

Nell inhaled her beer, laughing and sputtering so it spilled down her front. Angel laughed too and their eyes met. Nell really had amazing eyes. Their arms brushed and a shiver caught Angel's breath in her throat. She drank her punch, swirling the fruity drink against her taste buds, senses alive.

Arousal lit up Nell's face and Angel saw her avert her gaze.

"Glad to see you kids getting along," said Maddie, noting the look on Nell's face and Angel's sheepish grin. She kicked the kitchen door closed with her foot and maneuvered through the room carrying a lopsided cake alight with six candles. All the children dashed up, their shrieks filling the tiny room.

"Here it is," exclaimed Maddie. "Contains all the food groups: sugar, fat and more sugar."

When they sat down to serve the cake Nell ended up next to Angel and got to listen to her enthusiastic but slightly off-key rendering of the happy birthday song. She watched her help the mothers pass out small pieces of cake to the children as she tried to sort out her feelings.

They were seated at small child-sized tables and benches that Maddie had rented. As the children ate and a relative quiet descended, Nell saw Angel take her piece and slip out onto the patio. She chose one of the director's chairs set up around a makeshift barbecue and set her cake down on a small side table. She was in profile. Nell watched her lift her chin and sniff the air, ever so slightly, then close her eyes as if straining to hear the rhythmic crashing of waves out beyond the headlands. The tide was ebbing leaving dank, pungent mud flats, tender and vulnerable looking. Nell sensed Angel's body's heat and wondered how the curve of her back would fit against her hands.

When Nell thought about this later she realized she wasn't sure how she made the decision to leave the group and follow Angel onto the patio. All she remembered was finding herself in the chair next to her. A new fragrance teased her senses. This one was floral with a slightly woodsy undertone that suggested wild hot sex in the forest. "Sorry about the other day at the nursery," she heard herself say.

"Apology accepted."

"You know your plants."

"Sometimes." Nell couldn't tell if Angel was bluffing but didn't care.

"You okay? Need anything?" Nell inquired.

"No, just an insulin drip." Angel forked another mouthful of cake loaded with ice cream.

She was funny. Nell liked that. Funny and incredibly sexy. Out of her peripheral vision she could see the rise and fall of Angel's breasts. It was now or never.

"So what about you working with me?" Nell said, her voice louder than she'd intended. Angel turned to look at her. She said nothing but her eyes, huge and a dark smoky grey, met Nell's gaze. "Maybe you don't think that's a good idea…" Nell blustered. She stalled, wondering how to continue.

"I'm warming to the idea," Angel said at last, her full lips partly open so Nell could see the tip of her tongue. "Trying to figure out my fringe benefits."

"And what exactly did you have in mind?" Nell said awkwardly in an attempt at bravado.

"A free plant or two. Maybe some insights for my articles."

"Yes, Maddie told me about that. I could show you round some of the gardens if you like…" Nell blushed, preoccupied with how much she hated herself groveling like this and almost missed Angel's soft reply. *Did she really say "Okey dokey, when do I start?"*

CHAPTER SIX

Angel wearily lugged the last of the bags of potting soil into the back greenhouse and went to water some petunia starts. It was her first week on the job and surprisingly, she had to admit she was out of shape. Dancing was one thing, but these muscles hadn't been used in years. That and more recently too many late nights playing darts. That last round of drinks right before closing last night had been a fatal mistake.

"You look like death warmed over," said Nell.

"Well thank you and good morning to you too," replied Angel. Nell was wearing the stupid baseball cap again with her hair sprouting around the sides. Maybe she should suggest a good hairdresser.

"Want some coffee?" Nell got up and poured her a cup without waiting to hear the answer. Angel saw she added just the right amount of milk and one spoonful of sugar.

"Thanks," said Angel grudgingly. She was dying for a cigarette but was managing to limit herself to one a day now that the heartache over Yvonne was starting to subside.

"Why don't you go use my office and work on your stuff for the magazine?" Nell suggested, handing her a steaming cup. "It'll be nice and quiet and maybe you'll feel better. I can handle things out here."

"That's okay," Angel replied, inhaling the aroma and deciding coffee smelled much better than it tasted, "but thanks anyway." Nell had put a ginger snap cookie in the saucer. Angel wished she wasn't being so nice. It had surprised her that Nell was all right to work with after all. They had originally planned for Angel to just assist with Audrey's landscaping job, but it soon became clear once Isabel worked her last day that she was needed at the garden center too. It was spring and the Brits loved their gardens. Anyway, Nell turned out to be pretty good with the customers after all, quite funny actually, and Maddie was right. Nell was a terrific cook and brought all kinds of treats to work for everyone, including chocolate cupcakes (which Nell adorably called 'buns') once she knew they were Angel's favorite.

"Too much fun last night?"

"You could say that." Angel debated making something up just to make Nell blush, but headed for the potting shed instead. She sensed Nell's eyes on her butt and suddenly felt self-conscious.

About ten o'clock Maddie showed up with scones. She was disgustingly perky for this time in the morning and spoke several decibels too loudly. As they sat in the office eating the scones Maddie announced she had tickets to Trefarrow Gardens, a premier public garden on Angel's must-see list for the magazine. The garden managers had dropped them off at the inn, hoping to bring in some business with the tourists. Maddie stood up and waved imaginary tickets above her head. "For my new friend and my old friend," she declared.

Angel held her face between her hands and then covered her eyes. "Maddie, what are we going to do with you?" Nell looked on and shook her head slowly, trying to frown, but smiling anyway.

"Just love me. And be grateful." Maddie stood up and kissed Angel on the top of the head and then went over to do the same to Nell. "Come into the Ships tonight," she added, addressing Angel. "You too Nell, if you like. I'm working and it'll be slow." Her voice was still much too loud. "Miss having you stay with us now that you're back at the cottage," she added, ruffling Angel's hair.

As Angel shuffled back to work she approached Nell unloading bags of manure into the covered area by the showroom. Nell had taken off her hoodie and her forearms rippled as she lifted the heavy bags. Her athletic body looked stunning in those jeans that hugged her muscular thighs so nicely too. A thought flittered across Angel's brain that maybe lust was like chocolate: the more you had in your life, the more you desired. "Here, you're all sweaty." Angel handed Nell a tissue.

"Right, day's heating up."

"But you know what they say," said Angel, shielding her face with her hand and smiling. The sugar had definitely helped lift her mood. "Don't sweat the petty things. Pet the sweaty things."

Nell snorted and almost dropped the bag. Their eyes locked and Angel touched her arm. Nell's skin was hot and electricity sparked between them. For a split second she wanted to feel Nell's mouth on hers.

Nell jumped away as if scalded and got up, reaching for her work gloves. "Somebody has to work for a living," she said awkwardly.

Angel was silent for once, caught between embarrassment at the slight and irritation that Nell could go from being so appealing to such a drag so quickly. For a moment it had seemed they had connected on some new level that was quite sexy. Angel stifled the thought and got up wearily, realizing it was more disappointment she felt than anything else.

* * *

Nell couldn't settle. She had tried working in the office for a while, worrying mostly over bills and realized she couldn't concentrate. They'd got close. Angel felt something for her. She knew she did and then Nell had blown it again. She was such an idiot. Might as well head out for home, maybe call at the Three Ships. Nell caught sight of herself in the mirror and realized she was nothing but a lovesick fool.

"Just ask her out for goodness sake." It was Maddie across the bar getting Nell a beer and looking at her sheepishly. After Julia's party she'd told Nell that Angel dated women and explained her past history with Lucas. It had been good news at the time.

"Bloody hell Maddie, give me a break." Nell frowned and accepted the beer. "Is it that obvious?"

"Well, since you asked." Maddie laughed at the look on her face. "Yes, you're obvious. Although probably only to me," she added, giving Nell a knowing look. "So what's stopping you?"

"Lots of things. We're so different for one."

"She grew up in Seattle for goodness sake," insisted Maddie before Nell could protest. "Oh, you think maybe she's a Muslim too?"

"No!"

"No? You mean the thought hadn't crossed your mind?"

"Well, yes—"

"Sorry to disappoint," interrupted Maddie with that annoying told-you-so look on her face. "She's not. Has never even been to the Middle East and her mother is Scottish."

"No," insisted Nell again. "It's not like that. But I think," she added, pausing to choose her words carefully, "it might be interesting if she was a believer." Nell checked herself and was rewarded with a strong sense of satisfaction that it wouldn't have mattered either way. She honestly could say she didn't care about these things, only that Angel seemed like a good person, whatever she believed. This insight pleased her. It was a personal triumph in being open-minded and accepting, even if the look on Maddie's face and the reputation Maddie had of her suggested otherwise.

"Anyway," added Maddie affectionately, willing now to give Nell the benefit of the doubt, "you don't have to worry about Lucas anymore."

"I don't?" replied Nell, sounding more nonchalant than she felt.

"Yes. I don't think she'd mind if I told you she went up to see him in London for the day. She used the word 'disappointment,' if I remember rightly."

"Oh she did?" murmured Nell, still trying not to look too interested, but feeling like some grey cloud had just blown away and the sun had come out. She resisted the urge to hug Maddie and took a drink of beer instead.

"And she said he lacked intellectual curiosity."

"Is that right?"

"Yes, so it's going nowhere, you mark my words." Maddie suddenly looked serious and took a deep breath. "And you know how Lucas is." She wiped her forehead with her arm and drank from a tumbler of water below the counter.

"You of all people know how he is," insisted Nell angrily, tilting the beer in her glass for something to do with her hands. "I hate that sod. I should've let him know what I thought of him the first time he hurt you."

Maddie laughed at the outburst. "Oh come on, Nell, lighten up. You and your 'shoulds.' I can take care of myself. Anyway, I had a good lunch with Angel the other day. She's sorting that cottage like nobody's business. We spent an afternoon going through antique stores in Port Arrow and she found some cheap bits and pieces even though she's just here for another couple of months. The woman has a great eye for color, I'll say that. Funny as hell too. We had a great time. I'd love to see her have a reason to stay here a while longer," Maddie declared, raising her eyebrows. "And oh, I almost forgot. The funniest thing," she added quickly, "is Angel said she wanted to creep into that place in London that Lucas rents and mess everything up. That he's a neat freak," she added, chuckling to herself, "which of course I already knew."

Nell could imagine Angel having the nerve to do that and smiled to herself, thinking how at home Angel would be in her untidy house. It was a warm and comforting thought. Nell sat at the bar finishing up her beer, feeling a hundred percent better. Lucas was definitely on the way out. Maddie had as much as said so and Maddie was always right, at least almost always.

Nell watched Maddie take an order for a Cosmopolitan, cocktail, pouring it into a martini glass and adding a lime wedge for garnish. As she stared at the translucent pink color of the drink, it reminded Nell of Angel's earrings: tiny pearl studs with dangly pink crystal drops. Who else but Angel would wear earrings like that to work in a nursery?

"So how's business?" asked Maddie, rousing Nell from thoughts about Angel.

"Better," Nell said. "Much better, actually."

"Ah, I knew it. Didn't I say people would soon get tired of Walmart? It was just a novelty and people were curious." Maddie tugged at a loose tendril of hair and pushed it back into her clip, all the while keeping an eye on the patrons around the bar. "They soon figured out the plants there have a two week expiration date."

Nell laughed at the thought. "Actually I think Angel really helps. People like her. I wasn't sure at first because you know how small-minded people can be around here and her being so…you know, different and well, American, but she wins everyone over."

Maddie gave a self-righteous smile with the "I told you so" look on her face. "Good," she said simply. "That's really good news."

"And Bill?" asked Nell, as Maddie started to leave. "He been bothering you? I saw him at the Jewel the other day and was this close to laying him out. There he was spouting off about how you robbed him of the cottage your grandparents left *you*. How they'd be rolling in their graves if they knew what you'd done." Nell clenched her fist in mock attack and punched the air. "Such bullshit! Gave him a piece of my mind instead. Lazy bugger. If he got himself a job and figured out how to keep it, you'd all be better off. You sure you don't want him here doing the work he should be doing to keep the inn going?"

"No way. I'm definitely better off without having to interact with him and his drinking every day. Still hasn't paid me for his share of the last three months on the mortgage for the inn. He's still taking his share of the profits, what little they are," replied

Maddie, anxiety flooding her face. "So you can see his being all miffed about the cottage is the least of my problems. Anyway, I was hoping he'd have a check for me when he dropped off Justin for Julia's party, but no sign. Maybe next month if I'm lucky."

Despite the support of their regular customers, the inn barely broke even, and then only in the summer at the height of the tourist season. The siblings had developed financial problems over the last few years, so much so that Maddie and Bill as co-owners had to take on a mortgage to keep the place afloat. Maddie's father had died a few years before her grandparents, so the inheritance had skipped her mother, who never really got on with her in-laws anyway. It was a tangled financial and emotional mess and it was taking its toll. Maddie gave a weak smile and turned to fill an order. "Okay time's up. Gotta get back to work. Ask her out," she added as Nell got up to leave. "Just do it."

* * *

Once home Nell tried watching television, but kept replaying the scenario with Angel in the yard over and again in her head. All the elation after hearing about Angel and Lucas and the patting herself on the back about being open-minded had dissolved into anxiety and instead she couldn't stop admonishing herself for not acting on what was increasingly obvious. Not only had Angel provided an opening, but now Nell understood why. And she'd blown it with that stupid comment about having to get back to work.

About seven o'clock Nell decided to go back out even though it was getting late. Not the Three Ships again, despite the invitation. She didn't need Maddie psychoanalyzing her, or worse still, running into Angel. No, she'd go to the Hare and Hounds. On the edge of the village green, it catered to a different crowd and had snooker tables in the back room. Snooker was her specialty and she loved the sight of those green baize-covered tables and the sound of balls thudding into the pockets. She'd even been known to bring her own cue. Old friends from way back usually hung out there on weeknights. Ready-made company without having to say much.

Despite the hour, the roads were surprisingly busy and it took Nell longer than usual to navigate the drive into the village from her home on the edge of the moor above Cumberland Bay. The road curved down steeply, banked on one side by rocky cliffs and with sweeping views over the moors on the other. Nell braked as several sheep dithered in the road, trying to find a way back over the wall to join the flock. She slowed and drummed the steering wheel as they scurried away.

The sea was turning molten as darkness gathered. A sliver of moon was just starting to climb, its gilt edge hanging in the sky. Soon lights appeared ahead and before she knew it Nell was backing the pickup into a too-small space over by the sea wall adjoining the village green. Yellow light poured out of the open door of the Hare and Hounds, its raucous din audible over the sound of the waves. Shrieks pierced the air, followed by cascading laughter.

Picking her way across the gravel, she saw a woman sitting on the end of the sea wall talking with old Dora Gallagher whom everyone called Mrs. Dora. She roamed the village, rain and shine, selling flowers to tourists, or locals if the tourists weren't biting, one ragged flower at a time that she always tried to pin on your clothes or in your hair. Many people found her annoying and several local businesses had lately been complaining. The woman let Mrs. Dora put a droopy carnation through a buttonhole on her jacket and then Nell watched as the woman gave her some coins. Unaccustomed to kindness, Mrs. Dora eagerly accepted and shook the woman's hand.

By the time Nell reached them, she realized the woman was Angel. *Bloody hell.* She was waving a small goodbye to Mrs. Dora and her back was to her, but she'd recognize that sweet *derriere* on the wall anywhere. Nell was just about to sneak back, hoping she hadn't been seen, when Angel spun around, suddenly alert, her dark face silhouetted against the sky. Her mouth was slightly open and her eyes, huge in the dim light, looked into Nell's. She could see pinpoints of moving light in Angel's pupils as she inhaled the salt air.

"You scared me," she said.

Nell gazed at Angel sitting before her in those stupid tight jeans and those ridiculous clunky shoes and realized she'd never seen her so beautiful. Nell's legs felt wobbly and she broke out in a sweat.

"What're you doing here?" said Angel. "Got a hot date?"

"That'll be the day." Nell couldn't read Angel's face, but sensed a flicker of relief in her eyes that made her heart lurch. Sodding hell, maybe she was going crazy. There was an awkward silence as they looked at each other.

Nell was the first to speak. "So what're you doing here?" she said at last. "I thought you'd be hanging out with Maddie."

"I was, until a big tour bus arrived and it got crazy."

Nell nodded and stepped aside as a noisy drunken couple staggered up the steps by the sea wall. They narrowly missed colliding with a man on his way across the green to the pub. Shouts reverberated across the parking lot as the man careened along the path, yelling to some friends nearby. "Party city here tonight," Angel said, watching the revelers over her shoulder.

"Yes, the place is dangerously hopping this time of night," Nell responded, suddenly aware of the admonishment in the words. She didn't mean for it to sound like she was chastising Angel for being out alone and hoped that wasn't what Angel thought. But instead Angel shrugged noncommittally, her dark grey eyes watching Nell impassively. Nell hesitated, uncertain about whether to stay or leave.

She took the plunge. "Do you want to go for a walk?" Nell suggested gingerly, trying not to sound completely foolish and only just hearing Angel's "All right," barely audible over the beating of her own heart.

They left the green and sauntered out on the harbor path that wove steeply down toward the sea. Nell settled down and pointed out wheeling birds called stonechats nesting against the rocks. Together they scanned the horizon, looking for the ponies the National Trust had introduced to graze on the gorse beyond the harbor. Cumberland Bay was bounded by rocks and then scraggly gorse moorland scrub reaching out beyond the village as far as the eye could see.

Nell started down the narrow path to the beach and reached back to take Angel's hand, helping her down the incline. She felt the softness of her fingers and tried to keep herself from falling apart on the spot. Just to touch Angel was like a blow to the senses. It sent Nell's mind spinning.

Eventually they came to a level sheltered spot with the cliff at their backs and the beautiful golden sands below. Nell sat down on the coarse grass and hoped Angel would join her. She did. She was so close Nell could sense the rise and fall of her full breasts inside her jacket. Nell sat on her hands, aching to touch Angel's body. Feel the softness she knew would greet her. They made small talk about the village and London and Angel's almost-degree in horticulture.

As the sun was setting and a chill settling into their bones, Nell screwed up her courage and suggested they go down and explore the wide, sandy beach below. As Angel nodded her assent, they climbed down farther onto the gravelly sand, watching cormorants bobbing hopefully in the waves. After a while they found a long strand of seaweed discarded by the waves. Angel taught Nell to skip, or jump rope as Angel called it. "No, jump now," she said, laughing uproariously as the slimy wet strand hit Nell's legs time and again. "How did you miss learning to do this?" she implored.

"Easy," explained Nell. "I was raised as the boy in the family. With all my sisters, my dad was happy to imagine I was the son he never had. Didn't quite live up to his dreams of me playing football though."

"Weak defense," laughed Angel, winging the seaweed off into the ocean. She threw off her shoes, pulled up her jeans and ran into the surf again, her jacket flapping in the wind. The tide was coming in and sea foam littered the jagged path of the waves on the wet sand. With the light behind her, she looked gorgeous, dancing through the waves. The tight jeans accentuated her wide hips and her breasts bounced as she ran.

"I love the ocean!" she screamed into the wind.

"And I just might love *you*," Nell whispered under her breath. *Oh my God, let this not be the biggest mistake of my life.*

* * *

After Nell had walked Angel home to Tulip Cottage, she retraced her steps back to the Hare and Hounds. It felt like a pub crawl, but going home was not an option. She was much too wound up. Nell spied some friends waving madly from a corner table and was soon enveloped by the jostling crowd.

"Frank, you really suck tonight," someone joked as Nell picked up a snooker cue and attempted another turn. "You'll be sinking that cue ball any minute, I dare say, whether you want to or not." Sure enough Nell sent the ball skidding into a side pocket as the group exploded in laughter. Usually she played snooker the same way she lived her life: efficient, no-nonsense and in control. Although they were enjoying the joke at her expense, Nell had other things on her mind. She felt like she had some sort of high school crush when you think of all the things you're going to say, rehearse them in the bathroom mirror and then your mouth has a mind of its own and you say something stupid. She hadn't exactly said anything completely idiotic that evening, but knew she hadn't been scintillating, witty company either. She wondered what Angel really thought.

When the bartender gave the last call, Nell realized she couldn't avoid herself any longer. It was time to go home. She climbed into her truck, turned on the ignition and wondered what the hell she was doing. She felt completely sober. Senses on high alert, she noticed every detail in her path. Driving out of her way up past the Three Ships toward Borman Lane, she saw the lights still on in Angel's cottage. She was there somewhere. In bed? Taking a bath? Mortified by thoughts about Angel's body and the fact she was getting aroused just thinking these things, Nell swung the pickup truck around and wearily set off toward home.

When she arrived everything was pitch black. Not bothering to turn on the lights, she threw her keys in the dish by the door and went through the living room and out onto the deck where Gruff bounded to greet her. She gratefully fondled his silky fur and looked out across the bay. From the light of the new moon she could just make out the rocky shoreline and hear the waves crashing in the distance. She paced the deck with the dog at her heels, rehashing the day and tormenting herself with thoughts of Angel. Eventually she got down on her knees and prayed, asking for guidance and confessing the day's personal humiliations in an attempt at cleansing her soul and starting afresh. Afterwards she poured herself a small glass of scotch, straight up. As the liquor coursed through her tired body she relaxed, even though the sight of Angel's smoky grey eyes still stirred her mind.

CHAPTER SEVEN

"This work okay? In this pot?" A young woman held up a coleus plant with deep green and maroon leaves edged in orange. "It's so pretty." She pointed to a shiny ceramic planter wedged in her cart next to a chubby baby in its car seat.

Angel quickly put on her sales assistant face. "Nice to see you again. And you too," she said, smiling as the baby waved its tiny fists in the air. She remembered the customer from several days ago. "That should work fine, but this plant likes shade and so if you're mixing it with sun-loving plants and putting it in full sun, it probably won't do so well."

"Oh," said the customer. "Thanks, no shade on my balcony." Regretfully she put the coleus back down, stroking its bold leaves.

"Here, let's look at these," said Angel, leading her out toward another greenhouse, explaining the different plants as they walked.

"You should teach this stuff," the customer declared as she selected some wave petunias and marigolds. "Really, it would help us clueless no end." She picked up a six-pack of zinnias and dropped them in her cart with the others.

"Thanks. I appreciate that, although I've a lot to learn too." Standing by the cart Angel took off her gloves and reached out so the baby grasped her finger. The dimpled little hand encircled her pinky as the baby gave a slow toothless grin.

"Well anyways," insisted the woman, "I came back because you helped me out before." She lifted a bulging diaper bag and rifled around looking for her wallet. "Don't get that at Walmart, you know. It's worth not buying wrong stuff that doesn't last two minutes in your garden."

Angel smiled goodbye as they headed for the checkout. Amazing how some of what she'd learned in her college classes (the days she'd dragged herself out of bed and shown up) had actually lodged in her brain. Even more amazing was the percolating knowledge from childhood memories. She'd spent hours following her father around the yard, pottering in the shed and digging in the dirt. She hadn't realized until now just how much he'd taught her: general things about when and how to plant and what went where in the garden. Things she took for granted that transferred pretty well from the Pacific Northwest, where she'd grown up, to this part of the world.

Angel thought about her father and what a good man he'd been. He was devoted to her mother and worked hard to provide for their family. She felt tears pricking at her eyes, thankful he hadn't seen her flunk out of college. He was so proud of his girls and how well they'd done in school, especially Kate of course, who was always the academic star.

Angel pushed a strand of hair out of her eyes and turned to thin a batch of cabbage starts. Hands deep in the loamy soil, her thoughts turned to Nell. They had stayed out of each other's way since what she liked to think of the manure bag incident, where her touch had so disconcerted Nell, although the irony of that wasn't lost on her. The truth was she wasn't used to being turned down. Well, it wasn't as if she'd actually been turned down. Maybe it was more like Nell didn't pick up, even if they did have a nice walk on the beach later.

They were at an impasse and Angel felt intuitively that Nell had to make the next move. She sensed anything else would backfire on her. Still, it was hard because over the last few weeks she'd come to see Nell as something forbidden and slightly decadent that she craved. Like ice cream that's in the freezer and you know it's there and you think, just one spoonful and the next thing you know you're standing at the counter with the carton open and a jar of peanut butter next to it making yourself sick. That was how she felt about Nell. Any interest in Lucas paled in comparison to this. He was still in London and just as well. Deep in thought, Angel heaved the hose between the seedlings ready to be watered.

As she finished watering the cabbage and coiled the hose back into place, Angel thought about Trefarrow Gardens. Nell had the tickets. She hoped Nell would invite her to the gardens because they were a must-see for the magazine article. And even though Nell supposedly knew the place like the back of her hand, Angel would have to go alone if the invitation didn't come soon.

As Angel came around the corner, she saw Nell in the showroom stacking brightly colored packets of seeds on a display board. Behind her the annuals blazed in masses of rainbow colors. The thought of Nell as her assistant for the day, helping her put stuff together for the magazine, was rather sexy.

Nell turned and their eyes met. "Wait a minute…" Nell mouthed.

Angel caught up with her in the narrow passageway between the showroom and the greenhouse. Nell's violet eyes looked navy blue, pupils dilating in the low light. Angel could see Nell's collar was tucked under at one side and resisted the urge to straighten it. Their faces were inches apart. Neither of them moved and no one said anything. Angel imagined Nell's mouth on hers. Kiss me, she thought.

"Nell, you there? Got a minute?" A voice reverberated across the showroom. It was Annie, Nell's part-time office manager who handled publicity for the center and doubled as the bookkeeper. Annie's glasses bobbed precariously on top of her head and she held a sheaf of papers. She was trying to help a customer, an elderly woman who ran a B and B in the village and had a gardening magazine in her hand.

"Hello Mrs. King, how are you? Can I help you find something?" Nell stammered, turning to greet the customer as Annie slipped back into her office.

"Oh thanks love," replied Mrs. King, smiling sheepishly but glancing toward Angel. "Actually I was hoping to talk with your lady friend here. Hope that's all right." Angel stifled a giggle as Nell reddened, mumbled her assent and retreated into the greenhouse.

"Oh dear, I think I just upset Nell," said Mrs. King, fiddling with the magazine.

"I don't think so," said Angel, smiling reassuringly. "She'll get over it. You know how the boss gets."

Mrs. King laughed and showed Angel a picture in the magazine. Soon they were deep in conversation about replanting a perennial bed and paving a patio. Accompanying Mrs. King to the hardscape area and chatting about hardy annuals and whether they'd winter over in her sheltered garden, Angel's thoughts turned to Nell and her astonished embarrassment. Was it because a valued customer had sought her out first or was it the "lady friend" comment? Of course everyone knew she was a lesbian. How could they not? She wished Nell could just get over it. The thought made her pause and Angel wondered just how much this burden was preventing Nell from being more open about the two of them.

When Mrs. King had left with her purchases, Angel returned to the watering, thinking about Nell and remembering how cute she'd looked when her ears turned bright red. Angel felt something stir and half-heartedly tried to suppress the thought, despite the smile that was playing on her lips. Hesitating, Angel thought about whether to go and see if they could pick up from where they'd left off, or just let it be.

Eventually she could stand it no longer and went over to Nell's office, knocking quietly and then peeping inside. "What did you want to talk with me about," she asked, looking at Nell sitting at her desk, chewing on a pen. Angel debated whether to just take things into her own hands and kiss that mouth. "You started to say something," she said instead, jiggling the doorknob. She waited and idly kicked a scuff in the torn linoleum, hoping Nell would get up and embrace her, right there in the office.

"Oh." Embarrassment clouded Nell's face and her ears started to redden again. "I was going to say," she coughed slightly and cleared her throat, refusing to meet Angel's eyes. Nell looked tortured. "I was going to say that it's really good having you here and I appreciate all you're doing to help out."

"It's really my pleasure," Angel stammered, wondering what the hell was going on. She looked into Nell's astonishingly blue eyes, unwilling to show the disappointment she felt. What was it with this woman? There was something about the way she looked at Angel that made her all gooey inside. Gooey was a strange word to use in a relationship, but that's how it felt. Nell made her feel soft and lush, full of warm urges. The earnest way Nell talked with Annie and the customers, the way she walked into a room and pulled the bottom of her left ear when she was deep in thought. How when Maddie, as a last resort, dropped off Bill's little boy Justin because the child wasn't feeling well and his mother was frantic and couldn't take time off work. Justin was terribly cranky, plonked in front of a computer alone in the office playing video games. The little boy really perked up when Nell came in and kindly had him keep her company in the greenhouse.

And Nell smelled good. She had noticed this weeks ago at Julia's party when she'd still thought Nell a pain in the ass. Not to mention her accent was so adorable that Angel would make her say stuff just to hear her pronounce certain things. All those long vowels and clipped consonants and her funny choice of words. It was a constant source of amusement. Really, how could she have wormed her way into Angel's heart like this so quickly? She didn't know what it was about Nell. Sure she had a great athletic body and was pretty good looking with that golden hair and those incredibly blue eyes, but there was something else. Maybe it was the way she got a particular look on her face, a look of need rather than desire somehow. Sometimes she caught a glimpse of interest in Nell's eyes, followed by a blush or guilty response to the passion she thought and hoped, might be burning in her heart.

Angel wanted her.

But sadly Nell stayed out of Angel's way for the next few days, exacerbated by the fact that Angel only had a few shifts at the garden center and was spending a good bit of time on research for the magazine. Angel tried not to be offended by the lack of attention on Nell's part and wondered if it was because she'd gained weight and wasn't that attractive anymore. But she tried not to become too miserable and focused on her work instead. It was almost May and the weather had turned. Sunshine and showers with almost daily rainbows over the headlands. Trees were budding out and flowers bloomed in the mild climate.

* * *

One evening some weeks later, Angel had just returned from the grocery store when she heard someone pulling up by her cottage.

"Brought you a present…was going to give it you at work but I hadn't seen you in a while and thought I'd come by instead. Since I was in the neighborhood."

There was Nell with her outrageously tousled hair and violet eyes standing on Angel's doorstep, and looking apologetic. The look on her face was a mixture of pure longing and absolute torture. At her feet was a large, beautiful hydrangea. Its foliage was green and glossy with promising bluish buds soon to be its crowning glory.

"Wow! Thank you," said Angel, touched by the kindness and the irony of it all considering their first interaction over the very same plant. "Can you come in?"

Nell hesitated, looking down at her mud-encrusted boots. The sight of them made Angel smile which caused Nell to rake a hand through her hair and then reposition her hat. "I'm filthy," she said, "and probably should be going…"

Nell was halfway down the path when she turned to face Angel and spoke again. "If you'd like, I mean, if you're not too busy, how about we do Trefarrow Gardens tomorrow?"

CHAPTER EIGHT

Nell was worried about this trip to Trefarrow Gardens. She slowed down on a tight corner and waved to a neighbor, shifting into second gear for an uphill stretch before the long downhill into Cumberland Bay. She had spoken with Father Joseph who'd given his usual "Go with your heart, but remember to keep a space for God" lecture, a counsel he gave all couples struggling with issues of intimacy about keeping yourself pure in heart and mind. Nell interpreted this as being honest with yourself and others and living with purpose and integrity.

But Angel was taxing her resolve about the purity bit. Not that it meant being chaste. Nell had never thought that. It was about moral purity and self-respect. You could never avoid the sins of being mortal, but you could control what was in your heart, your intentions and the way you treated others. Nell knew sometimes Father Joseph's sermons just made her feel guilty, something Maddie never tired of pointing out. Maddie had even sent her a card saying faith is a journey, not a guilt trip, which Nell had to admit, was a very good point.

Nell pulled onto Borman Lane feeling cranky, barely resisting the urge to just keep driving up to the garden center and fake an emergency there. She slammed her open palm into the top of the steering wheel and felt herself perspiring. Even if they did have free tickets and it was more like a work trip, she'd be confined in the truck with Angel for several hours. The thought both excited and scared her. Nell knew she was going to make a fool of herself. She just knew it. She raked her hand through her hair one more time and tried to steady the feeling that she was losing control. Dutifully she pulled alongside Tulip Cottage, grimacing into the rear view mirror to check her teeth and to breathe into a cupped hand to make sure she didn't have coffee breath. She jerked on the handbrake, got out and slammed the door.

To make matters worse, the house across the street from Tulip Cottage was where her high school crush, Ramona, had lived. She had parked her old car right here all through her upper sixth year in grammar school. Nell was trying to seduce her, or at least get her to notice that she existed, since seduction implied she actually had some knowledge or a plan.

Parking here felt natural, as was the agonizing rush of adrenaline that reminded her of the moment when Ramona appeared in her doorway. She would walk the few steps to the street with a sexy smirk on her face and then look to make sure her mother wasn't watching through the window before she rolled up the waistband of her school uniform so that the skirt barely covered her thighs. Nell smiled remembering how all the girls (except her, of course) had used to do that and how the nuns would get out their tape measures and routinely send them into the lavatories to change before handing out the demerits. Somehow Ramona managed to roll hers up and down, just at the right times.

The thought got Nell all hot and bothered and made her feel seventeen again. It did nothing to squelch the anxiety seeping through her body, not to mention the guilt that always accompanied the memory since Camille had been sweet on her at the time, even then. The fact that Ramona peaked early, married the captain of the football team and had three children before she turned twenty-five and was now divorced and living who knows where, did nothing to make her feel any better.

Angel had already seen the truck and came out of the cottage, locking the door behind her. What a sight. Clingy, pinkish-colored top with tight blue jeans and ridiculous high-heeled shoes given where they were going. She bent over to pluck a few weeds from the gravel and Nell was rewarded with a full view of her shapely bum. She'd hoped Angel would have her hair loose, but it was tied back with some contraption or other. A pair of oversized sunglasses covered her eyes and she carried a big shoulder bag.

"Let's take my car," Angel announced. "Save on gas, or petrol as you so quaintly call it." Nell hesitated, unwilling to be driven by her, but it was too late. She was already heading for that piece of junk she called a car, rewarding Nell with another view of her bottom as she leaned into the back seat and tossed her bag inside.

"Are you okay?" she asked, watching Nell's face. Nell reluctantly murmured her assent, picked up her jacket and climbed into the passenger seat.

Nell fiddled with her seatbelt.

"Shoot, it's stuck..." Angel extracted the seatbelt caught under the seat and attempted to buckle Nell in.

"I can do it." said Nell emphatically.

"Are you dissing my car?" said Angel, peering over the top of her rhinestone-studded sunglasses. "I'll have you know this trusty car, old and battered as it might be, is the perfect vehicle. And" she said playfully, wagging her finger, "it's paid for and that's worth its weight in gold."

"Right, if you say so."

"I do say so. Anyway, you give me a raise and I just might replace it."

Nell felt her color rise.

"I'm joking!" insisted Angel.

"I know," stammered Nell. Angel hesitated, gave her a long look over the top of her sunglasses and then started the car. "You know how to drive on the left-hand side of the road?" said Nell as they barreled along the top road toward the coast.

"You're kidding? I've been here for years and I always drive on the right." She looked at Nell sideways, and laughed. "Nobody seems to mind."

"Humph." Nell tried to ignore the fact that her chest was a hand's width away. She rolled down the window to avoid Angel's perfume. Like her, it was just a bit too much, but extraordinarily sexy at the same time.

They drove in silence, heading southwest with the sea, a glossy slate, grey and smooth, with just a few breakers here and there, bursting into view as they wound along the coastline. It was low tide. Sunshine streamed heroically from behind clouds gathered on the horizon and poured in through the windshield. Angel was driving too fast.

"Watch this corner up here. Bit tight," Nell said, breaking the silence and clenching her fists.

"If you're going to be such a backseat driver I might have to ask you to sit in the back," said Angel playfully.

"That sounds terrible," said Nell, ignoring her comment and reaching to change the radio station. She was referring to the static noise filling the car.

"Here, let's play a CD." Angel pointed to a stack of music in the glove box and indicated the top one. "You'll like that one, sort of country."

"Sort of?" laughed Nell as slide guitars and fiddles fought for who could make the most racket and a deep voice sang 'whose bed have your boots been under?' She snorted at the ridiculous lyrics but found herself suddenly wishing that her boots were under Angel's bed. Permanently. Soon they lapsed back into a friendly silence, not counting a slight hum as Angel tried to keep up with the melody. The traffic was getting thicker.

Half an hour later they stopped at a roadside café for take-away drinks. Angel leaned against the car, peering up into the hazy sun and holding her tea in both hands to warm herself. Nell sipped her coffee and tried to keep her eyes from Angel's cleavage. It almost tumbled out of her top when she bent down to pat a little black and white dog that came up to visit.

"Oh, you are too cute," exclaimed Angel, scratching the dog's ears. "I can't wait to get my own place so I can get a dog," she added. "Just like you." The little dog looked up at her and would most likely have left with her too if she'd asked it. Nell watched Angel charming the dog and chatting with its owner, a young man in his twenties or so. They were deep in conversation about the merits of exercise for pet health, talking as if they'd known each other for years rather than two minutes.

Nell's spirits soared listening to Angel talk about her love for dogs. As far as she was concerned canines were family and this was a very good sign. Still, she registered the look in the dog owner's eyes and felt momentarily jealous. With her it was like moths to a flame. Everyone was attracted to her. Nell had seen it with customers at the nursery and among the regulars at the Three Ships. It wasn't just her body, Nell decided, although that might be enough. She watched her chat with the dog owner and tried to recall the word she was searching for. As Angel waved her goodbye and reached to pat the dog's head one last time, Nell realized it was charisma. That's what she had.

Nell was glad when they were back on the road and could sit side by side without her having to look into Angel's eyes. They were traveling deep into the most south-western part of the county, hugging the coast road to enjoy the panoramic views out across the Channel. Nell rolled down the window, took a deep breath and tasted the salty air. Even living here all her life, Nell was still entranced by the beauty of this spectacular coastline.

Crossing several estuaries where rivers flowed down from surrounding moorland and emptied into the sea, they saw large coastal lakes shimmering in the afternoon sun. Tattered grasses waved on marsh islands surrounded by swells of water. At one point Nell pointed out various spots where she'd fished for brown trout, including a river where salmon were making a reappearance. They pulled over to look at osprey fishing in the sound and saw the bright plumage of a kingfisher darting into view. And there was a peregrine falcon sitting on a post and eying its dinner. Nell looked at the birds, glad for the distraction from Angel's breasts, which were just a hand's length from her own.

* * *

Nothing is as sexy in a woman as talent and Angel was beginning to think maybe Nell had quite a bit, even if her conversational skills lacked. She was a mine of information about the natural history of the countryside and looked pretty good in that faded denim shirt, which made her eyes look so intensely blue. She watched Nell's ass as she strode toward the ticket booth at Trefarrow Gardens. Nice, tight and firm, just the way she liked it.

Angel grabbed her bag and camera case, locked the car and set off after Nell, eager to see the renowned waterside garden with its mild maritime climate. She was so looking forward to this and hoped she hadn't been too much of a chatterbox in the car. It would be nice not to do that when she got nervous. It would be great if she could be calm and confident for a change. Like Maddie.

They showed their tickets and strode over to the office where Angel picked up all the literature they had about the place. The brochure described it as a "sub-tropical ravine garden with a stunning coastal backdrop," originally established over a century ago and "designed through the years to represent its present glory." Spring canopies bursting with exotic blooms beckoned from the gardens as trees and plants from all over the world formed vibrant tunnels of color glinting in the sunshine. Angel was dying to see the famous ponds with their Japanese koi.

"You want to head toward the pergola?" suggested Nell, pointing along a ravine laced with azaleas. "Really pretty." She looked like she had her groove back after being so awkward during the ride down in the car.

As they walked toward the azaleas, Angel took multiple photos from all angles of the beautiful blooms, pinks and lavenders, white and deep red hues. She exclaimed at the sight of an orange, peachy-colored bloom with a delicately spicy, lemon-scented fragrance. "They make wine out of azalea blossoms in Korea," she said, snapping a photo.

"It's called 'tugy–on-something,'" said Nell. "Can't remember the exact name, but there's another reason to grow them, I suppose."

Tugyonju. That was the name of the Korean wine. Angel had learned about it a lifetime ago in school. It was one of the few things she remembered, probably because it had to do with alcohol.

"Oh my," said Angel, looking out across a valley of rhododendrons that bordered the ravine. The gorgeous blooms formed a spectacular palette stretching as far as the eye could see. "Fond memories of you in the garden in your wellies," she said, poking Nell in the ribs. She pointed to an expanse of hydrangeas that would look gorgeous in a couple of months. "And these are my favorites too, but I hear they need good drainage. Someone told me they can't tolerate wet feet."

"You'll never let me live that down," said Nell with a wry grin.

Angel smiled smugly and turned to look at the map of the garden. "I'd really like to see the koi pond and bog garden."

"You don't say?" said Nell sarcastically, having listened to Angel go on about ponds umpteen times.

"Stop being cheeky," Angel said, playfully slapping Nell on the butt.

Nell laughed and caught Angel's hand in mid-air, bringing it to her side and holding it there. Her hand felt rough against Angel's palm. *Was this really happening?* Angel felt suddenly light-headed and reminded herself to breath. The world seemed to shift and tilt. She tried to concentrate on putting one foot in front of the other as they walked along the pea gravel path skirting the valley of azaleas and rhododendrons. Nell's hand was solid curled around her own.

Hand in hand, they continued to walk along a route where the blooms created masses of vibrant color. Carefully picking their way along the path, they skirted beds of perennials that would put on a powerful show in the summer. Eventually they left the blaze of spring blooms behind and started on the downhill path toward the woods. Angel took off her sunglasses as they walked into the shaded woods where sycamores ruled.

Bluebells created a dazzling carpet dotted with a few late daffodils gently swaying in the breeze. A giant swath of blue covered the ground, escaping from the woods and running out along the ridge toward the horizon—a sea of periwinkle melting into the sky. They found patches of late snowdrops punctuated with a few remaining crocuses thrusting out of the ground, ravenous for sunlight.

Pausing amidst the lilac haze of bluebells, Nell and Angel looked into each other's eyes. Their bodies almost touched as they stared at each other, thinking and wanting, Angel hoped, the same thing. Desire sparked and time seemed to stand still. Angel held her breath, anticipation keen as Nell tenderly traced her cheek with soft fingertips, eventually letting a finger rest against her lips.

Angel saw Nell's eyes darken and her knees went weak as Nell gently bent to her mouth and brushed the lightest of kisses on her lips. Nell seemed to hesitate then and when Angel didn't pull away, Nell lingered and kissed her softly again. Her tongue shyly traced Angel's bottom lip, gently slipping inside. Nell's mouth was warm and sure and she tasted like heaven.

It was a sweet kiss, full of meaning the way first kisses are.

At last.

Angel's heart fluttered in excitement. She was on cloud nine. The kiss was sweet and gentle. She had let Nell make the first move and now she wanted more. Her hands were in Nell's hair pulling her close, enough that Nell took her mouth again. Frantic hands pulled Angel closer, molding their bodies together. It was a sensation unlike anything Angel had experienced. Her body simply melted into Nell's. All her senses came alive at once and she knew she had never been kissed like this before. Not with such tenderness and reverence. Nell kept on kissing her until a small crowd of schoolchildren entered the woods, shouting in the distance. Nell held Angel close and they smiled into each other's eyes.

Still reeling from the encounter amidst the bluebells, and feeling giddy and light-headed, Angel took Nell's hand and together they sauntered out of the woods and toward the spectacular grove for which Trefarrow was best known. Angel took a deep breath and exhaled slowly, looking up into dense leafy canopies. She knew flowering plants but really had very little knowledge about exotic trees.

"Wow," was all she could say, reluctantly dropping Nell's hand to snap a series of photographs. These were spectacular and perfect for the magazine. At one point Angel got down on her knees and pointed her camera straight up toward the top of a Chusan Palm swaying in the breeze at the edge of the path. A sign explained it was native to China and known as a windmill palm. She looked up into the fan of leaves and understood how it got its name.

"Nell. Quick, come here," Angel exclaimed, rounding another corner. "Incredible." Towering above her stood the famed Ghost Tree covered with floating white bracts sheathing reddish-brown fruit. Angel felt its huge trunk and touched the beautiful white flowers, reading the information about this exotic specimen. "Okay, Ms. Garden Center," she said playfully, blocking Nell's view of the sign. "Let's see if you can answer this million dollar two-part question. "Where does this tree originate from and what is its family name?" She hummed the theme tune to the television show *Jeopardy*, all the while waving her fingers in tune to the music.

"Easy," said Nell. "China and dogwood."

"Oh, you are so right on the first count," she said, pausing for emphasis. "I'm sorry you're wrong on the second." She made the sound of a buzzer.

"What! It is a dogwood," said Nell indignantly.

"Ah—aa," said Angel. "*Davidia*."

"Well, that's wrong," Nell said again, threading her fingers through her hair and stepping over to look at the sign. "They're wrong."

Angel laughed at Nell's annoyance. "Shall we cross it out and write in the proper answer on the sign? I might have a red crayon in my bag."

"Not funny. They're wrong," insisted Nell.

"Okay, take it easy," said Angel, laughing at her irritation.

"All right Ms Know-it-all," said Nell, ignoring the comment. "You have to answer the thousand pound question over in the flowering perennials." They had reached the pergola and were looking out toward the ravine.

"Oh, yes? Bring it on." Angel got up and shook Nell's hand. "If I get more right than wrong I get to have my way with you. If I get more wrong than right, then you get to have your way with me."

"Bloody hell," Nell spluttered, a half-smile playing on her lips. "I can't believe you just said that." Her blue eyes widened and Angel realized she was fiddling with the gold cross at her throat as she spoke. Maybe the last thing Nell really wanted was to go beyond a kiss with someone like her.

"Okay. What's that? Where does it come from and what family?" asked Nell, looking back toward the plants.

"Hmm, I'm going to guess *echium*," said Angel. "As for the second question I have no idea and for the third, I'll say borage family." Nell feigned horror, but Angel could see Nell was impressed that she'd got lucky with the botanical name of this exotic plant and knew its family.

"And this one." Nell pointed to another plant with a tall arching flowering stem.

"Oh, that's too easy," Angel murmured. "Mexican lily, *agave* family. You forget I lived in California. And this one," she exclaimed, pointing to a low shrub, "maybe from Japan or China. Heather family. *Enkianthus*." She was so bad. When Nell's back was turned Angel had read the botanical name on the sign and announced it as if she knew it all along. Really she'd had no idea.

Silently Nell continued walking along the path. Angel caught up with her and saw the vulnerability in her eyes. For a split second Angel considered fessing up to reading the sign, but stopped when she saw how childishly Nell was behaving. "What's wrong?" she said gently, reaching out to touch Nell's hand.

"Nothing," Nell pulled away her hand as if she'd been burned, much to Angel's dismay, her head still full of their kiss. Nell's ears had reddened and she seemed unable to meet Angel's eyes.

"Look, I'm going to see the water garden before we get locked up in here," Angel announced quietly. How could they have gone from a sweet, tender kiss—one she had hoped for and imagined ever since she saw those violet eyes in the garden—to this weirdness so quickly?

Reluctantly Nell got up and followed her. 'I'm sorry," Nell said to Angel's retreating back. "I don't know what came over me back there."

"I do," said Angel, irritation rising. She saw Nell start to disagree and held up her hand to stop. "You can't stand being the one who doesn't know everything. You're insecure and you're intimidated by me. Me, who doesn't have a degree or any kind of training you respect!"

"That's not true. I do respect you. But you're the one who thinks they know everything." Nell was lashing out, trying to protect herself, but the quiver in her voice showed she was floundering. She'd missed her mark.

"I can see it in your eyes," Angel persisted. "You can't imagine that I might know something you don't. Am I right? That I have this body you like to look at but can't reconcile with someone who has brains. I mean, you're like those men who think there are two kinds of women: those you fuck–excuse the French—and then those who are actually worthy of respect." Angel paused, wondering where this had come from. She had said too much and spoiled everything. It was too late. She turned and headed for the water garden leaving Nell standing alone on the path.

When she arrived at the pond Angel realized she was trembling, whether from anger or disappointment she couldn't tell. She tried to reconcile that mouth on hers and the feel of Nell's touch with what had just happened. She sighed and tried to calm herself by focusing on the natural springs flowing over rocks and falling into two beautiful pools surrounded by lush vegetation. Yellow-speared skunk cabbage was growing rampant and glossy lilies floated on the water. When she looked up she saw Nell walking toward her, it looked like Nell was still smarting from their heated exchange. The late afternoon sun glinted off the decal on her old baseball cap and blended with her golden hair as she shuffled along the path that wound between the tranquil pools into a shady dell of ferns and ancient tree stumps.

Angel picked up her pace and met Nell by a waterfall gently cascading into the koi pond. Flashes of orange, grey and white filled the pool as fish darted among the swaying water plants. Bamboo framed the ponds with gold, green and brown canes towering over the other shrubbery.

Nell turned to face her. "I'm sorry," she said, anxiously shredding the garden brochure in her hands. "You're right. I'm insecure. And I'm an idiot."

"You're not, at least not an idiot. We'll keep working on the insecurity part."

A long moment passed.

"Right you have it," said Nell at last, rewarding Angel with the smallest of smiles.

They drove home in awkward silence. Several ponies grazing up on the moor came into view and Nell was glad of the distraction to point them out to Angel.

"You hungry?" Nell said, trying to sound casual. There were a couple of restaurants on the way where hopefully they wouldn't run into people she knew. Not that she feared being seen with Angel, just that it was easier to not have to deal with people talking.

"I can make us dinner," Angel replied. "That's if you don't mind me cooking some pasta and opening a jar of spaghetti sauce and a bag of salad. I've got some nice wine though."

Nell looked at her profile as Angel drove. "You're inviting me for dinner?" She wasn't sure how she felt about that.

"Looks like it. No promises it'll taste any good though." Nell nodded and continued to look out of the window. "I was joking," said Angel. "You're supposed to say 'I'm sure it will taste good.'"

Nell tried to laugh and hoped she wasn't going to make a complete fool of herself. Perhaps a public place would be a safer bet. Too late now. Angel was fumbling around for her house keys, leaning over into the back seat and reaching into her bag.

"What?" Angel inquired, realizing Nell was looking at her. "Did you say something?"

"No, I was just thinking maybe I should..." Nell was losing her nerve.

"You're not going to bail on me now," Angel said quietly.

"Well," Nell started to object, but felt Angel reach over to place a finger on her lips. She was leading Nell up the path both literally and metaphorically. Once inside, she cheerfully showed Nell around the cottage. It was nice. Small and a bit messy, but she'd fixed it up quite well.

"Glad you like it," Angel said. "Here, have a beer." She reached into the fridge and handed Nell a bottle, then poured herself some wine. She leaned against the kitchen counter and took a sip, her eyes on Nell's face. Her hair was loose around her shoulders now and the makeup from earlier in the day had faded. Nell liked her better this way. The pink top was tight around her breasts and she could just see the outline of her nipples under the fabric.

Nell felt herself getting aroused and made an excuse to go to the loo. "Back in a minute," she said, hoping to get herself under control. When she returned Angel was sitting at the kitchen table with a small grey tabby cat on her lap, crooning into its ear. It was kneading her thighs and rubbing its face against her hands "I thought you couldn't have pets?"

"I can't. He's not mine," said Angel, gently rubbing the cat's head. "He lives next door. Just visiting. I love cats—sorry about this kitty," said Angel covering the cat's ears, "but I'm really a dog person. And that little black and white dog today, well, I could have brought him home that's for sure..." She lifted the cat off her lap and got up to wash her hands before getting out the salad.

Nell shook her head at Angel's nerve and reached to help with the salad. "You're a terrible renter," she said jokingly, her mind racing with thoughts about how much Angel would enjoy Gruff. As Nell imagined such a domestic scene in her own kitchen, the two of them happily cooking together with the dog napping by the stove, Angel moved to the fridge and brushed

Nell's shoulders. The touch sent a tingle all the way to Nell's toes and she felt the energy spark between them. Angel's hand lingered on her shoulder and time stood still.

Anticipation of her mouth on Angel's once more, of her hands touching that soft flesh, flooded Nell's brain. She tried to remain composed. It had seemed easier in the woods but here in her cottage there was no limit on what they could do. The thought both excited and mortified her. She knew she was going to make a complete fool of herself and wondered if she should leave before the opportunity arose. "Mmm" was what she heard herself say instead. She shifted her posture against Angel's fingers and continued to grate, glad of having something to do to steady her hands and her nerves.

Nell registered the soft caress but wished she could see Angel's face. When she could stand it no longer she whirled to face her. She looked into Angel's eyes, dark like the deepest part of the ocean and saw Angel's open mouth, tongue between her lips. And then Nell was on her, kissing her hard on the mouth and reaching to cup both breasts in her hands. It was dizzying. She was soft under Nell's hands and smelled like apples. Nell heard her gasp and move toward her. "Is this okay?" asked Nell, searching Angel's face.

"Thought you'd never ask," Angel replied, gently pushing Nell against the counter and kissing her back. As Angel's hands roamed Nell's body, Nell felt liquid desire pool in her hips. Then there was a loud hiss and Nell realized the pasta was boiling all over the stove.

"Shoot," said Angel. "Hang on a minute." She disentangled herself from Nell's arms and grabbed the pan, pouring off some water into the sink. Then the microwave beeped, indicating the spaghetti sauce was ready. "Oh well, night's still young," Angel said cheekily, rearranging her clothes.

Dinner was almost fun. Angel rattled on about this and that. They cleaned their plates, mopping up the sauce with white bread she'd toasted and buttered and sprinkled with garlic powder. "Thanks for helping," Angel said, tipping back the last of her wine. "That was great. We cook a mean plate of spaghetti."

"Loved it," said Nell warmly. "Made with care and eaten with appreciation." It was true. She loved Angel's down-to-earth approach to cooking. "I mean, if you don't have good Italian *ciabatta* dipped in garlic-infused olive oil and laced with black olives, why not just go for the honest sliced bread and garlic salt? Works for me."

Angel looked at Nell doubtfully and then laughed. "I'm trying to figure out if that's the back-handed compliment I think it is."

"No," Nell said earnestly, suddenly horrified that it had come out all wrong. "I meant it. I love the way you cook. And eat."

"Eat? You like a good eater?"

"I do indeed," Nell said seriously. "Camille picked at her food all the time and couldn't eat this or that, or had to take the cheese off everything. It was a nightmare making her food."

"Well, I've got my issues too, as you've no doubt noticed," replied Angel. "I just eat well and then whine about how fat I'm getting. I'd probably do better if I did a bit more picking like your ex and less wolfing down everything in sight." She dabbed at her mouth with the paper serviette and then reached over to touch Nell's hand. It was an intimate gesture and Nell felt the touch reverberate through her body. Immobilized, she watched the curve of Angel's lips and the heaviness of her breasts in her tight top. Nell startled, feeling Angel kneading her fingers and gently massaging her hand.

"So what's our next course?" Angel asked suggestively. "I might have something sweet."

"I bet you do." It came out gruffer than she'd intended but Angel ignored any admonishment and instead got up and came toward Nell, settling herself on her lap and draping an arm around her shoulder. Nell felt the full weight of her and cradled the soft cheek of her bottom. It was a very sensual move and made Nell feel like she was back in high school again with Ramona and Camille. Not that she'd ever got anywhere with Ramona, who was out of her league. Nell was thinking these things as she felt Angel's hands in her hair, her lips on her mouth. Their tongues touched, tasting and gently probing.

They sat entwined, both fully clothed and with Angel on Nell's lap, under the bright fluorescent lights of the kitchen. They kissed and stroked each other's faces, slow, deliberate and exquisite, kissing and kneading, savoring each touch and caress with sweet reverence. Nell was aware of blood pounding in her temples and the room felt hot despite the chilly evening.

Nell could tell Angel was waiting to let her make the next move and wasn't sure she could do it. Truth was she hadn't really been with anyone since Camille and she wasn't sure how she was supposed to act. *Loss follows love.*

It was the story of her life whenever she'd let herself love so completely, so unconditionally. Nell could remember a time when her love for Camille was so tender that all it took was a simple gesture—something like seeing her concentrating with her tongue sticking out—to bring tears to her eyes. And Trevor. Her very own little boy. She would have given anything, including her life, to keep him safe. No, it felt like when things were really good, when she was off her guard or wasn't paying enough attention, something bad would happen. Better not tempt fate again. She wasn't sure she could cope with more loss. As these thoughts sped through her brain, Nell froze, anxiety rising. "You okay?" said Angel, sensing Nell's mood shift. "We don't need to do this."

"I know, it's just—"

"Just what?"

"I'm not used to—"

"It being so easy?" Angel asked flippantly. She looked at Nell long and slow.

Nell met her eyes and then looked away. "No, it's—"

"Against your sense of decorum?" Nell thought she saw Angel's eyes slide to the gold cross hanging at her throat. "Okay, no problem," Angel sighed, slipping off Nell's lap and pulling down her top to cover her bare midriff.

Nell looked away, confused about her feelings. It was true she sometimes wished she wasn't gay—it would be so much easier to live and love if she wasn't. Father Joseph had said as much in his last sermon, which Nell had to admit wasn't exactly about homosexuality but more about his interpretation of family:

more or less the same thing. She also knew these immobilizing thoughts, which made her insecure and got her into trouble like right now with Angel, were about fear of involvement in another relationship. That it would cause her and others more pain. And deep down Nell worried maybe these two things were connected. That it was because she was a lesbian that things never worked out.

"I'm sorry," was all she could say out loud. "This is not about you. I promise."

Angel did not look as if she believed her.

"There are things about me—about my past—you don't know," Nell insisted.

"There are things about me too," Angel said quietly.

Nell didn't know what to say, but stood up and moved the dishes into the sink for something to do to avoid Angel's eyes. "I should go, it's late," came out of her mouth.

"Leave them," said Angel. "Just go. Please."

"Can we do something tomorrow then?" Nell heard herself say. "I could pick you up and we could go down the coast. Play tourist."

Angel paused and looked at Nell quizzically, obviously not sure if she was reading her correctly. "Let's talk in the morning," Angel said finally, following Nell out to the truck.

When they got to the road, Nell saw Angel check her post. Among the junk fliers was a shiny postcard. Bordered with the colors and stripes of the Union Jack with "From London" in multiple fonts, the postcard had a punk rocker with multiple piercings and a weird Mohawk hairdo grimacing into the camera. When Angel turned it over Nell could just make out the large-printed scrawl that filled the card: "Wanted you to be the first to see my new look. Home tomorrow. Dinner? L." *Damn.* To complicate everything it looked like Lucas had not given up on her yet. Did she feel the same way about him? Nell's heart sank and she knew she'd blown it yet once more.

CHAPTER NINE

Angel smudged dark shadow on her lids and a little kohl around her eyes, peering in the mirror to survey her work. Yvonne loved this look and would call it her 'harem face': a terribly politically incorrect comment, but one that always amused them nonetheless. Unlike Kate, who looked like their mother with her blondish hair and light skin, Angel had inherited the buxom dark genes from her Lebanese grandmother. Trust Kate to get lucky and resemble the slender aunts and cousins on her maternal Scottish side. Hardly fair, she would often pun. But as for the smoky-eyed and sultry look she'd got that market cornered.

Time to go. Touch of lipstick, spritz of cologne and she was on her way, grabbing her bag and keys on the way out. Within two minutes Lucas's black BMW drew up to the curb outside the cottage and she was sliding into the passenger seat. It was Friday night and she was claiming the wine and dine rain check. Why not enjoy an outing with Lucas? Angel hoped to forget the evening in the cottage with Nell. It embarrassed her to think about it. She'd tried ignoring Nell at work and the awkwardness between them was palpable. Nell had approached her a couple of times, once quite sweetly, wringing her cap in her hands and pleading. She'd tried to kiss her once too, out in the greenhouse. Angel had really wanted to smile and make it okay again, but something had stopped her. Like being taken over by a familiar dark mood that felt like an old friend. She was in a funk and it was settling into her bones. Rejection was never easy. Better to push someone away than get rejected all over again.

"Mmm, you look good," Lucas said, reaching over to kiss her cheek.

"Ha, flattery will get you everywhere," she said, giving him a peck on the cheek. She dropped her bag by her feet and reached to buckle the seatbelt.

"Who would have thought?" He caught her arm, gently pulled her toward him and gazed into her eyes.

"Thought what?"

"That when I first met you, a little girl of fourteen, you seemed light years away from me. And now you've grown into this amazing woman who…"

"Who…?" Angel prompted, curious about the unspoken.

"Who is smart, great-looking and smells really good."

"Actually I was only thirteen, but who's counting?"

Lucas sniffed her hair and inhaled deeply. "Well, anyway, I've missed you," he declared.

"You did? Now why do I think that's an overstatement?" she murmured, deflecting the compliment and leaning back into the comfortable leather seat.

"I swear," he responded, stroking his chin with delicate fingertips, the other hand on the stick shift. "I thought about you every day." He reached over and patted her leg before continuing. "How about the little bar at East Cove? We can have a drink there first. The view from the restaurant is quite spectacular. Then maybe head down to Port Arrow and have some dinner at the Blue Olive. Italian okay?"

"Italian's great." Angel smiled. Any food was her favorite. She tried this time to rein in her chatter, remembering having heard a French club owner allude to the open, friendly earnestness of Americans. He said they were like naive children. She'd taken this as an insult at the time but the notion stayed with her. Maybe that was one another reason Nell was turned off after the trip to Trefarrow Gardens.

These thoughts filled her mind as the engine surged and they left Cumberland Bay behind. He drove fast and expertly through the countryside, heading west into the setting sun. Angel looked at his hands on the steering wheel as he slowed to navigate a tight turn. They were almost like women's hands: fine, with perfectly manicured nails and certainly more feminine than Nell's. He'd rolled back his shirt cuffs again. Angel had to admit he had a sense of movement about him that was very classy.

Pink-infused streaks of cirrus clouds raced along the horizon as the sun dropped lower in the sky. They rounded a corner and the craggy rocks of East Cove edged out into the sea, creating two steep coves on either side. There was a long promontory with a profusion of gulls circling the farthest reaches of the rocks. She caught sight of a restaurant nestled in a dip on the far side of East Cove and gasped her delight at the view beyond.

"Here we are." Lucas parked the car and helped her out as wind whipped across the parking lot making Angel hold onto the hem of her jacket and tuck her head against the salty gusts. Lucas reached for her arm and guided her along the gravel path toward the bar.

They were greeted and led over to a perfect table overlooking the craggy shoreline with a fabulous view of the thundering waves. Lucas ordered chilled white wine and *hors d'oeuvres* of steamed clams with butter, garlic and parsley. Angel had never really cared for clams, but was a good sport and dipped the crusty bread in the clam sauce. It was pretty good once you got past the gritty texture. And very sexy as appetizers went.

"To Tulip Cottage," Lucas lifted his glass and clinked it against Angel's. They toasted and she took a sip of her wine. His smile was wicked and moved over her like quicksilver. He was wearing a stylish grey suit with a striped turquoise silk tie knotted loosely at the neck. He was definitely very hot if you were into men. At least several women in the restaurant seemed to think so. It was especially amusing to see two young bleached blondes dressed to the nines and propping up the bar even at this early hour, who couldn't take their eyes off him. Angel noticed all this and felt almost happy. It was nice to be on a date again. She had enjoyed the anticipation, the getting ready and feeling sexy and the attention that came with looking good and being with someone who looks good too. She regarded their attractive image in the large plate glass mirror behind their table. As she registered the scent of his cologne she felt the wine going to her head. "So, did you close the deal on Friday?" she asked, trying not to slur her words.

Close the deal?" Lucas looked at her quizzically. "Oh, you mean the clients in London? No." He feigned a miserable look. "I spent hours with them but nothing certain. We'll see." He paused to watch Angel suck clam juice off her fingers. "Hmm," he said, pretending to fan his face.

"What?" Angel feigned innocence. This was like being back at the Cheeky Monkey.

"What you're doing."

She smiled slyly. "You like this?"

"I do. It brings new meaning to the word edible."

"You mean like this?" She licked and pouted and then sucked some more.

"Stop or I'm about to embarrass myself." He leaned across the table and kissed her softly on the mouth. It felt okay.

As she downed the last of her drink, scents and sensations threatened to overwhelm. The smack of sea air and the sweet smell of the wine. Angel stared at Lucas across the table. They had enjoyed a fun day in London, but truthfully seeing Sylvie had been the highlight of the trip and she'd been glad to be back on the train heading home. This felt different, though. Maybe it was the wine, or the stuff with Nell. She'd given in to her attraction and been rejected too many times. It was disappointing and it was humiliating. Angel realized with a start that she felt sexy and desirable again. That was it.

"Sounds like you and Maddie had a fun time at Julia's party," he said, reaching for a piece of bread and expertly dipping it in the clam sauce. He didn't spill a drop. Angel sighed and let the conversation drift to a safer zone, embellishing details about the party. "So you're working with Nell Frank." Lucas interrupted. As he spoke he raised his eyebrows just ever so disparagingly.

"I am."

"You're enjoying it."

"I am." She ignored his look–this was none of his business–and went on to talk about work at the garden center before sharing her progress on the magazine research. When they finished the food and she drained the last of her glass, he waved away her insistence on helping pay the bill and came around the table to help her up, holding her hand and lifting it to his lips. She swayed slightly but was sober enough to hope that he hadn't noticed.

Grateful that Lucas had chosen to drink sparingly, Angel tried to relax once they continued driving along the coast. Her senses were on high alert and even though the alcohol had made her a little foggy, a hundred thoughts flashed through her brain, not the least of which was whether she should give this up now before things got too messy. She tried to imagine having sex with him and could only return to some titillating teenage part of her mind. It was not a mature response and she knew it.

Angel looked out of the window as they approached the small town with its neat houses adorned with bed and breakfast signs swinging on manicured lawns and gift shops and other retail businesses lining the route. She recognized Port Arrow from the day out with Maddie. Soon they pulled up by a narrow building wedged between a flower shop and a dilapidated building advertising yoga and Pilates classes. The restaurant had three tiny tables in front topped with bright umbrellas and planter boxes on each side of the door overflowing with pansies. The hand-painted sign read "The Blue Olive."

A young woman wearing a slinky black dress and an abundance of silver jewelry led them to a table on the enclosed terrace behind the main dining room. Lucas had asked for an outside table and the young woman gestured to a tiny one by the wall. Large heaters warmed the space and lamps glittered from hanging chains. It felt very festive. Port Arrow was a tourist town and the Blue Olive was a popular restaurant for couples looking for a romantic venue even on a weekday night.

"Sparkling water with a slice of lemon, please," said Angel in response to the drink request. No point in pushing her luck. He reached over, lightly brushing her leg, then letting his hand rest on the inside of her bare thigh. All around her couples laughed and flirted or talked together in low tones. She tried to keep things light.

When the food arrived they ate hungrily despite the appetizers less than an hour ago. The aroma of the creamy garlic-laced sauce of her mushroom *parmesa*, penne pasta with a roasted mushroom sauce and sun-dried tomatoes, encircled her in a steamy haze. Lucas had grilled shrimp *caprese* lightly covered with melted cheese. The marinated shrimp nestled in a bed of angel hair pasta with mozzarella, fresh basil and tomatoes. A bottle of *Aldo Conterno Barolo*, which Angel recognized as a premier and expensive Italian wine, duly appeared. All delicious.

As Angel looked up from her meal and met his eyes, Lucas began to speak French in a voice low and sultry. She hesitated for a moment as her brain switched from English. Haltingly at first, she was soon back into the rhythms of the language. The couple at the next table looked over, assuming they were French tourists. The conversation danced. Maybe this would be fun after all. He called her *doux amour*, saying she was the woman of his dreams and then moved on to what he wanted to do with her. This really was naughty. She let the erotic scenario of Lucas making love–ah, *faire l'amour*–to her. It sounded so much better in French and was almost believable.

By the time they ordered dessert, Angel was having a good old time, proud that she could still seduce this handsome man if she wanted to and in French, no less. She let him hold her hand across the table and then heard him suggest a hotel. Time stood still. Angel startled as buzzing filled her ears. She held her breath in the silence of the bubble around them even though the room was noisy and boisterous. She did not say yes, but she also did not say no. Fortunately they were interrupted by the arrival of tiramisu with its dense layers of sweet cheese and coffee and liquor-soaked biscuits. Angel ordered an Irish coffee to buy herself more time and it came thick and black, piping hot with a dollop of whipped cream.

Finally, as the crowd thinned out, Lucas asked for the check and Angel realized the Irish coffee had probably been a bad idea. The room slid about and walking straight suddenly seemed a challenge. She was thankful when they reached the car and she was finally able to lean her head back against the cool leather seat. No sooner had she closed her eyes than lights pierced the darkness and shook her awake. A hotel. *Now what?* Angel looked out into the lights and realized with relief that they were in her driveway. She'd slept all the way home. *Phew! Close call.*

* * *

It was still sunny in the yard, although just past closing time and the place was deserted. Angel had taken off her sweatshirt and was working in her tank top, a smear of sweat glistening on her brow. It was all wrong. She had woken with a thick head, embarrassed about the evening with Lucas. Now that made two evenings to be embarrassed about. It took the clear light of day to realize it. That and the fact she needed a therapist.

"You want some water?" Angel startled and realized Nell was standing over her, frowning, her blue eyes narrowed against the glare.

"Thanks," Angel said reaching for the drink. "Don't mind if I do."

Nell nodded and pointed to the plants Angel was arranging into hanging baskets. "You're good at that. Nice colors and texture."

"Hmm." Angel continued to jam the petunias into the basket. "If you say so." Her irritation grew. It was hot in the yard and she felt herself getting increasingly short-tempered. A long moment passed and neither of them spoke. Angel finished the basket and glanced up to see Nell still there, her mouth set in a grim line. Angel tried not to remember the memory of their kisses that seemed now like a lifetime ago.

"Look, let's clear the air for God's sake," Angel said at last, sitting back on her heels and returning Nell's blue gaze through outstretched fingers shaded against the sun. "I'm sorry if you think I came on to you. My mistake. Let's forget it so we can work together." She'd thought about going back to her old arrangement sponging off Kate and telling everyone in her life to go to hell. But it was an issue of pride. She'd finish what she started. And there was only a month or so left now.

"No, listen," Nell murmured. One piece of hair stuck straight up from where she'd taken off her hat. Angel stifled a desire to reach over and pat it down and instead wiped her hand across her own cheek, leaving what she knew was a small trace of dirt.

Nell caught the gesture and leaned in to wipe it away. Their eyes locked and Angel took Nell's hand before it reached her face. "I said forget it," she insisted, blocking Nell's touch.

Nell hesitated before she spoke. "I didn't turn you down because I don't find you attractive or because I didn't want more…" Her voice faltered and she wrung the cap one more time and put it back over her unruly hair. "Quite the opposite." She chewed on her bottom lip and rubbed her chin. It was evident in her face and in her posture that saying these words was incredibly hard for her. "I'm scared if you must know and I'm not sure about…" Nell paused and kicked at the gravel in the yard, "your intentions."

"Intentions?" Angel pulled her hair back into a ponytail, piling it up on top of her head with a rubber band as she considered the word. "And just what do you mean by that?" She stepped toward Nell and looked into her face. She was so close she could see the vulnerability in Nell's eyes. *Intentions!*

"I didn't mean it like that." Nell looked miserable and moved away from her, casting around for something else to say. Just as Angel thought Nell was about to retreat to her office she spun back around and faced Angel one more time. "I'm scared Angel. I usually screw things up and bring everyone down with me."

Angel stared into Nell's blue eyes and saw her distress. Her heart lurched and she remembered the tragedy of Nell's son and how her relationship ended. The irritation started to subside. "It doesn't have to be that way. We just take it a day at a time. We're consenting adults. We keep the lines of communication open, and we enjoy each other. It's as simple as that."

"And Lucas?" Nell took a swig of water and wiped her mouth on the back of her arm. "What about him? Or other blokes," she added quietly.

"Oh." Now Angel understood. The old switch-hitter thing, so to speak. "Look," she insisted feeling suddenly tired, "the fact that I went out with Lucas once doesn't make me untrustworthy or a sex addict." She watched Nell squirm. "I don't love women any less because I could date men, you know."

"I know that—" said Nell grudgingly.

"Plus," interrupted Angel, "we didn't screw if that's what you're thinking."

Nell flinched and looked away.

"What?" exclaimed Angel. Nell was so adorably prudish. Angel raised her eyebrows at Nell, hating to admit that she was enjoying seeing Nell shocked. "What's wrong with you and sex?"

"Well, I mean," Nell mumbled, "I just…I think there's lots of things about sex these days that causes problems. And that's not just because my church says so," she added after a pause.

"Like what?" Angel asked, leaning closer. "What kinds of problems?"

"Sex without love, for a start. I mean when two people come together and give equally, lovingly, then that's what we call noble or worthy. It's good. But just doing it without that intent, I'd have to say that's a problem. Some people call it a grave sin, but for me, it just feels wrong and kind of dirty, you know? That's what I meant by intentions."

"Okay," said Angel, unsure what Nell was getting at, but nevertheless intrigued. "And then what about *your* intentions? What about lust on your part or doesn't that count?"

Clearly embarrassed, Nell looked down at her feet, and scuffed at a rock amongst the pebbles in the yard. The question hung in the air. "I like you, Angel, really like you." A blush rose above her collar. "I don't think it is just lust, if you know what I mean."

Angel hesitated, unsure of her next move. Did Nell mean what Angel thought she meant? That maybe she was in love with her? As she looked into Nell's face and contemplated this, Angel realized with a start the irony of her name. If Nell really knew her and her past, she *would* see her as the fallen angel. Someone who had freely chosen sin. Her past would be unforgivable because of her moral failings. And then Nell's intentions would change. The thought made her catch her breath and a sharp pain pierced her heart.

"I hadn't noticed you being all that interested when it came right down to it," Angel said instead, trying to hide the feelings crowding her mind. "I thought maybe you preferred thin women," she said, unconsciously sucking in her tummy. "Or women who resembled you and didn't have a last name like Khoury."

"Angel, don't say that. First, you are, well, I think you're the most gorgeous woman I've ever met. How can you say that about yourself and then assume I'm not interested? And second, yes, you scared me at first because you're so...dark... but not because I didn't like that or thought it made you less of a person. Honestly. Our differences made me feel vulnerable and uncertain because they triggered all my fears about the unknown. It was never about you. They're my insecurities, right? I thought we settled that at Trefarrow the other day." Nell laughed for full effect and reached for Angel's hand.

Relief flooded Angel's face at Nell's words and sweet gesture. The air sparked between them.

"Well Ms. Frank," she said at last, "I'm listening but I have to say you're still giving me some mightily mixed messages." She tried to keep it light by pushing Nell playfully, but Nell caught her hand and brought it to her lips. Angel looked into the violet depths of Nell's eyes and held her penetrating stare.

"I just have one message for you, Ms. Khoury," said Nell shyly, gingerly putting her arms around Angel and pulling her so close she was talking into her hair. "I'm crazy for you, but I'm worried."

"What could you possibly be worried about?"

"Well, you and me, we're like what they call chalk and cheese."

"And what am I? The chalk or the cheese?"

"Oh, definitely the cheese," Nell exclaimed, laughing as if it was the most obvious thing on earth "You're like the richest, most decadent cheese ever. Maybe gorgonzola."

"That's stinky!"

"But good, really good." Color rose in Nell's face again. "I'm telling you, it's my problem,' she said finally. "The feelings I get about you are what worry me. The last time I felt like this it didn't end well."

"I'm so, so sorry," declared Angel looking deep into Nell's eyes. "We can never control the future. All we can do is live with hope and love. It's all anyone can ever do."

"I know you're right," said Nell blinking back tears and accepting Angel's hug.

They stood entwined for a long moment.

"Plus," insisted Nell, kissing the top of Angel's head, "whenever I see you all I really want to do is rip off your clothes. I think Father Joseph might see that as a sin!"

"Oh great," laughed Angel. "You do know that everyone gets like that, right? Even Father Joseph himself, I bet! I look at you in those work jeans and the word 'depravity' comes to mind." Nell blushed again. "And voracity," Angel continued. "Debauchery, wantonness and carnality. How's that for an earful?"

"Okay, I believe you," Nell said, laughing, "although I'm not so sure about the Father Joseph bit. But thanks for normalizing it for me anyway."

"You're welcome." Angel said impishly, trying to get a rise. She watched the smile fade from Nell's face. Nell would not meet her eyes.

"What else scares you?" said Angel after a while. Nell looked off into the distance and again refused to meet Angel's gaze. "Come on, tell me."

"If I'm being completely honest I don't want you to be shagging Lucas Therot. And it's not just because he's a man, or that I hate the guy or that I think it's a mortal sin to show lust. I guess I want you all to myself. There I said it." Nell hesitated, full of embarrassment. "Maybe I've said too much."

"No you haven't. It's okay," said Angel, wanting so badly to touch her. "Believe me, 'shagging' Lucas, as you so delicately put it, is the farthest thing from my mind. But how about if I shag another woman?"

"Angel, stop. You know what I mean. I really want you to myself."

A long moment passed. A dog barked in the distance and cars rumbled by on the road. "Oh Nell," said Angel easily, "I want you too. I'm not interested in shagging anyone but you." She laughed and Nell did too. "And, while we're being honest I'll tell you I'm not used to being turned down." She gently stroked Nell's hand, letting her fingers circle her knuckles and slip under her wrist. "I'm an insecure basket case. There I said it too."

"Well now we know where we stand," grinned Nell, leaning over and cautiously kissing Angel's mouth. "I couldn't turn you down now to save my life." They sat companionably on a bench by the back greenhouse, hand in hand and finished their drinks. It was getting late.

"One more thing," said Angel eventually. She paused, teetering on the brink of telling Nell about past, the dancing part. She feared rejection, but hated the dishonesty of it all.

"Oh, no! Are you going to tell me you were a bigamist in a former life that specialized in the mortal sin of fornication?" said Nell playfully, pulling Angel close.

"No." Angel faltered. She was losing her nerve. She stiffened and grew silent, letting Nell go on about the variety of grave sins that could excommunicate a saint. The sun sank below the horizon and she leaned against Nell's chest, knowing in her heart of hearts that she couldn't tell her. Not right now.

"Sorry, love. What were you going to say?" Nell inquired.

"I was thinking," she replied, knowing she was committing the sin of omission despite it being heartfelt, "that you and me are okay because we do have feelings...I mean, it is good what we have. Our intentions, that is."

Nell smiled then and squeezed her hand. "I know," she said simply. "That's what I was trying to say.

"You're looking good," Nell said after a while, glancing at Angel sideways with a mischievous smile on her face.

"I am? You like the sloppy garden center look?"

"I do, it's my favorite." Nell gave her another lopsided grin. "Actually as I said before it's imagining you out of those clothes that's really my favorite."

"Hmm, is that so? Shall we get out of here Ms. Frank?"

"We shall," said Nell, acting all proper. "Where shall we go?"

"How about the beach? You and me on a blanket, under the stars?"

"Now you're talking, Ms. Khoury."

They tottered, arms around each other, out to Nell's truck and then headed toward a secluded beach north of the village. They stopped by the store to buy soft drinks and chocolate, managing to avoid seeing anyone they knew. Soon they were back on the road.

Angel leaned against Nell in the cab of the pickup, her hand resting on the inside of Nell's thigh. She looked at Nell's strong profile, thrilled with anticipation, then reached out and touched the curve of her jaw, gently brushing her mouth. Nell's lips, pursed together in concentration as they traveled the winding road, opened as her fingers caressed them. When Nell caught her finger in her mouth and kissed it back, Angel left it there. She felt Nell suck slightly and smiled into the darkness of the truck. She steadied her breathing and savored the sexually charged air between them.

* * *

The beach was tiny and private, Nell's favorite and one she didn't share with many people. Silvery moonlight streamed across the ocean as small breaking waves moved rhythmically along the sand. It was a calm night and from the overlook on the lane where they left the truck, the sea looked like polished glass. Nell carried blankets and Angel had the bag with the drinks and snacks. Nell was suddenly anxious knowing they were going to the beach and what they'd most likely end up doing. It was the acknowledgment that they were going to have sex that made her break out in a cold sweat. Father Joseph's face flashed into her mind and Nell pushed it away.

These thoughts filled Nell's mind as she followed Angel's short sexy body through coarse dune grass that wound down through a sea of swaying fronds. Nell liked being behind her watching her bum sway and her ponytail bob up and down to the rhythm of her stride. She loved Angel's soft thighs and her full breasts. Nell felt the anxiety swell at the thought of those breasts, but made herself breathe and concentrated on Angel's bum moving in the dusky light instead.

After about five minutes the path emptied out onto a patch of pebbled beach and beyond that a broad sliver of sand thrown up by the sea. It wasn't quite high tide and they were able to find a soft dry spot sheltered by the bluff that looked out across the waves. The seclusion and silence of the place welled up around them. "Nirvana," said Angel, kicking off her shoes and smiling in wonder at the rising moon. The distant pitch and tumble of the ocean filled the air.

Nell loved this beach. It was magical. "Sit, I'm lonely," she said to Angel, patting the spot next to her on the blanket. Nell breathed deeply and closed her eyes, inhaling the wonderful tangy smell of sea, salt and Angel. The moon was rising rapidly and cast a silver beam across the waves as they gently rumbled onto the tiny beach. She started to feel better, lulled by the soothing sound of waves, her arms around Angel as they lay together on the blanket. As she relaxed into the calming rhythm, she lost track of where her body ended and Angel's began. They lay like this, listening to the waves and the beating of each other's hearts, until a milky smear of stars appeared. It was so peaceful Nell wished they could just stay like this forever. Uncomplicated. Easy.

"You asleep?" Nell was the first to stir, turning so she was looking down into Angel's face.

"Almost," Angel sighed.

"I thought you were," Nell sighed, touching Angel's closed eyelids with her fingertips. "Can I kiss you?" Stars had emerged one by one in the brightening sky and the moon shone above them. She could see Angel's profile in the moonlight and turned to stroke her face, letting her fingers trace Angel's jaw.

"Please, I'd like that," said Angel. Her eyes were still closed and she stifled a small giggle. Nell hesitated, unsure of herself and suddenly fearful. "No," insisted Angel, opening her eyes and taking Nell's face in her hands. "I mean I'd like that very much." She planted sweet kisses all along Nell's jaw and ended with one long, sloppy one on her lips. "There," she exclaimed, "I kissed you first. Okay?"

"Okay," said Nell bashfully.

After the kiss, Angel rolled Nell over and unbuttoned her shirt. Slowly Angel peeled it off and tossed it behind them and then reached inside Nell's bra and took her breasts in her hands. Nell gasped and responded by pulling the sweatshirt over Angel's head and unhooking her bra, kissing the warm skin on her shoulders. Nell's eyes grew wide as she saw Angel's nipples harden. When Angel pressed herself against Nell's chest, Nell felt their bodies touch in an agonizing tingle that electrified in one delicious sensation. She melted into Angel's touch.

"You're the perfect combination of beauty and brains," Nell said, admiring Angel's body and tracing hot kisses along the inside of her arms.

"Which do you prefer?" Angel asked coyly, moving to nibble Nell's ear and sliding her hands up and down her spine. It felt so deliciously good.

"Ah, that's a trick question," said Nell. "I know you thought I couldn't handle both in a woman, but I'm telling you I'm liking it very much. The combination, that is."

"No, choose," insisted Angel cheekily.

"Okay, your brains, of course," Nell replied. "Though the beauty is a nice added bonus."

Angel laughed then. "Right answer," she giggled. "And you've got a good combination going yourself." She turned to face Nell with parted lips. She tasted so sweet and hot at the same time.

They lay like this until Nell pulled away and gazed at Angel again. Her nipples were puckered now, waiting for Nell's attention. Nell held back and instead fluttered fingertips over Angel's throat and neck, feeling Angel moan and writhe beneath her. Aroused Nell reached to nibble Angel's earlobes, kissing her soft shoulders. Then, slowly, she took a nipple in her mouth, circling and sucking until desire, hot and thick, pooled in her groin. Angel arched her back as Nell brushed her thumb back and forth across the nipple several times and then took it in her mouth, rolling it beneath her tongue. It excited her to hear Angel cry loudly into the night.

Nell tried to still the tremors running through her, knowing she needed to relax, to try and breathe and listen to the ebb and flow of the waves. Angel caught Nell's mood and slowly fondled her through her jeans, smiling lazily. Time seemed to stand still. Eventually she unzipped Nell's jeans and, fiddling with her belt, managed to pull Nell's jeans over her hips, laughing as they caught at her ankles. Together they pulled them off. Then Angel touched her again through her panties, slowly running her hand through the dampness that lingered there. Nell heard herself groan and arched toward Angel's hand.

"Is that okay?" Angel asked tentatively as her fingers probed inside Nell's underwear.

"Oh," was all Nell could reply, glad of the darkness to hide her blush as she pressed herself against Angel's fingers.

"All right, I guess it is," whispered Angel, pulling off Nell's panties and delicately circling Nell's clitoris with her thumb while sliding a finger inside her. Nell groaned again and sensed Angel's smile. It felt so good. Angel had two fingers inside her now, sliding them in and out while gently tweaking her clitoris. It was so deliciously exquisite.

"Whoa," Nell said at last, desperation edging her voice. Maybe she should stop, but oh my God, if was so good. She felt blood pumping through her body and let her head loll back as Angel kissed her face and gently rubbed her until she was swollen and hot.

She thought she might come and felt panicked, but then sweet relief. Angel gave her one more caress and then looked into her eyes. "Too much?"

"Maybe," Nell said. "Okay if we slow down a bit? I'd like this to last."

"Of course. Here, I'm all yours. What do you want to do?" Angel lay back on the blanket, her head propped on her fist looking at Nell. She was the sexiest thing Nell had ever seen and she desperately wanted to see and touch the rest of her body. Slowly Nell reached out to Angel, undressing that luscious body. Angel read her mind, parting her thighs in invitation. Nell felt the slickness. Angel was hot and ever so wet. She struggled to contain her own arousal as Angel spread her legs wider still. Nell thought she might explode seeing Angel lying there, naked under the moon, ready for the taking.

Nell's eyes widened as Angel's legs encircled her waist, her sex open in front of Nell's eyes. Slowly and deliberately Nell traced her finger along the top of Angel's thigh, letting it linger in Angel's soft, damp folds. When Angel gasped and moved against her hand, Nell brushed the swollen clitoris until Angel trembled and tightened, a deep sigh catching in her throat. When Angel cried out, her body trembling, Nell held her breath to absorb every note of pleasure. She wanted to remember this moment forever.

As they lay together, Nell took her in her arms and felt Angel's eyelashes against her skin. Then her mouth was on Angel's again as she rolled her so Angel was on top. They were off the blanket now on the edge of the sand where waves spilled onto the beach. Nell caught her breath as soft wet sand hit her back, the chill receding as they sought each other's mouths, lost in the heat of their desire.

Sand covered their bodies but it didn't matter. The cold stung and made them cling together for warmth, each searching for the other's mouth. Damp curls, tangled in wind and sand, tumbled down on Nell's shoulders and chest. At some point Nell lost track of time again. All she knew was the sounds of Angel's desire, her cries and her sweet release. At the sound, Nell felt waves of intense pleasure rippling through her and thought she might die right there on the beach in the moonlight. Their bodies quivered, locked in a relentless rhythm as the air pulsed with their fierce longing for each other. They came together, exquisite waves of release in tune with the sea around them.

"Oh my." Angel sighed and looked up into the broad canopy above them. Stars twinkled and a bright planet blazed overhead. They stretched out together, feeling the flow of the ocean until their bodies grew soft and quiet. "That was pretty good," she said quietly.

"You could say that." Nell didn't know what to feel. It was crazy. *Had this really happened?* "Here," she said at last. "Let's move so we can lean against the rocks." Angel followed her lead, teeth chattering as she scrambled over toward the cliff face. "Brr, it's getting cold. Grab this," Nell said, tossing Angel a blanket. They wound the fleece around their damp bodies and rocked together until the fuzzy warmth stilled their shivering.

"Let's get you home," Nell said suddenly, rubbing Angel's shoulders to try and warm her. "It might stop us both getting double pneumonia." She could see that Angel was unable to stop shaking. They dressed, gathered their things and shuffled back along the path to the truck, arms around each other, blankets trailing in the sand.

When they arrived home, Nell watched Angel sleepily take in the large double doors and twin pillars. Then, as they came to a stop, she caught sight of the glittering sea behind the house and gasped. "Amazing house."

"Glad you like it." It always had this effect on people, especially in the daytime. But the moonlight on the ocean was spectacular. Nell looked out over the shining waves and suddenly felt the enormity of what they'd done. Maybe everything was going too fast. But Angel was already climbing out of the truck and mounting the stairs. Then she was leaning against Nell as they crossed the threshold and turned on the kitchen lights. Angel chose a stool by the counter and exclaimed as Gruff bounded up with a wet nose and a wagging tail. Was Angel really sitting on a stool in her kitchen in the middle of the night and smiling at Gruff?

"Oh, sweet dog," cooed Angel, kneeling to stroke Nell's old buddy. "I've seen you before, I think. Wasn't he in the truck with you one time when you pretended not to see me—"

"Oh don't remind me," interrupted Nell. "Listen, he can talk." The dog sat down obediently and looked at Nell, his tail wagging madly.

"No, speak," said Nell, laughing.

"He's shy," cooed Angel, patting his head. "I like you." Gruff sat obediently and looked lovingly up into her face. "Speak," she said.

"Woof," he barked on cue. "Woof, woof," he continued, running circles around the kitchen.

"Yeh!" exclaimed Angel. "See? Good boy. So how did he get the name Gruff, as he seems anything but?"

Sadness clouded Nell's eyes. "My son Trevor named him." The memory seared through Nell like a knife.

Angel stopped petting the dog and met her eyes. "Oh Nell, I'm so sorry," she said. "I can't imagine…"

"I know," Nell said dejectedly, trying to smile. "Here, want some tea? Or something stronger?"

"Tea, please and then what I'd really like is a hot shower," Angel replied. "With you if that's possible," she added, giving Nell a soft, sleepy smile.

"I think we can arrange that," Nell responded, her heart lurching madly.

"Now that shower," Angel said as they trooped back into the kitchen.

"Yes, your royal highness," responded Nell, leading her up the stairs to the bathroom. "Hope it's not too messy. The bathroom, that is."

"Hey, messy is my middle name, fortunately," Angel replied, panting in Nell's ear as they bounded up the steps. Nell remembered the comment about Angel wanting to mess up Lucas Therot's place just for the hell of it and managed a smile. Yes, it was going to be okay.

"Mmm, this feels so great," exclaimed Angel as the hot water cascaded over her gorgeous body. Nell agreed, feeling the warmth seep into her bones. They gently soaped each other and watched the sand flow from their skin, leaving small gritty piles in the bottom of the shower. Nell nipped at Angel's shoulder under the water and heard her squeal. Yes, it really was going to be okay.

In bed Nell could hardly believe what was happening. What *had* happened. Entwined and propped against pillows, they drank tea and looked up through the skylight at the moon and stars blazoned in the night sky. Angel still smelled like sea and salt and flowery shampoo. Nell was excruciatingly conscious of the fact this woman was naked in her bed. Completely naked. She reached to kiss her and let the weight of Angel's breasts rest in her hands. They were heavy and incredibly soft, the nipples flushed dark. Nell lowered her head, closed her hungry mouth around the nipple and sucked. She felt it harden again, puckering under her tongue.

Nell's hand slipped between Angel's thighs and felt the dampness. "You want to make love again?" she asked, marveling at Angel's responsiveness. When Angel moaned and shook her head, Nell saw she was starting to fall asleep. Make love? She realized with a shock the enormity of the phrase. Intentions, indeed.

CHAPTER TEN

"Yes," exclaimed Angel, pumping the air with her fist. "I got it!" She slipped the phone back into her purse with a flourish and jumped up from the table, doing a happy hula dance as Maddie looked on, a big grin on her face. The editors at *Country Escapes* were so impressed with Angel's work they had just offered a second assignment for another three months. Angel had submitted ahead of schedule and they especially liked the photos.

"You got it, you got it," shouted Julia, doing circles around the table and tripping over the neighbor's cat who had taken up permanent residence at Angel's cottage. Pigtails bobbing, Julia knocked over a basket of dirty laundry by the door.

"Julia, sit," said Maddie sternly. "Now," she added as Julia paused and decided whether to mind her mother.

"Sorry," said Angel. "I'm a bad influence aren't I?"

"No," exclaimed Julia, climbing back into her chair and reaching to give Angel a kiss. "We love you. You're fun." She gave a little pout and sucked on her straw. "More fun than mum anyway," she murmured, slyly looking at her mother and hoping for a rise.

"That's enough Julia," said Maddie. "No one is impressed when you talk like that, not even Angel."

"Right young lady, especially me." Angel gave Julia a wink and pushed the rest of the cookie at her. "Here," she said, "finish this cookie and please be nice to your mum."

"That's a biscuit," laughed Julia. "It's not a cookie."

"I know," said Angel, "whatever it is, just do me a favor and finish it. I'm having problems zipping up my jeans." Julia giggled and sidled away with her bounty. Soon she was playing with Lego on the living room floor. "She's something else," said Angel, smiling over at Julia. "I'm envious."

"Six going on sixteen if you ask me," replied Maddie, looking at her friend. "Envious? What are you envious of?"

"You. Motherhood. You know, the old biological clock and all that." Angel gave Maddie a goofy smile. "Well, one day at a time. I got the new assignment, so that's good. And Nell will be glad I think." That was an understatement. They had spent the last two weeks together in one giddy round of work, drinking and playing darts at the Three Ships and bed. Lots of bed. Mostly at Nell's place but they'd had their share of fun in almost all the rooms and on various surfaces in her cottage too. Angel wasn't sure when she had felt quite so blissful.

"Glad? She'll be ecstatic." Maddie poked Angel playfully as she spoke. "She's crazy about you and now you'll have more time together to…" Maddie paused and took a sip of tea before continuing. "Now you'll have time to figure out what you two want to do."

"What we want to do?" Angel raised her eyebrows.

"Yes, your future," said Maddie solemnly. "Together, love, those babies you're so envious about."

"Well, we'll have to see," said Angel, doubtfully. She poured more water in the teapot and leaned back in her chair. "She is very sweet and I'm definitely falling for her charms—"

"Don't say I didn't tell you so."

Angel grinned at her friend, but then her face got serious. "She definitely doesn't want children, so I'm not sure about the babies bit."

"*Says* she doesn't want children," corrected Maddie. "That woman doesn't know what she wants.

"And Camille is bugging her almost every day so she's having lots of reminders about that awful mess."

"No surprise."

"And I hate to say, but it's driving me crazy, her phoning and texting Nell all the time." Angel poured herself another cup of tea and added sweetener. "I mean sometimes it's financial stuff that seems like it really needs sorting out, but most of the time it's stupid things like her car won't start or she needs a light bulb screwed in."

"You're making that up?"

"Yes, a bit." Angel laughed half-heartedly, trying to see the humor in it. "At least the light bulb part. But really, she's calling or texting every day."

"You're jealous." Maddie hit the nail on the head. "That's reasonable. I would be too."

"I suppose so. But I don't like myself like this." Angel thought how she'd been disparaging of Camille during a conversation with Nell the other evening. Her comment was spiteful, even if it was true. Jealousy rearing its ugly head.

"Camille's always been high maintenance," said Maddie reassuringly. "She sensed Nell was moving on and she was probably having trouble with that. We all know women like that," she added, "men too actually. It's probably part of the human condition. Hopefully she'll soon find someone else to annoy, you never know. But how's Nell handling it?"

"Oh, she's being very Nell about it: stoic and trying to do the right thing."

"Well she got the worst of both worlds," said Maddie thoughtfully. "She thought of herself as married even though it wasn't legal then. And now she goes and beats herself up when the marriage fails because it's a sin."

"Yes exactly. But I'm trying to be tolerant about the whole religion thing," declared Angel. "Especially once I figured her out." It was true. Over the last couple of months Angel had realized Nell had two things going on: her internalized homophobia fueled by the community at St. Theresa's, and her fears about the future, especially when love was involved. Love meant danger and made her feel vulnerable. Really it came down to Nell not loving herself enough to have the confidence to feel that she could love others and deserved to be loved. These two things were connected and they were complicated. But things were looking up. "Did I tell you I've been going to mass with her these past few weeks?"

"Good for you."

"Yes, and I refuse to let them judge us. My plan is to win them all over—especially Father Joseph—with pure kindness and to act as if I think they're completely accepting of our relationship." Angel smiled sweetly to underscore the point.

"And how's that going?" asked Maddie doubtfully.

"Actually great," insisted Angel. "It's hard for them to behave otherwise under the circumstances. They act as if accepting us was their idea all along."

"No way!"

"Seriously. You wouldn't believe it. They even invited me to help run the youth group."

"No Kidding. Nell must be relieved...But that reminds me..." Maddie's voice trailed off and Angel wondered what was coming. "Have you told her about, you know, your dancing and all that?"

Angel screwed up her face and looked out the window. There was no avoiding the question. "No, I've come so close a couple of times but never quite had the right moment." She stirred her tea and licked the spoon. "It's no big deal. I keep forgetting, actually."

"Angel," Maddie looked at her knowingly, "if it was no big deal you'd have already talked about it."

"Yes, I suppose you're right," she admitted grudgingly. "I guess I just like the way things are going. I don't want to rock the boat. Plus," she shrugged and tapped her fingernails against the tabletop, "she's not the exotic dancer support club kind of girlfriend."

"Well that's true, but you might be surprised."

"I know you're right, but I'm scared how she'll take it. You know how judgmental she gets." Angel put down her drink and looked directly at Maddie before she continued. "I didn't tell you this, but the other day we were driving out toward Truro and she got her knickers in a twist over a new strip club that was going up over by the old Marks and Spencer's building."

"Oh dear."

"Yes, there was a big sign, you know, with triple X, live girls kind of thing. She was so disparaging and called it disgusting. There was such contempt in her voice. She said next there'd be drug deals going down and the world as we know it would end. Well, that's a slight exaggeration."

"Oh dear—"

"So I told her not to be ridiculous, that they were strippers for goodness sake, not drug dealers. And then her exact words were 'Bloody hell, Angel, I didn't realize you cared so much.' She looked at me like I was crazy."

"Oh," Maddie repeated. "I see what you mean. But still, you don't want her to think you're holding some secret that's more important than it really is." Angel knew in her heart of hearts that Maddie was right. She did need to tell Nell even if Nell took it badly. It was nothing to be ashamed of.

"So how's work?" said Maddie, changing the subject.

Angel took a deep breath, glad to have the conversation on safer ground. "It's doing all right, all things considered. Nell checked the books and we're okay. Of course June is always the busiest, but this month's takings are more than last year and it isn't over yet."

"Hmm, 'we,'" said Maddie, noticing Angel's choice of pronouns. "Nice."

Angel waved away the comment before continuing. "Actually," she paused, gauging Maddie's reaction, fearful that this good fortune might depress her given Maddie's dodgy financial predicament with the inn. "We've been talking about working together. A joint venture. I have this idea that's quite exciting really—"

"What?" interrupted Maddie. Always perceptive, she had noticed the change in Angel's tone.

Angel took a deep breath and fidgeted with her toast before continuing. She realized these plans were half-baked and felt suddenly self-conscious, but barreled on anyway. "Sylvie said something on the phone the other night that resonated with me. She said how I'd changed for the better since I was working with plants again. That it was a crime to ignore my calling. Rather melodramatic, you know Sylvie, but sweet."

Maddie nodded emphatically. "And she's right."

"Thanks," said Angel, reassured. "So I found this link for a new business in south London doing garden design for small urban spaces. It's really interesting looking at their business and what services they offer. Great website. I realized that we could do something like that and I'd be interested to hear what you think,"

"We?"

"Well yes, me and Nell."

"Ah, I like the sound of that."

"It's just a business venture."

"If you say so." Maddie looked smug.

"I was having trouble sleeping the other night—"

"I bet you were."

"Maddie will you focus!" exclaimed Angel. "Or I won't tell you my idea." She shook her head playfully before continuing. "So I was lying there and kept getting up and writing notes so I wouldn't forget things. Lots of ideas kept popping into my head."

"Like what?"

"Like a consulting business doing online custom landscape design, maybe specializing in cottage gardens or small urban spaces. I could do 'webinars' or online seminars with a 'how-to' focus on lots of stuff like, you know, terracing sloping gardens or building a backyard pond or growing espaliers—"

"What's that?"

"Oh, fruit trees you grow flat against a wall rather than letting them grow into a regular tree."

"Oh," said Maddie doubtfully. "Go on."

"What do you think? I even came up with a name. Clarity Designs."

"I like it! Great name. What does Nell think?"

"She likes it too, but she's cautious. That's Nell, of course."

"She doesn't take to change easily."

"Right, but she can see the merit in it," said Angel, finishing her toast. "And she likes to think I need her expertise of course."

"Do you?"

"What do you think?" giggled Angel. "Shit, what do I know? I'm just the crazy, risk-taking idea-woman."

"Well that's a good start."

"Until I get to the business plan bit where I get out of my depth and you and Nell come in," Angel admitted. "I'm good with the vision and pretty useless with the nuts and bolts of making any money. Have no idea how to run an actual business."

"I might not be the best person to help you with that."

"Are things okay?"

Maddie looked into her cup and shook her head. "Bloody awful actually. I mean Bill is such a bollocks of a brother." Angel exploded with laughter, but gestured between snorts for Maddie to continue.

"You okay? Where was I?"

"Your bollocks of a brother." Angel snorted again.

"Right, I'm dipping into my inheritance to pay the mortgage on the inn every month. Okay for now, but not sustainable in the long run. Bill has already ripped through his money with all his stupid schemes and drinking and all." She looked over at Julia to make sure she was out of earshot before continuing. "He's such an idiot and his wife's totally under his thumb. I worry about her because Bill drinks so much and he's got such anger management issues. And then there's Justin to think about too, of course."

Angel grew serious again recalling the chubby little boy and wondered how he was doing. She remembered Nell's kindness and thought how difficult it must be to have a parent like Bill. Maddie read her mind. "Much be awful having Bill for a father, poor little mite." She shook her head slowly and started packing up Julia's stuff. "Two minutes," she said to her daughter. "We're almost ready to leave, love, okay?"

"No."

"Yes Julia," responded Maddie. "Little sod," she whispered, rolling her eyes before turning to Angel again. "But your idea," she said to Angel, "is the best. I love it."

"Thanks and if it doesn't work out, me and Nell, I mean, I can do this from anywhere."

"It'll work out," insisted Maddie.

"We'll see," said Angel, getting up and hugging her friend. "As I said before, one day at a time."

They gathered up the rest of the gear and herded Julia out to the car. "Better get home and bring the washing in," said Maddie, looking at the darkening sky as a few rain drops started to fall. "And then I need to get to work."

No sooner had Maddie and Julia left and Angel set to sorting the laundry than she heard Nell's voice by the backdoor. She turned and there was Nell smiling sheepishly at her.

"I missed you," she was saying.

"But you just saw me this morning," laughed Angel, kissing her full on the lips.

"I know. I can't get enough of you. I just wanted to see you here in this domestic bliss."

Angel laughed, picking up a stray sock from the floor and tossing it in the washing machine. "Really? Why do I think you had something else planned?"

"I have no idea. A dirty mind, most likely." Nell's eyes darkened as she stroked Angel's hair.

Angel laughed and carefully added detergent to the washer. As she reached to put the basket back on the floor Nell moved behind her, tugging the t-shirt from her sweatpants and kneading the skin around her waist. "Mmm, that feels good," Angel said approvingly as Nell lifted her shirt and kissed the length of her back. Angel leaned over the washing machine as Nell pulled her sweatpants down around her hips and her shirt up to her shoulders. Angel felt soft kisses along her spine and shivered with anticipation, moaning at the sweet pleasure of it all.

They looked at the clock. Barely enough time. "Better be a quick one," said Nell, turning Angel to face her, knowing they were both wet and eager.

"All right, if you insist," Angel crooned. "Fastest fuck ever, excuse my French."

"What? You are such a bad influence on me," Nell quipped as Angel pulled down her jeans and reached inside her panties. As Angel's fingers touched the soft curls in Nell's groin, she heard moans, not knowing if they were Nell's or her own. Nell was incredibly wet and her clitoris throbbed as Angel slipped her fingers inside. Angel felt Nell close around her fingers and arch against her hand. She looked into Nell's violet eyes and thought she might drown in her love for her. Then with eyes closed, Angel moved her fingers to the rhythm of Nell's body, bringing her to a sweet, thundering release.

"Wow, we weren't kidding about the fast fuck, were we?"

"Ha!" responded Nell, opening her eyes and moving to pull off Angel's t-shirt. Angel sighed approvingly as Nell's hands caressed her body. She gave Angel a long look before advancing again and slowly circling each nipple with a pointed tongue. When Angel gasped and fell into her, Nell dropped her hand between Angel's thighs.

"Oh, oh, oh," Angel cried as Nell tore off her panties and felt her sex. "Oh," said Angel again. "Nice, that's the spot."

"Oh, my," sighed Nell, gently backing her up against the washer, her hands in Angel's hair and her mouth on hers. Nell shifted her hips and wedged a leg between Angel's thighs. Angel felt the muscles in Nell's toned stomach flex as Nell's hands glided over her hips and between her legs. Nell groaned as she lifted Angel up onto the washer and gently spread her thighs. Angel quivered and threw her head back, opening her legs so Nell could probe her with a pointed tongue. It raked across Angel's swollen clitoris and sent shudders through her body. Nell tasted and sucked until Angel could contain it no more. It was full and perfect, sweet and bold, hot and gentle all at once.

From Nell's perspective, this was the woman of her dreams. As she took Angel in her arms, gently rocking her, she felt tears pricking behind her eyes and blinked them away. Her love for Angel was raw and tender, terribly vulnerable. She looked at the dusky skin of Angel's neck and buried her face in the damp tendrils of hair curling there. As Nell kissed that soft tender spot between Angel's shoulder blades, she heard Angel moan softly. She knew that sound. "Again?" Nell asked, marveling at Angel's ability to have so many orgasms in succession. She could count on one hand the number of times she'd ever had more than one orgasm, mostly grateful for the ones she did have. These were Nell's thoughts as she lifted the hair from Angel's face and saw a small smile lingering there.

"Maybe," replied Angel coyly. "Sorry, it feels so good."

"No apology necessary," murmured Nell, gathering her tightly. "Here, wrap your legs around me again." Nell maneuvered Angel's body so that she was straddling her again with just enough distance that she could easily slide her fingers up and into Angel's sex. Her clitoris was hard and swollen and heat poured off her. Nell felt Angel shift and squeeze, slowly grinding, raising and lowering herself until she cried out again, eyes half-closed and her wild, curly hair covering her face.

As Angel's body stilled, Nell took her in her arms and kissed her again, and then they started to laugh.

"I'm sorry," Angel said. "I was so noisy."

"You were perfect," Nell replied, "but that was quite a howl you had going."

"I'm sorry," she said, laughing again. "It's all your fault. You and that sexy body of yours."

"Oh no, don't you dare give me that," joked Nell, stroking Angel's back and inhaling her scent, mixed as it was with the smell of laundry detergent. "You invented the word voluptuous."

"You sure that isn't just another way of saying I'm fat?"

"Angel! I'll have to spank you if you don't stop that."

"Oh, then I'm really fat. Grossly gargantuan, morbidly obese."

"Oh dear, look what you're going to make me do," said Nell, pretending to pull the belt from her jeans.

"Ah!" Angel squealed, jumping up and running naked out of the kitchen with Nell in hot pursuit.

Nell caught up with her by the living room sofa and they collapsed again in a hot tangle. They lay together until their breathing slowed. Time seemed to stand still. Angel felt solid and real, her heavy breasts against Nell's chest. "Such wild hair." She stroked Angel's curls.

"Listen who's talking about wild hair," murmured Angel dreamily.

"Should I change it?" Nell asked, anxiety creeping into the question.

"No," Angel cried emphatically, her voice muffled against Nell's neck. "It's too sexy for words."

That was hard to believe, whichever way you looked at it.

* * *

"I hate petunias!" yelled Angel to Annie, Nell's manager, as she passed by the doorway of the greenhouse. Angel wished she were back having hot sex in the laundry room.

"What've they done to you?" said Annie. "I'd say a petunia is a relatively harmless flower."

"Oh I'm just sick of watering them," said Angel. "Maybe we can offer a free petunia to anyone who shops here. How's that for a good idea?"

"I like it," said Annie, stooping to deadhead a marigold. "Hey," she said suddenly. "There was a phone message earlier from some bloke wanting to talk with you. I didn't give anything away," she insisted, winking at Angel, "given you-know-who and all that." Angel had given Annie the low-down on Yvonne and the trouble with the collection agencies. "So not to worry. I left him a message back that you didn't work here anymore."

"Thanks." When would she ever be free of Yvonne or would this stuff keep following her around for the rest of her days? What was it with ex-girlfriends? Camille wasn't giving them a break either.

"Here, why don't you let me finish these?" Annie said, waving Angel away and grabbing the water hose. "Go find Nell and tell her to stop worrying. She's in the office working on the computer and grinding her teeth."

Angel laughed and headed over to Nell's office. Sure enough, there she was with a frown on her face, peering at the screen. "What're you doing?"

Nell looked over at Angel standing by the door. Her blue eyes softened as she lifted her baseball cap, revealing a tousled mass of hair. Angel got goose bumps looking at her and thinking about what they had been doing less than an hour ago on the washing machine. As Angel reached the desk, Nell's cell phone rang.

"Bugger, Camille again," said Nell, noting the number. She hesitated and Angel could tell she was torn over answering it. Camille had called yesterday when they were working on Audrey's front deck and they had ignored it, causing her to phone again when they were in bed. She was very annoying.

"Best get it over with," exclaimed Nell, irritated at the interruption. She headed out into the foyer, cradling the phone against her neck as she walked.

Angel watched Nell's tight butt edge through the door and tried to squelch feelings of jealousy. Like she'd told Maddie that morning, it was a relatively new emotion for her. She liked to think of herself as a free spirit who didn't want to be tied down. It just went against everything she'd spent all those years crafting in herself.

Another problem was that Camille was positively gorgeous and that fact made Angel feel inadequate. Small and blond—everything she wasn't. Maddie had never come straight out and said this, except once early on when she'd described the young Camille to Angel as a "blond bombshell," but she'd seen a couple of photos at Nell's. They weren't close-ups, but there was no mistaking they looked to be a very cute couple. The sight of the person she loved smiling with her arms around a beautiful woman made her heart beat wildly. She'd felt her pulse throbbing in her ears, leaving her face hot and tight. She'd made an excuse and slipped into the bathroom, splashing cold water on herself and trying to calm her anxiety. She tried to remember that she had no need to compare herself to Camille and that this part of Nell's life was over. But it still left her with deep nagging doubts. The fact that it had affected her so was the worst part of how she felt and she hated to admit it.

She was in deep, no mistaking it. Last night they'd talked about Trevor's accident and she'd held Nell in her arms as she'd talked tearfully about the life she'd lost. Nell had cried then, and despite the anguish, Angel realized this was the glue that bound them together. Made their relationship stronger. She tingled with thoughts of Nell with her small, firm breasts, naked except for a towel slung sexily around her hips.

Was this normal? She smiled to herself remembering how she'd felt with her first girlfriend in ninth grade when she'd sat behind her in Spanish class and tried to synchronize her breathing to hers. And then with a few other special loves through college, and Yvonne, at least at first. But this, this was different.

Angel chewed on a sandwich and tried to ignore the feelings threatening to burst out and make her a green-eyed monster. Wearily she returned to the greenhouse and moved the last of the newly-started purple salvia seedlings, barricading them with plastic tape so they could be shipped to Audrey's without being sold.

Nell was back in her office, still talking on the phone, so Angel drifted into the tiny break room, no more than a closet really, to refocus and work on plans for Clarity Designs. The website was up and running with help from one of Kate's friends. Sweet serendipity, another friend had also connected her with an extension service in California to provide a webinar on pond construction. It was amazing to Angel that she could be sitting in Cornwall and have her video streamed across the world. She balanced her laptop on her knees and sipped from a can of diet soda as she worked.

"Okay, I think I've got it." Annie appeared in the doorway with a pad of paper, chewing the end of her pencil and frowning as she spoke.

"Got what?"

"Your 'In the Garden' spots,'" said Annie, reminding Angel of an earlier conversation. After plans for Clarity began to take shape, Nell and Angel had realized that some of the web sessions could also be done in person at the garden center. Everyone thought this a good idea and Annie had the brilliant suggestion that maybe they could stream the video locally if someone figured out the technicalities. But for the moment they were planning on advertising the sessions as "In the Garden Workshops" and encouraging a drop-in crowd at the center itself. "Let's hope they do drop in and hopefully drop some cash while they're at it," was Nell's comment.

Annie sidled over to Angel and showed her a list of topics she'd come up with. "Plus they get a petunia–your idea," Annie added with a smile.

"Better Blooming Roses. Patio Ponds. Fabulous Fountains. Outrageous Orchids. Nice alliteration," exclaimed Angel. "Totally tantalizing topics and titles!"

Annie, engrossed in her plans, missed the joke. "And we can have Priceless Perennials too," she said, adding it to her list. "And then there are the autumn themes and a Christmas focus like making your own wreaths."

"Riveting wreaths?" suggested Angel. She suddenly realized she'd never planned to be here in the autumn, never mind Christmas.

Annie looked up quickly. "Oh it's too corny?" she said, suddenly deflated.

"No not at all," reassured Angel, worried that she'd offended. "I love the titles. And I could definitely do the pond one as I have to plan that one first for the extension service in California. That is if this thing ever gets off the ground."

"It will." Annie's face lit up again and she gave Angel a grin. She pushed a lock of wavy brown hair behind her ears and stuck the pencil after it. "Okay, I'm going in," she said, grimacing and heading for Nell's office. "She'll think these topics are perfect or I'll have to kick her in the bum."

"You go girl," exclaimed Angel. "She needs a good kick."

CHAPTER ELEVEN

Light peeped around the edges of the curtains as Angel strained to see the clock. Five twenty-three. It was too early to rise, but Angel felt surprisingly awake. And alive. It was heaven to be lying here next to Nell, feeling her solid, muscled body and listening to her soft snoring.

Nell was curled toward Angel, her hand against her face. Angel was overcome with love for her and caressed the curve of her hip as she slept. Her skin was soft and warm against Angel's touch. Such a simple touch, yet it caused Angel's heart to race, caused her breath to catch. Aroused, Angel brushed her lips along that precious curve below Nell's waist, letting her fingers rest in the soft hollow of Nell's groin. Nell made a small sound and flung her arm over the pillow. Angel tensed, her heart pounding so loudly she felt it would surely wake her. Desire pooled in her as she imagined Nell's touch. She never knew her body could be so aroused by the thought of another's caress, never knew she could be transported to such levels of ecstasy just from Nell's mouth on her. Yes, it was so right to have Nell loving her.

Angel trailed her fingers along Nell's back, hoping she might wake, hoping that mouth she knew so well might hungrily find hers and give her sweet relief. Body primed, she realized she was holding her breath and tried to relax to the rhythm of Nell's soft breathing. She turned onto her back and lifted her breast away from her side to get more comfortable. Sometimes having such large breasts was a major hazard. As she touched herself she felt the nipple pucker and continued to brush her thumb across it. It felt good. Angel slid her hands between her thighs, feeling the growing dampness. She parted her flesh and rubbed her clitoris which grew under her touch. Moaning softly she slid her fingers through the slickness of her sex, rubbing herself until she felt hot and swollen. Pressure mounted as she slipped a finger inside herself, then two and squeezed, feeling the soft, thick walls of her vagina closing in. Eyes closed and rocking slightly, Angel imagined Nell's mouth on her and heard herself gasp into the soft light of dawn.

Nell was deep in a dream about a flood at the garden center when she was roused by a soft sound. She opened her eyes and looked toward Angel who was quietly moaning. At first Nell startled, thinking there was something wrong, but quickly realized what was happening. Nell's eyes focused and she caught her breath. There was Angel, her legs open and her sex exposed, running her fingers though the slick folds. Her eyes were closed and there was a small smile lingering on her lips. Nell's breath stopped in her throat. It was light in the bedroom and she could see the tawny flesh like soft petals of the most beautiful flower she had ever seen. Transfixed, Nell watched as Angel bent her knees and slid her fingers inside herself. Nell heard herself gasp as Angel's soft moans increased. Never had she seen a woman pleasure herself like this. *Wow*. It was one of the most erotic things she had ever experienced.

Angel's moans were increasing and Nell realized Angel was about to climax. Nell reached out to touch Angel's soft belly, but stopped herself, overcome by the sight of this woman she loved experiencing such heights of pleasure. It was amazing. As the soft sounds increased, Angel threw back her head on the pillow and Nell saw Angel's body tense and then relax. A satisfied smile appeared on Angel's lips and she turned slowly to grab Nell, pulling her close.

"Oh, my," said Nell. "That was quite something. Sorry I missed most of it."

"Mmm, me too," said Angel, slipping her hand between Nell's thighs. "Ah, what do we have here?" she said cheekily, holding up her hand to check the dampness there.

"Well, what do you expect? My God, Angel, you were really rocking."

They laughed then until Angel slipped down under the sheets and nuzzled into Nell's groin. Nell's eyes widened and she felt blood pumping through her body. She let her head loll back as Angel kissed and gently rubbed her round and round. Full of hot need, she let Angel part her thighs and cried out as she felt Angel's mouth on her.

"Mmm, you like this," Angel said, coming up for air and reaching to roll Nell's nipple between her thumb and forefinger. "I really like it too." With those words she moved to slip her fingers—the ones that were still wet from her own body—inside Nell. *Oh, sweet agony*. Nell's body tingled and she cried out, her orgasm racking her body in one long delicious release.

Half an hour later and Nell and Angel tumbled out of each other's arms, staggering from the sheer delight of it all and dashed for the bathroom. Angel got there first and was soon in the shower letting the hot water tumble over her body. Life was good. Her mind switched to the day ahead and it was a full one. She had an interview with the local newspaper about the new business venture and then she was doing the "Better Blooming Roses" workshop at the garden center.

"Shoot, I forgot to do the handouts on black spot," she said once they were down in the kitchen eating cereal. "Too much sex and not enough focus."

"Terrible problem," said Nell, reading a magazine.

Angel ignored Nell, her mind on the tasks ahead. "We'll have the pictures from the website," she murmured, "but I wanted to have something for them to take away."

Nell was biting into a piece of toast and looked to be trying not to drip marmalade on her shirt. "Oh," she said, glancing up from the magazine, "did you say something?"

"Maybe you can do it for me?" Angel gave Nell her puppy-dog look. "Make the copies."

"Yes, of course," said Nell, registering the conversation. "I aim to please." She reached over to plant a kiss as Angel dropped her cereal bowl in the sink. "Bye, love," Nell said, "and good luck with the interview. Go do us proud!"

* * *

The sun was rising high and it promised to be a gloriously sunny spring day. Annie had done a great job advertising the "Better Blooming Roses" seminar and the chairs under the marquee were starting to fill up. She had arranged several teapots on a side table accompanied by a plate piled high with chocolate biscuits. They were just about ready to start.

"Hi. Good morning everyone! Very nice to see you all here." Angel worked the tent, greeting regular customers and introducing herself to new people. Nell watched with admiration. Some of it was because she was an American, Nell thought. Angel had that open, assertive, casual way of being with people and they warmed to her. Nell had to admit there was a short period when some people, and especially those who didn't care for Americans, were a bit stand-offish and a few seemed hostile probably because Angel looked different, but as soon as they met her, everything seemed to change. Nell wasn't sure if Angel was aware of that switch, but most likely she was used to it. Nell was reminded of her own prejudices and pushed the thoughts away.

"Mrs. Johnson, how good to see you again." Angel gestured at an elderly woman in the front row and handed her a cup of tea. "Would you like a biscuit?"

"Yes please dear." The woman gripped Angel's hand in gratitude as Nell looked on. It didn't matter if nobody bought anything. Just the publicity and good will for the community were enough. As she watched, Nell grew envious of Angel's way with people and couldn't help comparing it to herself. She always felt more comfortable with plants than with customers.

At ten o'clock Angel started her program. She talked about the different varieties of roses and which did well in different climates. She had several large potted roses which did best in Cornwall. Nell watched her navigate several websites, telling the audience she'd put the links on the garden center website. Nell ran her hand through her hair, feeling more stupid by the moment. She could never do this in private, never mind off the cuff in a public setting. She felt herself perspiring just at the thought of it.

And then Angel switched to a YouTube clip on pruning. What if the website didn't work? What if that buffering thing happened when everything freezes? She found herself becoming anxious just at the thought and couldn't help comparing herself again to Angel who seemed calm and collected and even looked to be enjoying herself. The whole idea of public speaking made Nell quake in her boots.

After the presentation Angel asked for questions and took each as if it was the most interesting and insightful query she'd ever heard. She was so good. Nell watched Angel reassure, flatter and yet also establish her credibility. How did she do it all so easily? As Angel soared, Nell found herself feeling increasingly stupid, old-fashioned, out of date and just plain boring.

The questions petered out eventually and Angel reached for her clippers. "Anyone want to try?" she asked, pointing to a ragged potted rose bush. "I know this is a bit late, or early depending how you look at it, but your roses will need this sooner or later."

A young woman at the back volunteered and Nell watched Angel lead her through the basics of pruning roses. The group gave the volunteer a round of applause at the end and the woman glowed with pleasure.

"And now black spot," Nell heard Angel say. "A very nasty fungus that we've all seen on our roses." She turned to the computer, "I have a good website on this I'd like to show you."

She clicked on a link as the image froze. Okay, thought Nell triumphantly before catching herself, aghast at what she was feeling.

"Sorry, technical difficulties." Angel rushed over to the computer and typed in several commands. Annie tried unplugging and restarting the thing, but they'd lost the connection. "I'm sorry, I don't think this is going to work," said Angel as the crowd got restless. Nell hated that it pleased her just a bit to see Angel flustered. Suddenly Angel turned to Nell standing in the corner and waved her hand. "Nell, do you have the handouts, please?"

"Handouts?" She'd forgotten to make the damn copies.

"Yes, the handouts on black spot." The assembled group turned to look at her.

Nell froze. Her embarrassment turned to irritation rising like bile in her throat. *This is my garden center.* She looked at the accusatory faces staring at her, wanting to just shut them out. "No, who do you think I am? Your secretary?" Nell spoke the words harshly, a crude attempt at a joke, but one immediately regretted.

Angel turned to her, her color rising. The audience tittered politely. Annie shot Nell a look of pure disgust and ran to make the copies. Nell stood there, frozen. Firstly, she couldn't believe she'd forgotten to do the photocopying, but more importantly she was aghast at saying something so senseless and inane. *Why had she done that?* Angel looked embarrassed, but carried on, answering the audience's questions before Annie returned. Nell saw that Angel would not make eye contact with her. *Damn.*

Annie passed around the handouts and the group was soon deep in conversation about organic methods for treating black spot. By the time they'd got to aphid control, Angel was back in her element. Nell leaned against the side of the tent, still mortified by her behavior. *What is wrong with me?*

It didn't help that Nell had deliveries most of the afternoon and when she got back Angel acted like it had never happened, like everything was fine. But everything wasn't. Worse still, Angel was spending the evening with Maddie and a couple of her girlfriends, leaving right after work. Angel had already told her she'd be spending the night at her cottage in the village as they'd surely be drinking and she didn't want to have to drive the winding lanes to Nell's place. They were having some kind of make-up/beauty products party and then they were going to plan a get-together for the fortieth birthday of a friend of Maddie's, which Nell was going to miss because of work.

Nell had been invited to the beauty party, but had turned it down. Too much estrogen and hysterics for the likes of her, not to mention the make-up, which she never wore anyway. Now she wished she'd accepted the invitation, just so she could be near Angel and wouldn't be alone with her own crazy thoughts. No doubt she would be the talk of the evening. And with women that she used to call her friends. *How did I end up the outsider?* Not being there was an invitation for them all to gossip about her. Stomach lurching, Nell felt desperately that she needed to talk with Angel and have everything be right again.

It was the most miserable evening. Nell tried to watch football on television and drank too much scotch. The room was spinning and she staggered off to bed. As she was getting out of her clothes, her phone rang. *Let it be Angel.* It was Camille.

"Where's your girlfriend?"

"Out with Maddie." She realized she was slurring her words.

"Oh." There was a pause that seemed to go on far too long.

"You want company? I'm at my mother's right now."

She was drunk and her ex-partner, ex-wife really, was inviting herself over. She steadied herself, lulled by the familiar voice. Nell wanted to be included, appreciated, loved and forgiven.

"You there, Nelly?" *Oh, the old familiar voice.* The room was starting to spin again.

Nell leaned against the wall to get her bearings. "Yes, I'm here." Her mouth was dry and her voice sounded weird. Words gushed out, Nell eager to talk to anyone, even Camille, to alleviate her pain. She rambled on and on incoherently, inappropriately and what she would come to realize later, regretfully.

"Let me come over," Camille said after a while, interrupting the avalanche. "It'll make you feel better. I know you and I know what you need."

Nell caught sight of herself in the bathroom mirror and saw her scared face looking back. "Camille don't do this." She was reasonably inebriated but sober enough to know it was a bad idea. She was also sober enough to know she was overreacting about Angel and angry at herself for feeling so messed up about the whole thing.

"Don't do what? You're the one who's been spilling their guts for the last half hour."

"I'm drunk. You caught me in a bad place."

"Well exactly, that's my point."

Nell could just imagine her. Tiny, blond hair framing her face, turned up nose and pale blue eyes. She had loved her. She was Nell's first love, not counting Ramona, and her memories of being a teenager were tangled with her memories of Camille. She had been Nell's one constant and there was a time when Nell couldn't have imagined life without her. They'd been good parents together and good companions, and maybe Camille was right: they deserved to be friends after all they'd been through.

"Okay, I'll see you in a few minutes." *Did she really say that?*

Downstairs in the kitchen Nell reached into the refrigerator, suddenly hungry. There was Angel's six-pack of diet cola. The thought of Angel roused her and she put her free hand to her forehead, cradling the phone in the other. She leaned against the refrigerator. *What am I doing?*

"Nelly, you there?" When she heard the voice in the hall, Nell's heart sank. Camille still had a key.

"Look at you," Camille said when she entered the kitchen, reaching over to smooth Nell's hair. Nell suddenly realized she had taken off her jeans at some point in the evening and was in her boxer shorts.

"Sit down and let me make you some coffee," murmured Camille softly. Nell watched as she moved busily around the kitchen. It was too familiar and she wondered if she was dreaming. At some point the coffee appeared in front of her and she felt Camille's hand stroke her cheek. In her drunken stupor she wasn't sure if she'd been asleep and how much time had passed, but the next thing she knew Camille had pulled her stool up next to hers and had her arms around her. Nell breathed in the familiar scent of her, lilies of the valley, and let her head loll against Camille's shoulder. Camille pushed the hair out of Nell's eyes and kissed her softly on the forehead. The kind gesture was more than she could bear. The pain of all her losses, compounded by her stupidity with Angel, bubbled up. She felt a sob rising and tried to stifle it.

Too late. Camille knew her every gesture and patted her back. "Let it out," she said quietly. "Just let it out."

An image of Trevor, when he was about two, sitting in his playpen over by the window, flashed before Nell. She remembered him smacking a toy on the head with a little wooden hammer and how they'd both laughed until he smacked his thumb and Camille had picked him up and twirled him around the kitchen, singing quietly in that same soothing voice she was using right now. The dam broke and tears flooded Nell's face. Sobs racked her body as she cried for her son and her relationship and the sorry person she'd become.

Camille held her and wiped away her tears.

"I'm sorry," Nell sputtered.

"You don't ever have to say sorry to me," Camille soothed, gently stroking Nell's face. "Here, let's sit outside. The stars are beautiful."

Nell nodded, reluctantly following Camille's small shapely bum out onto the deck. She noticed Camille had gained a bit of weight and was looking good. Nell dozed and couldn't say how long they sat in companionable silence.

"Want to go to bed? It's getting late." Camille's voice was so low Nell almost missed the words.

"What?"

"Want to make love?" Camille said, "for old times' sake. I've missed you."

"Sorry—"

"You don't find me attractive. Is that it?"

"No, you look great. You always look great."

"Then what is it? Worried you'll have to confess to Father What's-His-Name?" Despite the fact she had problems focusing, Nell looked at Camille and realized why this relationship had faltered. Deep down she knew that although Camille had loved her and was happy for her successes and for things that gave her pleasure, Camille didn't really respect her core values. Nell's passions were always discredited because Camille showed no interest. Like her faith. Nell's eyes opened wide at the insight and for a fleeting moment she felt completely sober until the fuzz in her brain descended again.

Minutes passed. It was probably the middle of the night now for all she knew.

"Come on. I know what you like." Camille reached over and touched Nell's knee, rousing her from her stupor by running a soft hand up the insides of Nell's bare thighs and then letting it lie there, fingers gently probing. She fondled Nell through the thin fabric of her boxers, pulling the fabric aside so she could touch her sex. "That's more like it," she said, watching Nell's face. "Mmm, you like that, no?" she murmured, finding Nell's mouth and nipping her lips.

Nell felt like she was having an out-of-body experience, enjoying the erotic sensation though watching it from above. At some point she looked down and saw Camille's blond head in her crotch. *It was all wrong*. "No," she gasped, pulling away, although the tension of her movements heightened the feel of Camille's hands on her and her lips sucking and licking. She thought she might come and tried half-heartedly to pull away again.

"You want me to stop," Camille said, coming up for air.

"Yes, no, I don't know what I want," Nell gasped, holding the chair rails as the deck rolled around her like an ocean liner.

"I'll stop then," Camille said petulantly. "Unless you want me to tie you up." Nell could hear Camille chuckling to herself, but her voice sounded miles away. Nell cringed at the memory when once, and only once, Camille had bound her hands, and she'd liked it. She was too embarrassed now, even in this pathetic drunken state, to admit it. Instead she closed her eyes so that the floor might stop moving.

"I can if you want," Camille persisted.

"Shit no," Nell said sleepily, eyes still closed. "Don't say that." Nell heard Camille laugh again and wasn't sure how long they lay there together. But it felt good. Very, very good to just keep her eyes closed and do nothing. A delicious, cool breeze wafted across her body and eventually stirred her enough to open her eyes. Camille was sitting by her side, wearing only her push-up bra and a tiny little thong that barely covered her. She looked so vulnerable, so small and delicate.

Camille turned lazily and reached for Nell's breast. Nell tried to get up and leave, but her legs did not seem to be connected to the rest of her body.

"Nice," Nell heard Camille say as she unhooked her bra and climbed into Nell's lap so her breasts were in Nell's face. Those small, perfect round breasts she knew so well. Camille was moving her hips against her.

"Camille I can't do this."

"Mmm," she said, her face buried in Nell's hair.

"I mean it," she said, trying to lift her off her lap. "This isn't right."

"What do you mean, this isn't right? I thought in the eyes of the church commitment was a sacrament, even if it is a bit queer—"

"Stop it." Nell managed to extract Camille from her lap and sat up straight. The deck was rolling around again and the pain at her temples was thunderous.

"How can you turn this down? After all you've put me through. I'd say you owe me being nice, at least." She had taken off her thong so that Nell could feel her sex against her groin. Camille was eager for her.

Nell waited and let Camille move against her. She could tell Camille was getting excited and listened to those soft cries she'd heard a million times. "All right," she said at last, trying not to slur her words. "You've worn me down. But this is just for you." Nell was resolute. She would relieve Camille's lust if that's what she wanted. It was true. Camille probably deserved it given the promise of ''til death us do part,' they'd once made together, not to mention putting up with her over the years and then what had happened to Trevor. She just wasn't going to share this act and certainly would not enjoy it. She felt almost clinical about it. Her arousal had subsided and all that was left was doing what needed to be done for Camille.

"Thanks," Camille said cheekily, opening her legs wide so that Nell could touch her. Camille moaned as she came and Nell looked into her eyes. She wondered then what the hell she was doing.

CHAPTER TWELVE

It didn't seem so bad in the morning. The girls-night-out had processed what happened with Nell during the 'Better Blooming Roses' gig and the women had gleefully analyzed it from every possible angle. This work rivalry was Nell's problem, they decided—her problem and hers alone. Now in the light of day, Angel was ready to agree with them. It was nothing, just a bump in the road.

The sun streamed through the window, caught a dangling crystal she'd strung up and sent dazzling beams across the room. It felt good to be in her own bed again. Angel stretched, turned and then snuggled back down, pulling the covers around her ears.

She thought again about last night. Maddie's friend, Janine, had spoken harshly about men who always wanted to be on top, could never let down their guard and had problems expressing their feelings. Manly men, she called them, insinuating that Nell fell into this bag too, even if she was a woman, or barely a woman if you caught Janine's subtext. Maddie was protective of Nell and pointed out that Janine's ex-husband actually had been a controlling jerk and Nell wasn't like that all. Angel was grateful for that because she wanted to forgive Nell and move on. Or move back into the blissful bubble they'd erected around themselves.

Angel lay there thinking about Nell and how much she loved her. But she knew love was really like a flimsy plastic bag. Sometimes the bottom falls out when you least expect it. Or like a soufflé. Opening your mouth, like opening the oven door, can make it all collapse. Angel lay on her back watching the sunlight dance across the room, thinking of all the clichéd similes for love. She was deciding whether to get up when she heard the sound of a dog barking insistently. It was her cell phone ringing in her purse downstairs. The bark was Nell's ring—to remind you of my puppy love, she'd said. Loyal as a pooch.

Angel listened to the message. It was a subdued-sounding Nell, almost pleading. Wanted to meet at the Jewel at eleven. She texted Nell back and jumped in the shower.

The electric kettle switched off and steam filled the tiny kitchen. Angel poured herself a cup of tea, added a generous helping of sweetener to kill her hunger pangs and tried to avoid the muffins the women had shared that were right now staring at her, covered in plastic. If she was going to meet Nell for a late breakfast at the Jewel, she'd better save herself.

On her way out Angel lingered on her doorstep and breathed in the sweet aromas of the garden. Damp dirt was the number one scent, although with an undercurrent of something sweeter coming from the new perennial bed. Whatever else was going on, there was always peace to be found here. Life was good and she realized with a pang that she didn't miss London at all anymore, except for Sylvie. Even images of Yvonne had disappeared from her mind and the few that remained were innocuous at this point. Best of all she hadn't been tempted to sneak a smoke in weeks.

Angel saw Nell first. She was newly-showered with damp hair starting to spring up from her part. Angel noticed Nell's faded green and brown plaid shirt and the worn khaki trousers.

She needed some new clothes. Angel hesitated, trying to connect with the irritation she felt about this impossible woman. Nell looked to be turning the pages of the newspaper. She was adorably cute.

"Thanks for coming. I'm sorry, I messed up again," Nell said simply.

"Yes, you did," Angel responded, taking a seat next to her. Nell had behaved like an idiot, but Angel couldn't help wondering if she was overdoing the remorse. It didn't seem so important now. They'd get over this. Nell moved her chair closer and reached for Angel's hand, taking it in both of hers. Angel let it rest limply, but felt the rough warmth of Nell's hands cradling her palm. When she looked into Nell's eyes she could see vulnerability there. And sadness. "Let's order some food," Angel said, taking back her hand and reaching for her purse.

Nell nodded. "My treat."

"All right, I can go for that." They got up, left a jacket on the table to reserve it and greeted the barista at the counter. They were regulars at the Jewel now. Angel ordered the porridge, thick and creamy with plump raisins, and a scone. Nell got the special: a veggie omelet. Nell asked for a refill on her coffee and Angel ordered a cappuccino. They went back to the table with their drinks and Angel split the scone, taking a bite. "Where were we?" she asked.

"That I'm an idiot and about to lose the love of my life."

"Okay, that's a good place to start," replied Angel playfully.

Nell would not meet her eyes. "I shouldn't have said that to you yesterday. I don't know what came over me. I think I was trying to be funny—"

"It wasn't even close to funny, but it's okay. I know you didn't mean it," said Angel softly.

Nell threaded her fingers through her hair and then reached across the table for Angel's hand again. Her eyes were full of pain. And guilt. Angel could read guilt in her face. "Can you forgive me?"

"Of course I can forgive you. But I have to say," Angel paused and took another bite of scone, "this is twice now you've got weird. I wish you could handle my success"—she gestured, using air quotes around "success"–"without seeing it as your failure." Nell looked tearful and Angel wondered if she was coming on too strong. "I was embarrassed," she continued, "and for Annie too, because people thought your stupid comment about the secretary thing was aimed at her." Angel managed to keep her voice low so as not to attract attention, but still the couple at the next table noted the tension and glanced over. "Why do you do this when everything's going so well? It's almost as if you want to sabotage things."

Nell sat quietly, her head in her hands. She looked mortified. "I want you to do well," she stammered at last. "You don't know how proud I am of you." Angel raised her eyebrows, but let Nell continue. "You're such an amazing woman and I'm not sure what you see in me," she added. "I think that's what worries me. That you'll wake up and find me a fraud. That I'll disappoint you." The words came out wounded, curled around the edges.

"That's silly."

"I know, but it's true," said Nell, her blue eyes darkened with anxiety. Angel swallowed the last bite of scone, remembering the time they were at Trefarrow Gardens, a lifetime ago now. How Nell had got all bent out of shape because she felt insecure and intimidated.

Angel tried to remember a time when she'd felt like this, like an imposter whom everyone thinks is brilliant, but who knows deep down they can never live up to their reputation. Maybe when she first started dancing in the clubs in Paris—especially when the language challenged her—she had felt this way, but really, when she thought about it, she'd always felt entitled enough to know she belonged, even when she also knew she had lots to learn.

Poor love, Angel thought again, reaching across the table to touch Nell's face. "You're not a fraud and you don't disappoint me except when you act like this. The only thing disappointing me is your fear, which sometimes makes you lash out and hurt the people who love you."

At this Nell winced slightly and looked across the room. Angel followed her gaze and was relieved to notice the café had mostly cleared out and only a couple of young mothers and a handful of rowdy children remained in the vicinity of their table. The women had their hands full and Angel and Nell's intense conversation wasn't even close to being on their radar. "It's okay," said Angel, indicating they were as good as alone. "Is this too painful to talk about?"

"No, it's just that..." Nell's voice faltered and a look of anguish passed across her face. "So much of this comes back to Trevor." Angel reached across the table and took Nell's hand in both of hers and brought it to her lips. "And Camille. We got so messed up." Nell shook her head so forlornly that for a moment Angel thought she might cry. But there was something else in her face. Guilt, and something else.

She realized it was shame.

Nell continued, picking distractedly at several bread crusts on her plate. "We never got closure really. We just drifted apart. I think that's why Camille is calling me so much now. I mean and then..." Angel saw a tormented look flicker across her face.

"And then what? What aren't you telling me?" Angel saw it again in her eyes. She shifted her weight and felt herself catch her breath. "Tell me."

"No!" exclaimed Nell. "It's nothing." Her voice came out in a hoarse, breathless rush.

"Then what did you mean?" Angel could feel fear in the pit of her stomach and it terrified her. She wanted to leave but leaned back in her chair and crossed her arms instead, rooted to the spot.

Nell looked away from Angel's gaze but continued to speak, now almost in a whisper. "You've got to believe me Angel. Our relationship was over before we ever split up. If I'd been more mature. If I'd been forced to look at myself. If Trevor hadn't died and made everything so impossible and sad. If all these 'ifs' had happened I know we'd still have ended it, but maybe I wouldn't be so messed up." Nell paused and took to her habit of raking her fingers through her hair, refusing to meet Angel's gaze.

And then Nell dropped the bomb. "She called last night when I was on my own. I was so drunk and I don't remember what I said. I was sorry for myself and I was sad and mad about us. She wanted to come over." Angel's eyes got wide as she took in this new information, which explained why Nell seemed to be overdoing the forgiveness thing.

"I was so drunk," Nell repeated. "I'm such an idiot."

Angel felt the air sucked out of the place and got up quickly. She grabbed her bag and headed toward her car by the village green. She did not look back.

"Stop! Stop, Angel! Please." Nell caught up with her and grabbed her arm from behind. "Please," she implored. Her eyes were dark and hooded, but she there was pain lurking there.

Angel turned away, desperate not to look at those eyes again. Memories of Yvonne and all her affairs fueled her despair.

"Please Angel," Nell pleaded. She tried to get Angel to sit on a bench, but she resisted, reaching to punch Nell's arm. Nell caught her hand and held it against her chest, maneuvering Angel onto the bench.

Angel let herself sit, but looked out to sea, refusing to meet Nell's eyes. The squawking of gulls circling high above pierced the air, surf pounded on the rocks and a couple strolling the beach called their dogs. A wall of composure slid into her mind and with it detachment. The intense pain receded and moved away to gnaw around the edges of her vision, out on the horizon. She closed her eyes, reached into a soft, safe space inside herself and wished the pain gone.

The story came out in a series of gasps and sobs. Nell told her everything and Angel had to believe it. That she got drunk as a skunk and let Camille come over. That they made out, got naked together on Nell's deck and she tried to seduce her, but that they didn't actually have sex together even though Camille wanted to. Angel let the silence fall between them and hoped she'd survive this.

* * *

"It was awful." Angel was sitting at Maddie's kitchen table, her head in her hands.

"I'm so sorry. You don't deserve this." Maddie gave her a hug. "I can't believe Camille could do this." She hesitated before she spoke again. "Well actually I can if, truth's known. She knows how to get to Nell."

"It took two to tango," said Angel, bile rising in her throat again. "What about Nell? How could she do this? To me? To us? And we were doing so well." Angel shook her head woefully, new tears sprouting.

"Here, let's make us some tea," said Maddie by way of response. A loyal friend, she always took Nell's side, but Angel could see that this one had even her stumped. She sighed and accepted a piece of paper towel from Maddie, who'd run out of Kleenex. The towel felt rough on her eyes as she tried to blot away tears, careful not to smear mascara over her face.

"She was probably getting drunk and naked with Camille right when you were telling me to give her a break," Angel said, stirring her tea. "Jeez, I should've listened to Janine." She'd had so much tea she felt like she was about to float away, but the transition was helpful and the ritual priceless. After leaving the seafront and Nell still standing there, Angel had come straight to Maddie's.

Maddie smiled ruefully and looked into Angel's eyes as she spoke. "Look, I know Nell, and Camille too. That relationship *is* over. Seriously over." She patted Angel's arm reassuringly, but the shock of what Nell had had done clouded her eyes. "It's so like Camille to try something stupid like this. But Nell? Have to say this one has taken me by surprise. Thank God she managed to control herself in the end."

"But she still had Camille over. And on her deck." Angel felt herself starting to cry again and blew her nose loudly to stem the tears. "I can't believe I fell so quickly for her. That was my error."

"No, don't say that. Falling in love is almost never an error," said Maddie. "You know when I think about Nell and doing stupid shit, it's usually when she plays the martyr." She looked up to gauge Angel's reaction. "Nell's a master at that," she added. When Angel said nothing, Maddie tried another angle.

"If Nell felt something for Camille, which I'm almost a hundred per cent sure she doesn't, she'd hide it from you. That's what men do anyway," she added. "They don't come out and tell you." Maddie slowly stirred her tea and looked back at Angel. "Don't you think?"

Angel nodded. "I just don't know."

"What're you thinking?"

Angel was silent. "Look, you have to talk about this again," insisted Maddie quickly. "You've got to talk this through." Angel could see she was desperate that her friends should stay in love.

"Oh, it's too much," said Angel wearily, suddenly tired of the drama of it all. She cast around for something to change the subject. "Anything new with Bill?" she asked. There hadn't been an appropriate moment to bring up the question at the party, especially since they'd been having so much fun and Angel had not wanted to bring down the mood.

"No. Neither hide nor hair."

"Well good riddance to him," murmured Angel. "We'll figure something out," she added. They were not going to let Maddie lose her home or her livelihood. This stuff with Nell was small potatoes in comparison.

"Thanks," said Maddie gratefully as her daughter, with a freckled, red-headed friend in tow, scampered into the kitchen. The girls grew suddenly shy, giggling together. Julia had spent the night at her friend's house and the two were now inseparable.

"How's it going? How was the slumber party?" asked Angel. She loved listening to English children speak.

"It was really fun. This is my friend Jenny," Julia added proudly, looking at the little girl by her side before turning to her mother. "Can we go over to Jenny's house please, Mum? Our club's meeting."

"Okay love, but clean this mess up first." Maddie gestured at a discarded pile of toys in the living room.

"Cute," said Angel as the girls whirled away.

Maddie explained they had a 'J club' with five neighborhood girls whose names started with 'J.' "Well four actually and one who renamed herself Josephine—"

"Too funny—"

"Hey," interrupted Maddie suddenly. "How about we drown our sorrows and go do some shopping. Great therapy. I was thinking of maybe going into Truro." Truro was the nearest place with decent-sized shops. "Window shopping probably, but maybe it'll cheer us up. We could find something to wear for Ruby's fortieth do. What do you think?"

"Okay" said Angel wearily. "I suppose I could do with some new underwear."

"All right, that might bring you back together. Nell's going to like that."

"No, if she gets a chance she'll be lucky," said Angel savagely.

"Oh, I think Auntie Nell's going to like that," repeated Julia, sidling back up to her mother and enjoying the roar of laughter that followed.

* * *

When Angel got home from shopping it was midafternoon. She and Nell had talked briefly on the phone and Nell had been solicitous and very subdued. Angel was back at the cottage and trying to enjoy the solitude. *Damn her.* Now she felt out of sorts. There was stuff around the cottage to do, but she couldn't be bothered and so she headed for the kitchen to find something to make her feel better.

A pint of ice cream later when she felt slightly sick and disgusted with herself, Angel recalled a conversation from earlier in the week during dinner. Nell had given her an extra helping of dessert telling her she needed to keep her strength up. Angel had laughed at the time, knowing, as Nell did, that Angel's appetite was never a problem. "Love my women with some meat on their bones," Nell had said. But she was just fat. Fat and disgusting. No wonder Nell had been so easily seduced by that thin, blond, midget of an ex-wife of hers. Angel's face grew hot at the thought.

Angel tried replacing the thoughts with positive self-talk that a therapist had once taught her. Sometimes it worked and sometimes it didn't. Eventually she made herself work in the garden, intentionally leaving her cell phone inside. She was determined to ignore it.

It was almost June and summer was close. The hedgerows had sprouted new growth and her apple trees had shed their delicate pink blossoms. In the last couple of weeks she'd tidied, fed and mulched the rhododendrons and azaleas along the path and worked in the kitchen herb garden, weeding and planting. She'd dealt with the overgrown magnolia and was rewarded with a profusion of blooms. Enticed by the salvia, dianthus, calendula and coreopsis sitting seductively in rows in the greenhouse, she'd planted early. She'd also bought some vegetable starts—broccoli, red cabbage, cauliflower and kale, as well as several raspberry and gooseberry canes, still wrapped in burlap, plus rhubarb promising summer pies. The lawn was still weedy, but she'd painstakingly dug out a mass of dandelions and removed the moss. She'd got three months free rent for all her work and was mightily pleased.

But everything else in the garden paled when compared to her wisteria, which still hung on gallantly, its purple blooms fading. A month or so ago the gnarled grey vines had sprouted spectacular blue-lavender blossoms in a dramatic display along the front of the cottage. Amethyst, thought Angel. It was like a necklace of amethyst jewels dangling along the vine.

She pulled herself away from it and headed for her new perennial beds. The landlord had delivered top soil and now she was ready to plant. It was like working on a canvas, arranging colors and sorting them with compatible neighbors. Eager to get started, she looked at her array of pots lined up alongside the fence and paused, tilting her head and rubbing her neck, considering how to arrange the back row of the bed that would be in partial shade.

She imagined the rich pink foliage and tall feathery plumes of astilbe in front of the towering eupatorium with its rosy-purple flowers that attracted butterflies. She'd also bought several pots of monkshood that would also reach about four foot tall and hopefully produce huge, purple-blue hooded flowers on thick red stems. The ligularia with its orange daisy-like flowers and massive rounded purple leaves would also work in the shade and would give some color later in the summer.

By seven, Angel decided to call it a day and headed back inside. Her phone was flashing a new message. It sat there like an insistent friend. Angel ignored it and went upstairs to take a shower. Later she reluctantly opened the message: "Did u see paper? Need to talk?" What on earth was that all about? Nell's tone was surprising given everything, but then texts were deceiving that way. Still, she felt a new pang of desolation. This was all so tiring.

As she dressed, Angel wondered what Nell meant by the paper. And then it came to her. The interview she'd done for the Business Editor of the local newspaper. It was supposed to run today in the Sunday paper. Maybe that was what Nell had been searching for when she saw her at the Jewel. She'd forgotten about it.

Oh shit. It was the lead article on the front page of the business section. Titled "Online Gardening: The Future of the Business," the article began with a quote from Angel saying that online companies were the wave of the future. It looked like the author had taken one small aspect of what they'd talked about, the new online company and crafted the whole article around it. Plus she'd made it seem like it was Angel's business, and set in opposition to Nell's garden center, rather than a project she and Nell were doing together. Worse still, the word "obsolete" appeared several times in regards to traditional garden centers.

Angel was horrified. She'd never said such a thing. Yes, she might have said that online businesses represented future business enterprises, but she'd never implied they would replace, or make obsolete, traditional nurseries and garden centers like Nell's. And she had definitely said this was something she and Nell were doing together. The article made it sound like they had some competition going. *Shit.*

To make things worse there was a photo of her sitting with her laptop surrounded by bushy plants. The photo had been taken in one of Nell's greenhouses. The rest of the article was okay. The author had described her as smart and attractive, but she'd also written that Angel was "strong-willed" and "ambitious." It all made her sound unfeeling, especially given those earlier remarks.

Angel tried to decide what to do. This was really bad press and made her seem like a traitor in the village. Nell would be upset about this. If she was having trouble with Angel's success before, this would really put her over the edge. Angel needed to see Nell, now. Even though it was late and she was still pissed at Nell over everything else.

* * *

The newspaper article hit her in the solar plexus, but she felt surprisingly calm. It was what she deserved after last night with Camille. The conversation with Angel sat uneasily. What she'd said and what she hadn't said. Angel would never understand. She would lose her. It was so messed up. She could barely tolerate herself. The shame was palpable and was all she could think about. It was against all she believed for herself. How she should live as an ethical person. And as a Christian.

Someone must have taken the business section out of the copy at the Jewel or she would have seen it earlier. Nell felt glad for that, thankful at least for being saved public embarrassment. There Angel was in Nell's greenhouse saying the business, which she had spent over a decade building up, would soon be obsolete. She held her head in her hands and tried to focus. She found herself going down the road that painted Angel as the know-it-all interloper, who made her feel small and insignificant, who showed Nell to be the fool she was. She texted Angel, ready to open up that wound, to face the pain if that was the only course of action.

Stop! Nell took a deep breath and made herself change into running gear. Soon she was out on the top road huffing and puffing, her muscles burning. She filled her lungs and plodded on until she reached the top of the hill and the burning lessened and she knew she was over the worst part when you feel you have to stop. When you know you can't run another step, but then do it and find you really can survive. Her head cleared as she jogged downhill toward the woods on the edge of the moor. The afternoon light dimmed as shadows slipped by. As her mind cleared she focused on Angel's kindness and their vision for their new company. *No, this wasn't Angel. Not in a million years.*

"Loose, footloose, kick off your Sunday shoes." Nell was standing on her front lawn, stretching and cooling down, feeling virtuous after her run. She started at Maddie's dance tune ringtone.

"I don't want to talk with you about what you did. That's between you and Angel," said an angry voice. "And Camille," the voice added scornfully. "But just so you know, Angel did not say that stuff in the paper." It was out before Nell could say hello.

"She would never say that," repeated Maddie. "You accept this and you'll make the biggest mistake of your life."

"I know. You don't have to tell me that."

"Nell trust me on this." Did Maddie ever listen to anything she said? "Okay, we're busy over here. Gotta go." Nell was left holding her phone, her thoughts whirling at the mention of Camille. She wished she could confess all to Maddie, but just couldn't. And Father Joseph was out of the question. She blushed at the very thought. Still, she'd passed this minor test at least. Even if Angel had meant those things about the garden center, which she felt in her heart of hearts she did not, Nell knew she could offer forgiveness.

But there was no tranquility to be found. She couldn't settle at home so drove into the office to take her mind off things, late as it was. There was no shortage of last minute details for the final leg of the work at Audrey's place. Nell willed that this thing with the newspaper might be an equalizer of sorts, that her dismissal of negative intentions on Angel's part might act as a counter-balance to her stupidity with Camille. She knew of course that it could never be equal. Never.

Almost ready to call it a night, there was a tap on her office door. Nell's body tensed. Her hands shook. It was Camille, she knew it. Gingerly she went to the door and saw with a wave of relief that it was Angel. Nell checked herself. Even in the midst of this mess, relief was a sign of her love for Angel and the possibility that they could work things out.

Nell opened the door and looked into Angel's eyes, searching for her mouth before she could say anything. Her lips brushed Angel's once, twice and then fiercely met them. As her hands caressed Angel's neck and shoulders and stroked her damp hair, she felt Angel relax against her. She was so beautiful and Nell loved her so much. She wanted so badly to make it all right again.

"I went to the house but you weren't there and I was so worried. I didn't say—"

"I know," Nell interrupted, searching Angel's face. "I didn't believe it. Never. Not one bit."

"I'm sorry, I didn't—" Nell shushed Angel again and put her finger against those lips she knew so well. When Angel resisted, still trying to explain, Nell bent and kissed that soft mouth. Angel relaxed into her so that Nell was able to kiss her again and once more in the tender hollow at the base of Angel's throat. She pushed Angel's sweatshirt off one shoulder and nibbled the skin there. As Nell looked into Angel's eyes, she saw Angel shiver and reach for her mouth, her hands inside Nell's shirt. Angel's actions said everything. It was a long, slow, sexy kiss that relieved her soul. Almost.

They left the office and stumbled into the enclosed yard. Fortunately she hadn't locked the gate yet or Angel would not have been able to get in. Now Nell set the lock and looked back at Angel framed against the gate. It was growing dark and Nell couldn't make out Angel's face, but she could imagine it. Deep grey eyes, fringed with long lashes and arched brows, straight nose and that gorgeous mouth.

Angel led her to the heated greenhouse that housed the flowering vines. As they ducked into the hothouse the fragrance was overpowering. Sweet and spicy, fabulously floral and very feminine. They paused, hand in hand and breathed in the glorious smell. Bougainvillea and clematis vines clustered along the rows, interspersed with honeysuckle and jasmine. They approached a mature moon vine, a night-blooming morning glory plant with creamy white fragrant blooms. The large flowers glowed eerily in the dark.

"Here," Nell said, throwing the blanket they'd brought out from the office onto the ground near the moon vine. The greenhouse had plastic over peat moss in places, providing a soft dry place to arrange the blanket. The moon was visible against the darkening sky and gave them just enough light to see each other's face. "Sit with me." The magical fragrance of the greenhouse enveloped them as they talked and the air felt heavy and humid. Nell lifted the hair off the back of Angel's neck and kissed her there.

"Mmm," Nell said tentatively, "I need to say—"

"Not now," Angel said, gently touching Nell's lips with her finger. Angel lay back on the blanket and stared up at Nell, her grey eyes dark and intense. Then, in one fluid motion, Angel sat up and pulled the sweatshirt over her head, all the while gazing into Nell's eyes. Reaching out, she slowly unbuttoned Nell's shirt and let it slip off her arms. Then she pulled the sports bra over Nell's head and took her small, firm breasts in her hands, smiling as Nell's nipples hardened at the caress. Their bodies glowed against the shimmering white blossoms of the vine.

"How's that for expertise?" Nell stammered, focusing her attention on Angel's bra clasp in an attempt to disturb her mental vision of Camille's naked body that rose like a tower of shame. The front clasp of Angel's bra, which had once mystified her, popped open.

"Very slick, Ms. Frank," Angel replied, pressing her breasts against Nell's and running her fingertips up and down the ridges of her back. Nell fought her arousal. She did not deserve this. "Well this gives a whole new meaning to the notion of hot house," Angel said, giggling.

Nell tried to smile. Angel was the most beautiful woman she'd ever seen and she wanted her so badly. To feel and hold her and never let go. Tears pooled in her eyes and she willed them away, moving to hide her face in that glorious mass of hair.

"Oh Angel," she whispered. "I love you so much, so very much." Her pulse quickened and she felt fire coursing through her body. Trembling Nell held Angel close and inhaled her sweet smell. "I never want to betray you. I'm so sorry."

"I know. I love you too," Angel said, pulling away so they gazed at each other nose to nose. "You're everything to me." Angel's eyes, so dark and full of promise, seemed to look right through to Nell's soul. She must see the awful person lurking there, thought Nell, shame rising like bile in her throat at not telling the entire truth about her evening with Camille. As she looked into those eyes, intense and burning, Nell feared she would never be worthy of Angel's love.

Overcome with emotion, she smoothed the tangled hair from Angel's face. "I want you so much. Just let me love you," she murmured. "Oh please let me love you." Her need was deep and raw. "I want you," she said, struggling for breath.

As Nell watched Angel reach up and trace her fingers along Nell's face, smiling all the while, Angel's trust almost stilled Nell's heart. When she felt tears prickling her eyes, Nell turned and kissed Angel hard, her tongue probing and her hands in Angel's hair. Nell's hungry mouth took Angel's in a kiss both tender and ravenous. As she scooped the curly strands from the back of Angel's neck and kissed the soft skin there, she thought she might drown in her desire.

"Whoa, steady," Angel laughed, gently pushing Nell down on the blanket. She reached inside the waistband of Nell's jeans and pulled down the zipper. Angel's hands traced her sex through her panties and kissed along the inside of her thighs.

"No," Nell stiffened, fighting the ache and trying not to think about Camille kissing that very same spot. The memory of her blond head in Nell's groin was almost too much and caused a wave of nausea to rise in her throat. "Not right now. It's not you," Nell added in a soft murmur after seeing Angel's face. "This is me, really. I'm just not sure I'm up for it tonight."

"Okay," said Angel, smiling tentatively into her eyes. "Just so long as it's not something I did. You'd tell me, right?"

"Right." She made herself meet Angel's eyes and willed herself not to cry. A deep pain seemed firmly lodged in her heart.

"Okay, but let me cheer you up a bit." Angel rose as she spoke and then started to hum a tune. Her breasts were free and bounced as she got to her feet, but she still had her jeans on. Nell was transfixed. Angel slowly moved her hips, thrusting and whirling in a very sexy way, almost like a striptease dancer, unbuttoning her jeans as she moved. Nell was transfixed, needing to look away, to stop this, but wanting it so badly. But then Angel arched her back, twirling sideward so her breasts bounced again on her chest, the nipples large and firm. Nell felt herself gasp as Angel slid out of her jeans, tossing them aside with barely a movement and then turning so her bum was in the air and she was looking at Nell from between her legs.

Bloody hell. Nell wasn't sure what to think, although her body, which certainly wasn't thinking, was aroused fit to explode. She felt such shame in her arousal given the night with Camille, such longing and yet such guilt at the way her body responded to Angel's vulnerable flesh. Vulnerable because she was offering this to Nell–to cheer her up for goodness sake–when such nasty things lurked in Nell. She covered her eyes with her hand and tried to block out Father Joseph's words about moral purity that were screaming through her brain. And the way she was feeling watching Angel doing these things proved how awful a person she really was.

But it wasn't over yet. Smiling all the while and still humming softly, Angel put her fingers in her panties and lowered them up and down, twirling all the while. Her hair spun around her face and caught the light from the rising moon glinting through the glass. Soon she had her fingers inside her panties and was caressing herself, moaning. Nell felt herself quiver and thought she might come right there just watching Angel do these things. The realization and the disgust she felt at herself because of it, only slightly dampened the lust in her heart.

Soon the panties were on the ground and Angel was standing above Nell, her sex level with Nell's face, open to her hungry gaze. Angel paused then and the humming stopped. "Now this is just for you," she explained. "For us. Only us. Okay?"

"Okay," Nell said, confusion clouding her eyes. She wasn't sure what Angel meant. But all thoughts disappeared from her mind as Angel slowly parted her thighs, opening her vulva with two fingers from each hand so that her lips parted and Nell could see the soft, glistening flesh of her sex. Nell inhaled slowly and gasped, reaching out to her. Her heart pounded and her hand shook and she thought she might die until she felt Angel's clitoris, hard and swollen, with her fingertip. Ah, the very slightest of touches, feather light. She desperately wanted to kiss her there and suck the sweet juices she remembered so well. When she thought she might faint with the intensity of her need, Angel whirled away and danced naked some more.

Nell felt her body shudder, but she couldn't touch Angel again, she just couldn't. The memory of Camille stuck in her mind. She slipped her hand between her own thighs and pressed, hoping to get relief, but she couldn't do it in front of Angel and besides it wasn't what she wanted. She ached to have her body tightened around Angel, remembering the small noises she made deep in her throat when she came.

Now Angel sat down beside her, panting slightly. "How's that?"

"Oh," said Nell, hiding her face in Angel's hair. She had no words for what she was feeling.

"Looks like you were enjoying it," Angel said, kissing Nell hard on the mouth. When she came up for air, Nell groaned and let Angel fondle her breasts. Something like pain tingled through her body and she stiffened again. "Not tonight," Nell repeated. She couldn't do it. Not so soon.

"Well I wasn't…" Angel's voice trailed away and Nell saw confusion in her eyes. "I was just loving you, that's all," insisted Angel. "I wasn't expecting any more."

"I know. Just don't leave me," Nell said, watching Angel's face, soft in moonlight. "I don't ever want to lose you."

"You won't," whispered Angel. "You won't. I won't let you." She held on tight and Nell thought Angel might be crying too.

CHAPTER THIRTEEN

The place was just slightly creepy. A disco ball twirled above the tiny stage and flashing colored strobe lights, bouncing off the walls in sync with the thudding bass of the music, turned everyone's faces a strange green color. Maddie wished she was home in her jammies watching the telly, but tried to be a good sport. It was Ruby's fortieth birthday party and they were out on the town. In the Black Rabbit Club in the nearby city of Truro to be exact.

The moving light beams spilled across the floor and lit up several scantily-clad servers carrying trays of drinks. Stale smoke seeped from the walls and reminded Maddie of earlier times when her customers could chain smoke. Huge flat-screen television screens flashed music videos featuring gyrating women pouting into the camera.

"Bacardi and coke," Maddie replied when Angel motioned for her drink order. "Please," she added, her voice swallowed by thudding techno bass.

"Loud," said Maddie when Angel returned.

"What?" asked Angel, cupping her ear.

"Never mind," replied Maddie, laughing. But Angel had already turned away and was talking with Ruby, who wore a glittery tiara in her curly brown hair. Maddie watched as Angel finished her martini and ordered another. Just as well they had a hotel room for the evening.

The DJ was switching up the music and getting the crowd on their feet. The Black Rabbit Lounge catered to stag and hen parties as well as birthday celebrations and was known for featured performers, who came in to give shows. Tonight was Ladies' Night and supposedly a male dancing troupe was set to entertain.

Maddie sipped her drink and looked around. The show was about to begin. Angel smiled over at her and mouthed if she was okay. Maddie nodded and smiled back, then turned just in time to catch Ruby who swayed and grabbed the chair for support.

"Wow Ruby, steady girl," said Maddie, beckoning for her to sit down. But Ruby was determined to reach the dance floor and staggered on, dragging Angel and their friend Janine behind her. Angel raised her eyebrows but followed dutifully, supporting Ruby who stumbled again in her high platform heels. The music boomed and thumped as they reached the dance floor. They beckoned Maddie, but she waved them off. The lights were starting to give her a migraine.

Angel could certainly dance. Soon there was a circle around her and people were starting to look. Her body was one fluid motion: hips moving, swaying, turning. Her long hair looked crimson in the lights and spun around her face like a circling halo.

Maddie watched as several men approached Angel and were engulfed into the circle of dancers around her. Angel brought them in but would not dance alone with them. They had their eyes on her and tried to talk with her, but she avoided their gaze and their patter. Maddie could see that it was Ruby, Janine and the other women who were the focus of Angel's interest.

As the music switched to another beat, the dancers left the floor and headed back to their table. Angel made a slight bow to her admirers and gave a cheeky wave. She sat back against the leather seats of the booth and fanned herself, laughing gaily as Ruby talked drunkenly over the din of the music. She was exclaiming about Angel's dancing. Soon a couple of drinks materialized on their table and the waitress indicated two men at the bar grinning over at them.

"Leave them," insisted Angel as Ruby reached for a glass. "Never accept a drink that's been out of your sight. Seriously," she added as Janine raised her eyebrows at her. Ruby snorted and spilled her drink on her friend who started to dab at her skirt furiously.

The gesture made Maddie look up and catch sight of someone over by the bar who looked vaguely familiar. "Who's that?" she asked.

"Daphne Dubois," said Janine. "Haven't seen her in donkey's years. Wonder what she's doing here? Thought she'd moved back to France." Maddie registered the name and realized this was Lucas' ex or maybe current flame. Daphne was strikingly attractive, wearing a short miniskirt and high-heeled stiletto ankle boots. Hanging off the arm of an older man, she looked over at their table and gave a cheery wave. Janine waved back as Daphne sashayed onto the dance floor with her date. Maybe "ex" was right after all.

Thoughts about Daphne were soon chased away by the DJ announcing the evening's performance: a troupe of male strippers called the John Henrys. Soon seven gorgeous men strutted onto the stage. They wore tight shiny trousers and sequined shirts with matching jewel-toned ties. The crowd applauded as they danced their routine, swaying and gyrating to the beat. Several songs later they were down to their ties and briefs, grinding their pelvises and shaking their bums.

"The blond one on the end is very cute," giggled Angel as they cheered on the men. They laughed as the bloke winked at Angel, gave her a come-on wave and then proceeded to take off his tie and throw it at her. The crowd cheered again as Angel swung the tie above her head and did a little happy dance out in the audience.

As the music rose and the bass thundered off the walls, the John Henrys closed in on their finale. Laser lights danced around the room. The dancers removed their briefs and then continued to dance in sparkly jock straps. Again the crowd cheered and egged them on into giving an encore. By the time it was over the women were laughing hysterically, ordering more drinks and heading for the dance floor. Maddie could see Angel, her face flushed, dancing with Ruby, who could barely stand.

"What'll you have?" Angel was about to order another round.

"I'm okay," said Maddie, thinking that someone needed to stay sober.

"Okay Mum," said Angel, giving her a squeeze.

"Someone has to do it," replied Maddie good naturedly, standing up to find the loo.

When Maddie left the lavatory and was maneuvering her way back across the floor toward their booth, she heard the DJ announce the competition for the evening. The Black Rabbit Lounge was known to host competitions for karaoke and dancing and sometimes had some serious prize money. Tonight it seemed like the competition involved dancing with the John Henrys.

As Maddie approached their table, Janine was gesturing wildly to the DJ and pointing at Angel who was waving away the invitation.

"No you must," said Janine. "You're amazing. Make us proud."

"No I don't think so," said Angel, slinking down into the dark recesses of the booth. But the lights were on her and the crowd was chanting their enthusiastic support.

"Do it. Do it," they cried, clapping and cheering her on.

By the time Maddie reached the table, Janine and Ruby had hauled Angel up onto her feet and pushed her out onto the dance floor. The last thing Maddie heard was a roar of approval as Angel was hoisted up onto the stage and embraced by three of the John Henrys. One was on each side of her and one was dancing erotically behind her, his crotch up against her bum. The men had their tight trousers back on but were bare-chested except for their ties.

Oh my goodness. As the crowd applauded, Angel suddenly transformed from the shy girl pushed onto the stage to someone definitely in charge. She stepped out from behind the John Henrys, hesitated for a moment as she picked up their beat and then followed their moves step by step. Soon she was on center stage, playing off the men, pulling them toward her with their ties so their faces were in her cleavage. She spun and twirled, hitting the floor in an erotic downward move that spread her legs wide and then sliding back up, her behind in the air. The crowd gasped and then cheered her on again as she twirled and spun, her hair floating out behind her.

Maddie stood with her mouth open. *Wow.* It was very sexy, but also very athletic. She was in awe, but very anxious knowing Angel's past.

Now the crowd was chanting again. "Take it off. Take it off." They wanted Angel to strip right there on the stage. Maddie's eyes got huge.

Angel smiled as the chant continued and grabbed one of the men's shirts and sparkly waistcoat lying on the side of the stage. Without missing a beat she put them on over her clothes, added a tie for good measure and then danced a strip tease removing the men's clothes. To the delight of the crowd, she threw the garments to Ruby out on the dance floor.

Maddie breathed a huge sigh of relief to see Angel stay fully clothed. Soon the music was dying down and Angel was being lifted off the stage by two of the John Henrys and deposited back on the dance floor. She won. No one tried to match it.

* * *

Ping! Lucas was sitting in a hotel lobby waiting for a client when the text message appeared. "*La petite amie dans l'action* (The girlfriend in action)." Puzzled, he opened the attachment and frowned as a video started to play. He peered closer and then smiled an amused smile. It was Angel doing some striptease moves with what looked to be a group of male strippers. *Was it really Angel?* He peered at it again and moved toward the window to access better light. *Mon dieu, she's really good.* He smiled to himself and watched it through several times. As Lucas put the phone back in his pocket and rose to meet his client, he thought sadly how the girlfriend part was all wrong.

Nell was sitting in her kitchen eating cereal when she heard the announcement of a new text message. She didn't look at it, thinking it might be from Camille who unfortunately had been adding to her grief by refusing to leave her alone. Nell stretched and refilled her coffee cup and spooned the last of the milk from her bowl. It was Sunday morning and she was enjoying a few minutes' peace reading the paper before heading out to church. She'd planned to drive over to Plymouth later in the day to pick up stuff for Audrey's party and then to stay overnight with relatives. Angel was still in Truro with her girlfriends after their night out.

Nell was unlocking doors at the garden center when she saw her phone blinking insistently. She touched the screen and frowned when she saw the message wasn't from Camille after all. "Your employee in action," it read. "Thought you should know what she gets up to after hours." Nell didn't recognize the number and noticed no one had signed the message. Nell raked her hand through her hair and wondered why someone wanted her to know about Annie. Peering at the message he saw there was a video attached. *Bloody hell.*

Her heart lurched. Catching her breath and gasping, she held onto the door to steady herself. *Oh fuck.* It wasn't about Annie. It was Angel. Dancing with a bunch of half-naked men. *Is this some sort of sick joke?* She realized with a pang that it was no joke. There was Maddie and Janine and their other friend Ruby, all of them there in that sleazy night club in Truro. *Why? Why would she do this?* Nell looked again at the number but still didn't recognize it. She knew it was a cruel act, but was still grateful for the knowing.

* * *

"Hi. What's up?" It was Angel. She'd rung twice and Nell hadn't the heart to answer it, or listen to her messages. She'd missed church and driven on autopilot to pick Audrey's stuff. She was at her oldest sister Ellen's place, but she wished she was in the cool, quiet gloom of St. Theresa's. The afternoon was a blur. *Love always turns to loss.* Now she finally answered the call, her heart thudding in her chest.

"Hi! Been missing my main squeeze."

"Oh," croaked Nell.

"What's wrong? Is your phone working?" Nell couldn't speak and let the question hang in the air. "Are you okay?" Angel insisted.

"I don't know." Nell's voice came out gruff and edgy as if she hadn't spoken in days. "Is there something you should tell me?" She had a terrible headache and found herself holding onto the door for support.

"What?" There was surprise and anxiety in Angel's voice. "I don't understand."

"No, I'm the one who doesn't understand." Her heartbeat pounded in her ears as she gripped the doorframe. Despair rose like vomit in her throat. She tried to think what Father Joseph would think if he knew she was living with a stripper. What had happened to her moral compass? "Sounds like you had quite the time last night," she said instead.

"Yes, it was fun—"

"You call that fun? Doing a strip tease with men fawning all over you?"

"What—"

"In front of everyone. Making a fool of yourself. Of me," she added.

"Nell, it wasn't like that—"

"Taking your clothes off in front of everyone."

"No, I never did that," insisted Angel. "Listen—"

"No, I won't listen. I'm sick of listening." Nell's voice was shaking. She held onto her fear like a life vest.

"Please, I can explain." Angel's voice was low and pleading. "Please. Stop acting like a jerk," she said. "Just let me explain."

Nell let the silence linger between them. "I saw you online. Quite a history you have." The text message sender had also added a link to a YouTube video of Angel dancing in some sleazy nightclub called the "Cheeky Monkey." It had almost been too much to bear. Nell's voice wavered and she struggled to regain control. She was about to cry and put the phone down instead. A dog barked outside and Nell could hear television blaring in the next flat. She stared at the phone and wondered what she had done.

Several minutes later Nell startled as the phone rang again. She saw it was Angel and let it go to voice mail, still too upset to answer. Whether because of Angel's striptease or the depths of her own rage, she wasn't sure. Angel tried two more times and then it was silent.

Nell got a beer from Ellen's fridge and went outside and sat in the fading sunshine. She slammed her hand down on the armrest of the chair and watched as the wood cracked and fell off its base.

By the time the phone rang again Nell had wound herself into a frenzy of anger and self-loathing. She had made herself watch the YouTube video again of Angel dancing, naked with only a tiny G-string, to "Angel of the Morning." And although the dancer was called "Nebibi," it was definitely Angel twirling about naked on the screen. *Bloody hell, who was this woman she loved?* She'd almost thrown up.

In the silence that followed after she picked up the phone, she heard Angel say "Please Nell, say something." Blood pumped in her ears and shivers cascaded down her spine.

"You think I'm stupid?" Nell said at last. "How about the bloody Cheeky Monkey? Remember that? Who are you, anyway?"

"Please Nell—"

"Dancing for a bunch of men wanking themselves off!" Nell gasped, her blood churning at the humiliation she felt. "I knew I couldn't trust you." She heard Angel gasp and muffle a sob. Nell downed her beer and knew in her heart that what she had said was wrong. But still she couldn't stop. "It's disgusting," she persisted, oozing contempt, oiled by her own self-hatred. "You think you're some free-spirit but really you're a fucking slut who'll open her legs for anybody that comes sniffing around," she said, appalled at what she'd said, even as the words came out of her mouth.

"How can you say that to me?"

"How can I say it? I can say it because it's true. The Cheeky Monkey was clue number one! Plus the thing with that French git. Telling me you never screwed. Like hell you never screwed. That was clue number two. And then with me..." Nell was on a roll with pain and anger so deep and raw that she couldn't stop the tsunami of rage. "That was sodding clue number three—"

"Well fuck you too, you self-righteous ass."

Nell registered Angel's words and felt like someone had punched her. The line went dead. Angel had hung up on her. Nell ran her hand through her hair and looked out over shabby back alleys where washing flapped in the breeze and a few heroic shrubs struggled amidst the concrete. *What have I done?* The force of her anger and self-loathing scared her to the core. She tried to watch television but could not escape herself. When the phone rang again later in the evening Nell was paralyzed with fear. But then she saw it was Maddie.

"You're an idiot."

"Don't you get involved."

"I am involved."

"Shit Maddie, you saw what she did."

"I don't know what you heard."

"Saw. I have a video. Bunch of guys with their faces in her tits. And one from YouTube, triple-X rated."

"Videos?" Nell heard Maddie inhale sharply. "Where from?"

"Some kind soul sent them to me."

"Ah," said Maddie. "I think I might know who."

"Right, well I'm just glad to know what's going on."

"And just what is going on, Nell? Why are you behaving like this?" Nell hated it when Maddie got that tone in her voice. As if she was her mother. All self-satisfied and full of herself. "Look," persisted Maddie, "there are a couple of things you need to know. First, Angel loves you."

"Love, sod that. You've got to be kidding. If she loved me why would she humiliate me like this?"

"She's not humiliating you. If you'd stop acting like an idiot and get your facts straight, that would be a good start." Nell sloshed the beer around in her glass and tried to focus on a ship out on the horizon sailing across a sliver of ocean barely visible from Ellen's tiny balcony. Now the little performance in the greenhouse all made sense. Nell thought again that she was going to be sick. "We were having a good time," Maddie explained. "Everyone was having fun. There was a competition and she didn't want to do it but Janine and Ruby egged her on. She didn't take any clothes off either, so you're wrong about that. But you also need to know more about this past of hers you've discovered. It's not really like you think."

"Working in a sleazy strip joint?"

"If you weren't so pig-headed, narrow-minded and judgmental she'd have already shared this with you and then you'd have found out for yourself that it wasn't like that. And what you need to know," persisted Maddie, "is she kept it to herself not only because she thought you'd judge her, but because she didn't want to disappoint you."

"Well she succeeded in that."

"That's how much she loves you. She doesn't want to lose you."

Nell rubbed her eyes, trying to register the words. *Love?* She felt like someone had hit her. "Lose me? Well this is one way to do it," Nell heard herself say.

"She wanted me to tell you since you're not answering her calls anymore."

"What?"

Maddie sighed and started talking about Angel's past. "So now do you understand?"

"No," said Nell. "I don't understand and I don't care." The blood rose in her face and she knew she'd gone past the point of no return, just like the boat disappearing beyond the horizon. She felt sad and terribly alone.

CHAPTER FOURTEEN

Stage lights dazzled green and gold illuminating the massive backdrop on the set. Angel and Kate were at the Duke Theatre in London's West End enjoying a creative rendition of Shakespeare's *Midsummer Night's Dream*. The audience was enjoying the slapstick performance of the mischievous Puck turning Nick Bottom's head into that of a donkey. Titania was just about to fall in love with the donkey after having love juice put in her eyes.

"Okay?" mouthed Kate, reaching out in the dark and squeezing Angel's arm. Angel nodded and patted Kate's hand, happy to know she was loved. She was glad she'd followed Maddie's suggestion to get away for a few days and try to forget the terrible fight with Nell. It had to be Daphne. Maddie was right. It saddened her to think a woman was so jealous of her and so vindictive that she'd try and wreck as many relationships as possible.

"She'll come around," Maddie had said, speaking of Nell, but Angel wasn't so sure. The woman she'd once considered her soul mate was now ignoring her calls, leaving Angel so hurt and disappointed that maybe it was just as well. She knew she should have talked to Nell about her past before it came to this. Nell's words had wounded her deeply, especially when she had so little knowledge of the actual work that Angel did. She had probably done her own share of looking at naked women on the internet nonetheless.

But the worst was Nell's betrayal that moved Angel from the desolation of disappointment into full-blown rage. The village grapevine had been active. Camille had talked to Maddie about her encounter with Nell, and that had led Maddie to confront Nell with this other version of their evening together. Maddie had decided to tell Angel because she felt she needed to know, even though Angel knew it pained her to choose between her friends. Angel had been close to hysterical when she heard the story and then anger had set in. How dare Nell call *her* the slut?

Eventually, after much second-guessing herself and a significant amount of crying and moaning with Maddie, Angel had put it all in perspective. She would not let Nell's cruel words and actions affect her self-worth or ruin her life. Janine was right—Nell was a stupid jerk, an asshole. But deep down she knew it was more complicated than that. Sure Nell had internalized some shame associated with loving women because of her family and more recently with the church, but deep down Angel knew Nell's real problem was she didn't love herself.

Maybe at the end of the day they just weren't right for each other. Nell would be better off with some little religious mouse of a woman who fitted her version of perfection so she could live happily ever after. And maybe Camille was that person all along. It still hurt Angel to think about Nell and Camille back together and let go of her dreams of being with Nell: those short-lived happily-ever-after dreams. It was too bad she'd already extended the sublease on her flat and negotiated a few more months in the cottage after accepting the additional work with *Country Escapes*. Oh well, that couldn't be helped. She'd just have to write it off as a loss.

But the glitz and distractions of the city were working. And by one of those tricks of self-protection, Angel was starting to feel better. Today they'd taken the tube and done some shopping along Oxford Street, pottered around Knightsbridge and then had lunch at a little place they liked near Harrods. Angel had dragged Kate into the flower department just to see the wonderful displays and they'd shared tea and cream éclairs in the café there by the food court. They'd then dashed back to Kate's flat in Chelsea to change and now were at the theatre in the West End with Angel dying for a cigarette. The break-up with Nell had left her sneaking smokes again. Right when she thought she'd really called it quits.

"Good play eh?" said Kate as they headed for the ladies room at the intermission.

"A bit artsy-fartsy, but good. It's a fun way to do Shakespeare, that's for sure," replied Angel. They rounded the corner and she saw the long queue for the ladies'. Angel wondered if she had time to duck out for a quick smoke. "The men's room needs liberating" she said instead, reluctantly joining the other women as Kate jiggled impatiently. "God know why they don't just take a few of the men's stalls and put them in the ladies' loo. Help everyone out."

Very few people looking at the sisters would assume they were related. Kate was smaller, thin and willowy with glossy, shoulder-length hair. It was naturally light brown but was dyed the color of autumn wheat that reminded Angel of Nell every time she saw the light glinting off its golden highlights. In marked contrast to Angel's more feminine look Kate wore preppy clothes and angular snappy suits. Despite these differences, anyone spending a little more time with them would see the similarity in their gestures and in the way they laughed. They both had the same generous mouth and full lips, although at this moment Angel was wearing a deep plum-colored lipstick and Kate just a hint of lip gloss.

"Did you see Gillian?" asked Angel, peering into the mirrors lining the lobby and checking her makeup. Gillian was Robert's intern at the law office. She moonlighted as an extra when she could get work in the theatre. She was quite charismatic by all accounts, but might do well to stick to acting if stories about her messing up at the office were true.

"I think she was in that last crowd scene," said Kate, "but she looks different in a toga, so it's difficult to tell." She raised perfectly-shaped eyebrows and laughed. "Gillian in a toga: now that's worth seeing." Gillian was 'stacked' by all accounts. 'Stacked' not being Kate's exact words.

The sisters laughed as the queue edged slowly forward. "What do women do in there? I really need to go." Kate peered around the corner and saw they were almost at the front now. "What?" she said, noticing Angel hadn't spoken. "What're you thinking about?"

"Nothing," said Angel, glancing at the program again.

"Don't give me that," persisted Kate. "I know you better than that. You can't fool me."

"Oh it's pitiful," said Angel. "I just need the love juice washed out of *my* eyes, that's all." She smiled ruefully in an attempt not to cry. "Love is nothing but trouble."

"Well sorry to disappoint," said Kate, "but I think you're at your best when you're in love." She reached over and gave Angel a quick hug.

Kate's kindness precipitated tears that Angel blinked back as best she could. She twirled a strand of hair around her finger: a childhood gesture she often found herself affecting around her sister. "No, I'm sick of love," Angel said at last, holding open the door so they could slip into the ladies' room. "Give me 'no strings attached' any day."

"Hmm," said Kate, peering into Angel's face as they waited for a stall to open, "maybe you just call it 'no strings' to avoid the fact that you've been in love all along. You talk a good line, Angel, about being a free spirit and all, but I don't think you're really the 'no strings' type when it comes right down to it."

"Jeez, Kate, you sound like my shrink. Not that I actually have one."

"Well maybe you should get one. Or listen more to your sister." Kate caught Angel's eye in the bathroom mirror and tucked a stray strand back behind Angel's ear. "What I mean," she said haltingly, "is that you've spent years calling your relationships 'no strings' types of affairs, but really you fall into love like a ton of bricks."

"Ton of bricks?" Angel looked into the mirror and tried not to feel misunderstood. She felt the classic irritation with Kate, but then let it slip away knowing that her sister meant well. Whatever their differences of opinion, the most amazing thing was the change in Kate who used to get so weird whenever anything to do with her love life came up. Leaving the Cheeky Monkey and Yvonne, had helped the sisters' relationship no end. Plus Kate really cared and, when she saw Angel hurting, was one hundred per cent on her side.

"Anyway, call it what you want, love suits you," continued Kate. "And love is risky. You can't avoid that, you know." She looked like she thought she'd said too much and quickly slipped into the stall. "Good. I won't have to wet myself after all."

Angel was left standing waiting for the next stall to be free, her mind full of Kate's words about risk. Maybe Kate was right. She was fine with risk in her work life, but when it came to relationships, she did move into uber-self-protective mode, worried to show her true self in case she rocked the boat and lost love. If only she'd been honest with Nell about her past, she wouldn't be here now. But then if she had been honest and told Nell earlier, maybe the relationship would have pushed Nell away and right into Camille's arms. What a tangled mess.

After they left the theatre, the sisters walked arm in arm down Charing Cross Road toward Leicester Square in a throng of people emerging from the various West End venues. Neon lights glared from shops and restaurants, music spilled out onto the street. Taxis wove in and out between parked cars, and groups of drunken young men jostled each other playfully. London vibrated with the sounds and smells of nightlife. "So crowded," said Angel, remarking on the huge number of people out in the street. "Different from Cumberland Bay, that's for sure. Feels like I'm turning into a regular country gal down there."

"Yes I like you this way," laughed Kate, gesturing for a cab. "Like love, it suits you. And it's good to see some color in your cheeks. Nice and wholesome." Before Angel could think up a smart-assed reply, a taxi drew up and the sisters tumbled aboard.

"We could walk faster," declared Angel watching the waves of people from inside the car. The cabbie drummed his fingers impatiently on the steering wheel as they slowly inched along past Trafalgar Square. When the traffic lights turned green and Angel hoped they'd make it through the intersection before it turned red again, she noticed a text message from Lucas. He must have heard about her whereabouts through the rumor mill. She hadn't thought about him in a while and realized he must be in London again too.

"Just so you know, I didn't tell him you were here," insisted Kate.

"Thanks, but it's okay," said Angel, tucking her phone back in her bag.

"Does he know about–?"

"Nell? Most likely." Angel was still getting used to Kate being okay with her sister's sexuality. Maybe it had just taken time. That and the fact the culture around them had changed: there was masses of stuff on television these days helping people get over whatever shit was in their heads about gays.

"I tell you what," Kate paused and looked at her sister thoughtfully, "how about inviting him to the party on Saturday? It'll be a big enough crowd that you'll not have to be alone with him, unless you want to, of course," she added quickly. "Okay, then that's all set." It had obviously been a rhetorical question all along.

* * *

Angel loved London. She loved the hustle and bustle, the crowds and the clubs. She loved the museums and the people-watching. She'd had a fun evening out at the pub with old friends, although sadly Sylvie had moved up north to live with her cousin, having giving notice at the club. Angel missed seeing her. But now it was Saturday and the sisters were getting ready for the dinner party, the party that included Lucas. Angel had spoken to him on the phone and he'd flirted with her mercilessly. She found she didn't mind. It was the thing to do with Lucas after all and took her mind off all the other awful stuff with Nell.

They were in Kate's guest bedroom, standing by the old-fashioned wardrobe with its graceful full-length mirror, and deciding what to wear for the party. "What about this?" Angel modeled a sapphire blue silk shirt and flared charcoal-colored trousers. She twirled and looked at her butt in the mirror. "Not bad…too formal?"

Kate sat down on the bed and assessed the outfit. "Yes a bit severe."

"Hmm you're right," answered Angel, pulling off the clothes and leaving them in an untidy pile on the bed. "What about this?" She reached for a pale dusty rose top with a deep scoop neck.

"Not bad." It was a stretchy lace material subtly revealing a silky camisole. "Actually really nice," said Kate, tilting her head to get a full view. "If I had boobs like yours, I'd definitely go for it." She laughed and placed her hands over her small chest. "What about the bottoms? Your black pants?"

"Where are the damn things?" Angel rifled through piles on the bed. "Oh, here we go." She extracted a pair of black stretchy trousers and pulled them up over her thighs. "Flats or heels? What do you think?" She slipped on some ballerina flats. "Makes me look dumpy? I think I might need a heel to balance these child-bearing hips of mine."

Kate laughed. "I think they're perfect. Plus you'll be more comfortable."

"All right, comfort it is."

When Kate left to get changed, Angel did her hair and then finished her makeup, accentuating her eyes with smoky green eyeshadow. She put on a dab of pearly lipstick and was set to go.

By the time Angel got downstairs, Kate was fretting. She feared the baked brie *hors d'oeuvres* were overdone and the wild mushroom crostini wasn't quite right. Robert tasted the treats and declared them perfect, pouring her a glass of Shiraz to calm her nerves. Angel sidled up and kissed her sister, ate one of each of the *hors d'oeuvres* and seconded Robert's declaration. Kate, wearing a yellow striped apron and busy with dishes at the sink, gave Angel a grateful look.

"You look fabulous," said Kate. "And the apron's a ten."

"Thanks, you too," replied Angel, smiling over her shoulder as the doorbell rang and Kate went to greet the first guests. She saw Kate hug a young man and a woman she recognized immediately as Gillian from the theatre. Kate was right. She *was* stacked.

"I want you to meet my sister," said Kate, leading them into the kitchen.

"I can see beauty runs in the family," said Gillian holding out her hand to shake Angel's. It must run in her family too. Somewhere in her mid-twenties, Gillian looked good in a fitted lavender shirt and grey slacks. As she smiled, a lock of thick, wavy brown hair the color of nutmeg fell into her eyes, eyes that drooped slightly at the corners and reminded Angel of a cocker spaniel. Her friend was short and blond with a small straggly goatee.

As Angel made small talk with them and considered why anyone would grow a goatee, she heard Lucas' voice in the hall greeting Kate. She quickly gave an excuse to slip away from the group, check her lipstick and remove her apron. Kate was introducing him to a professor friend and her husband, a couple from the college where she worked. Angel took in the slim figure in the dark jacket, his black hair curling into his collar. Lucas had his back to her in handsome semi-profile.

"Lucas. How lovely you could join us," said Angel warmly. *And Nell can go to hell.*

"Ah Angel," he murmured, eyes softening at the sight of her. He smiled into her face and caught hold of her hand, lifting it to his lips. "I've missed you." As Angel raised her eyebrows at him in mock disbelief, he caught her arm and pulled her close. "Loved the awesome dirty dancing," he whispered.

Angel sat down and fanned herself, shaking her head in disbelief. "You too?"

"Too?"

"Well..."

"Trouble in paradise?" He gave a little pout and pretended to look forlorn.

"Paradise?" she said, laughing. "What planet do you live on?" True, the brief time with Nell *had* felt like paradise, but she should have known it would never last. Once they'd moved beyond infatuation and really had to face each other's dark sides and shortcomings. This focus on all the failed loves in her life made her think about Yvonne and the last time she'd seen her, golden and long-legged. She knew it was a ridiculously pathetic gesture to conjure up such a flawed relationship to help console herself about Nell.

"The same planet as you," Lucas quipped. "Come on, let's go drown our sorrows." Angel saw a shadow pass over his handsome face as he steered her toward the sideboard and poured them each a hefty gin and tonic.

"Daphne?" asked Angel, taking a sip.

"She refuses to accept our finale, unfortunately," he said wearily. "It's over between us, has been for months, but she's not willing to let go. I'm sorry she blames you," he added. "Hoped to humiliate you, of course and ruin your employment." His eyes softened. "Little did she know what she might actually be ruining."

"Well that's over now," said Angel.

Relief crept across his face. "Can't say I'm sorry about that. Nell Frank is what the English call a prig and the Americans uptight, yes? In French we say she's *très tendu.*"

Angel tried to smile, but despite everything felt a loyalty to Nell still. "It's all very complicated I'm afraid," she replied, looking to change the subject. "Here, let's go check out the appetizers," she said. "What would you like?"

"Mostly you. You look gorgeous tonight."

"Thanks, you don't look so bad yourself," Angel replied, smiling sweetly and kissing him on the cheek. When she looked up there was Gillian leaning against the wall watching them.

"To you and to us in London, city of splendor," he said, clinking a toast against her glass. "I have big plans and such very bad thoughts."

Angel looked into Lucas' big brown eyes, shaded by their gorgeous lashes that should be illegal on a man. "You don't say. What kind of plans might those be?"

He paused and then whispered in her ear. "Oh, a bit of real estate here and there, but mostly plans featuring you… and remembering you dancing in that G-string. The link that Daphne sent was very entertaining, I can tell you."

Angel started in alarm as Kate approached and asked her to help with a batch of stuffed mushrooms. Kate sensed she'd missed something saucy and turned to Lucas. "I hope you're not a bad influence on my sister," she said sternly.

"Who, me?" said Lucas coyly.

"Yes you," replied Kate. "*Especially* you." Angel left them playfully arguing over who was the worst influence on her and trooped back into the kitchen. As she left the room she saw Gillian, deep in conversation with the professor, register her departure with a slight movement of her head.

A few minutes later when she entered the hall, heading for the dining room again with a platter of mini quiches, she came face to face with Gillian. They did a little dance as each tried to move to let the other aside, eventually laughing as they collided and a few quiches slid off the plate. Gillian picked them up and pretended to dust them off, laughing as she put all but one back on the plate. "Three second rule," she declared, eyebrows raised in a mock grimace as she popped the quiche in her mouth. "Or is it five? Mmm, think I got a bit of extra protein on that one."

"Gross," said Angel, laughing.

"Sorry, didn't mean to creep you out." When she smiled her dimples puckered. Angel wondered quickly how old she was and figured she must be no more than twenty five. "You don't smoke do you?" Gillian asked suddenly, peering into Angel's eyes.

"Smoke? Why do you ask?" said Angel guiltily.

"I'm trying to stop," said Gillian, her spaniel eyes dancing, "but am in a total relapse right now. What do you say?" She gestured through the kitchen toward the brick back terrace. "Join me? I was just about to open this." She held up a bottle of wine in the other hand.

Angel felt suddenly giddy and before she knew it was seated on the back step next to Gillian. They chatted about the theatre and she told Angel about her work with Robert. Inhaling the forbidden cigarette, Angel felt her body relax right to the end of her toes. She had taken a big slug of the wine and that was racing through her system too, several seconds behind the nicotine, or so it seemed. "Mmm, nice," Angel murmured, eyes closed and her head against the door frame. "I'd forgotten how good—"

"Mmm, no kidding," interrupted Gillian slyly, her mouth against Angel's ear. Such belligerent smoking prompted old memories and Angel felt herself stir, lifting her lips briefly to brush Gillian's. The kiss was chaste and when they parted each smiled at the other. Angel took another drink and Gillian a drag on her cigarette, their eyes locked, each surveying the other. She realized Gillian was really very young and the thought was quite delicious. *Damn Nell. Damn Lucas if it came to that.*

Angel sighed softly as Gillian gently caressed her earlobe, fingering the earring and stroking her cheek. They kissed again wistfully, soft and light, fueled by the wine and cigarette highs. As Angel leaned back against the doorframe, Gillian played with her hair, letting the curls slide through her fingers. Angel dreamily closed her eyes to savor Gillian's light touch. They might have stayed like this for some time, but Angel was startled from her reverie when Kate's voice echoed through the kitchen. Quickly, they jumped apart, holding the cigarettes behind their backs like naughty children.

"Oh, there you are, Angel. I wondered where you were and Lucas is looking for you. We were just going to sit down for dinner." She gave them a quizzical look. "You okay, Gillian?" she added, looking suddenly stern.

When Kate left they giggled and stubbed out the forbidden smokes. Gillian put her fingers to her lips and indicated she would phone her. Angel hoped not, although it was a sweet gesture nonetheless.

Gillian sat across from Angel at dinner, gazing with barely concealed full-blown lust. No one seemed to notice except Lucas who glared back across the table at Gillian. Angel was enjoying herself. Why not? Let them duke it out for all she cared. They were all like animals really, territory marking and seeing who could pee the farthest.

Angel caught Kate's eye and felt her happy mood slip away. Still, she'd be damned if she let a woman spoil her life.

She returned to her grilled trout, lavishly smeared with lemon butter and almonds and accompanied by tiny new red potatoes. There was also a curried couscous and garbanzo bean dish and a large salad of baby greens. Kate was serving dinner on their mother's delicate chinaware. Edged in gold, the china suddenly reminded Angel of how their mom would let them use the cups and saucers and dessert plates for special teas served to their dolls and numerous stuffed animals. She felt a desolation creep into her heart. The sight of the dishes brought with it a melancholy so deep Angel found herself stifling a tear. She dabbed at herself, pretending she had something in her eye. Lucas sensed her mood. "Okay, *petite amie*?"

Angel felt his hand squeeze her thigh and rest there for a moment. He reached for the water jug, refilled her water glass and picked her napkin off the floor and rearranged it back on her lap. His chivalry was starting to irritate. As the meal came to an end, Angel watched Lucas' reflection in the mirror across the room. Candlelight glittered off the gilt edging, framing his handsome face and shadowing the sensitive mouth. She tried to rouse herself by imagining his mouth on hers, those elegant long fingers in her hair, his body against her own. But it was just like before: nothing. Lucas sensed her tension and reached out and touched her wrist. It was an offhand gesture, but Angel fought to stop herself from pulling her hand away.

But dessert was good. Kate served huge slices of raspberry meringue cake topped with chocolate buttercream. The crisp meringues, layered with raspberries and moist chocolate cake, were garnished with chocolate slivers and served with rich, dark cappuccinos. Angel took the first bite of her piece. It was heaven. She closed her eyes as the chocolate sweetened her tongue and temporarily blocked out her barrage of swirling thoughts. Registering the heaviness in her heart, she hoped the chocolate would get her back to a place where she could get through the rest of the evening.

After dinner they gathered in the living room. The party was still going strong and glasses were being refilled, but Gillian was saying her goodbyes. Another date lined up, most likely. As she waved to the group, Gillian caught Angel's eye and gave her a cheeky grin. Lucas ignored Gillian's departure and was deep in conversation with Kate's neighbor who worked in a boutique in town. "*Combien de temps avez-vous vécu en Angleterre?*" said the neighbor sweetly to Lucas, asking him how long he'd lived in England. When he responded in English, Angel saw the crestfallen look on the young woman's face. She remembered how annoying it was when you'd try and talk in French and they'd answer in English. It was so tiresome and made you feel stupid. Angel looked around, suddenly bored and realized her phone was ringing, muffled in her purse hanging on a peg by the kitchen door. She grabbed it and moved toward the window alcove in the hallway away from the crowd.

"Hi Maddie. What's up?" Maddie had been trying to reach her all day and they'd kept missing each other.

"Angel it's me." It was Nell. Startled, Angel felt her knees go weak and sat down heavily on the window seat wishing she hadn't deleted Nell's number in a moment of rage. At least then she would have had some warning for the call. Hot panic seared through her. Speechless, she felt the heat rise in her face. Turning her cheek against the cool of the windowpane, she tried to steady her breathing as she looked out onto the darkened London street.

"I'm sorry." Nell's words hung in the air. Angel hesitated, feeling caught between her body, staring out onto the street and her mind, hovering above the scene.

"I've been such a fool and I've thought about you all the time. I miss you so much." Angel heard Nell's voice crack, heavy with emotion. "You have no idea." *I do. All those empty days and sleepless nights.* The room started to tick around her one more time. Saucepans in the kitchen clanked, someone laughed and background music swelled and fell away. Before Angel could gather herself to speak, Nell rushed on, her voice hardly above a murmur. "I wanted to say I'm really sorry. I acted like a complete git and you didn't deserve that. I'm not sure that you'll forgive me. I'm not sure I could if I was you and I'm not sure if you even want to see me again after what I said to you…" Nell's voice faltered and Angel heard her catch her breath.

The silence grew as Angel struggled to respond. In her heart of hearts she wanted to reach out over the phone lines and tell Nell it was okay, it would always be okay, but the knowledge of her betrayal still stung.

"Angel, I'm sorry. Say something." It was *déjà vu*. She'd said that to Nell before calling her a fucking slut. The pain was deep and the sting of humiliation rushed back. *Why now?* Angel was just starting to come to terms with not having Nell in her life.

"I'm not sure what you want me to say," Angel stammered. "It's been awful." Her voice broke off in a whisper, continuing now soft and low. "Maddie told me everything."

"What did she tell you?" Nell's voice caught and Angel could tell she was stifling a sob.

Angel started haltingly. The betrayal was still so raw. She told Nell what Camille had shared with Maddie, and what Maddie had passed on to her. "I can't believe you made love to her and then lied to me about it. I can't decide which is worse."

"It wasn't like that," stammered Nell. Angel knew if she could see her that Nell's face would be as red as a beet. "It was never about love."

"Well what was it about?" Angel persisted until she got the whole story out of her, bit by bit, between her sobs and declarations of self-loathing. Angel needed to hear everything, every sordid detail. She tried to make sense of Nell telling her that she had felt guilt and pity and worry because Camille was so vulnerable.

"It meant nothing, believe me. I was so drunk I didn't know what I was doing."

"That's a cowardly excuse."

"I know."

Angel let the silence linger a moment before starting again. "What you said to me really hurt." She took a breath. "What a hypocrite! There you were calling me a slut when you'd been jacking Camille off. I mean, really. What a nerve. And you thought the worst of me. You said such cruel things and you didn't trust me. That hurt so much, that you would think such things—"

"I'm sorry," Nell exclaimed, her voice rising.

"No, let me finish. That you would think that my dancing, a job and something that I actually have some pride in, was something that I did for sexual pleasure. You must be joking. I mean, please. Have you ever been to a strip club?"

"I know. You don't need to tell me that. I hate myself for what I said. I'm sorry I blamed you and made it all about me. I felt so jealous." Nell paused and silence loomed. Eventually she spoke again. "Why didn't you just tell me?"

"I'll tell you why." Angel sighed loudly into the phone. "There were so many times I almost told you, but was scared you wouldn't understand. That you'd think less of me or reject me. Case in point."

"Well it's a lot to take in. I mean a pole dancer. Bloody hell."

Angel took a deep breath and tried to stay calm. "I know you've never had to deal with something like this before. It's all new and I know you've had losses I can't even imagine. And I think you're the kind of woman who needs to protect herself."

"No, don't say that. I'm not 'some kind of woman,'" Nell repeated. "We have a life together. Don't we?" she stammered.

"I thought so," retorted Angel, trying to steady her anger threatening to erupt again. "But you're the one who walked away." Angel hesitated, now deadly certain about what she was going to say. "I've spent the last week and a half trying to get over you. I might forgive you for the terribly mean things you said to me—"

"You must know I didn't mean it."

"Yes, but it's the stuff underneath, the judging me, that's the problem. You reek of that crap."

"I know I didn't get an 'A' in women's lib," Nell said sheepishly.

"Oh please, that's not helping your case one bit. This is not nineteen seventy five." Angel looked out into the night, watching couples strolling companionably along the road. A woman was walking her dog and two taxis flew by. Laughter spilled out from the next room. The party was still going.

"Look," she tried again, "it's not enough to say you're sorry and not say these things again if you still feel them deep down.

Do you understand what I mean?" She paused and waited for Nell to respond. The woman with the dog was turning the corner and was soon out of sight. Angel steadied her breathing and wished her life was ordinary, boring and ordinary.

"I'll try." Nell's voice was barely above a whisper. "I promise I'll try." Angel felt herself soften, her heart pounding. The connection she felt to Nell, the pull, some kind of electric charge crackled down the phone lines. *Damn her*.

"I'll do anything you want. Anything you need," Nell murmured, voice quaking with emotion. "I love you Angel, I want us to be together."

Love? Angel registered the words and tried to imagine her face: violet-blue eyes, tousled hair and that solid, athletic body. She sat in a bubble of light and ached to see her, to feel her. "I love you too," she said quietly, "even though you annoy the hell out of me." At this Nell laughed and she laughed too, the charge between them building again.

"Come home," Nell said. Angel registered the notion of home and smiled inside. "I miss you," Nell added, "and I want us to be together forever."

Angel was quiet for a moment, thinking about forever. "I miss you too," she said at last, "but there's something else I wanted to say if we're talking about forever."

"Something else?" Nell echoed.

"Yes." Angel paused and licked her lips. "Our fight," she said, "it got me thinking—"

"Anything. I love you," insisted Nell.

Angel looked out the window and watched a couple stroll by arms around each other. "You might not want to hear this, but I'm going to be honest if we're talking about our future. It's about babies. A baby to be more precise."

"Babies?" Angel heard Nell catch her breath. She couldn't stop the flood now if she'd wanted and this needed to be said if they did indeed have a forever.

"I want to have a baby. Not now of course, but sometime soon. I know you don't want kids and it's not fair to you and certainly not to me, to compromise." She heard laughter from the next room and this emboldened her somehow. "You can't compromise over children." There was a long silence. It was agonizing. Angel could imagine Nell pacing and running her hands through that disheveled hair of hers. It was pure agony.

"Are you still there?" Nell said eventually, voice full of trepidation.

"Yes," said Angel. "I'm still here."

"Let's try again, please." It came out in a rush and Angel realized Nell was crying. Nell, the stoic rock, was sobbing into the phone. "I know I get weird when I think my life is getting out of control and I don't know how things are going to end up, but I want to try." Angel heard her take a breath and stifle another sob, "And I'd like to change my feelings about having another child. With you."

These words made Angel's heart thump wildly. She felt her cheek grow hot and turned it to the cool windowpane once more, every nerve in her body on high alert. She saw the twinkling of streetlights and a tracery of headlights sweeping along the road outside. "I'd like that very much," Angel said softly.

Somehow Angel managed to bear what was left of the evening, glad to see the guests eventually getting their coats and saying goodbyes. Lucas lingered to the end and started to help them clean up, but Kate shooed him away, insisting the mess would be cleared up in the morning. Angel saw him to the door where he lightly trailed his fingers down her cheek. "No worries, my sweet." When she didn't reply he cupped her chin in his fingers. "*Vraiment, Angel,*" he said, "*je crois que je suis amoureux avec toi.*" Angel watched a flicker pass across his eyes, dark and smoldering in the low light and realized his words: he thought he was falling in love. With her. Angel had no energy to respond, but didn't need to. Lucas was out the door and giving her a wave as he jumped into a cab and disappeared around the corner.

CHAPTER FIFTEEN

Bloody hell. Startled, Nell looked into Angel's molten grey gaze and saw the furious desire there. She blinked, hardly able to believe her eyes. What was she doing back from Kate's so soon? They'd talked themselves to death over the last few days and Nell had expected her back tomorrow. But here was Angel, pushing her against the file cabinet, in her office. Angel's hands were on her and she kissed Nell hard on the mouth, nipping her ear. *Ouch*. She was playing rough. Nell grabbed and brushed her breast. It was soft, impossibly soft and Nell realized Angel was not wearing a bra. Her nipples showed through the silky material of her dress in little peaks. Nell's eyes went from her chest to her face, watching as Angel smiled a slow, wicked smile, then puckered her mouth and narrowed her eyes.

Angel must have taken an early train down from London and here she was wedging her thigh between Nell's legs. She watched the green, gauzy fabric of Angel's dress swirl and catch at her hip. Those wide hips, impossible curves. Nell licked her lips and swallowed, heat rising as fire burned through her veins.

Angel circled her hips, pressing against her. Nell reached for Angel and let her hand trail up her thigh, higher and higher. Her eyes widened as she touched Angel's warm bare skin. *No panties*!

"Just this once," Angel said. "Decided to give you a treat as well as a talking to." She smiled coyly and pushed Nell playfully. "I know that's naughty."

Naughty? Oh my God, did she say naughty? Nell laughed out loud and lifted her dress, burying herself in Angel's sex. She smelled sweet and earthy and tasted awfully good. Nell felt herself get hot and damp and smiled with relief as Angel opened her fly and caressed her there.

"I've missed you," Nell murmured. "I'm sorry. Please don't ever leave me again." She felt tears threatening to spill and blinked, terrified at the thought.

"Then don't ever do anything like that again. And never, ever, treat me that way," Angel said, nipping gently along Nell's jawline. "I mean it." She glared, daring her to disagree. Then she pushed Nell back against the file cabinet more roughly and kissed her again, biting her lower lip as their mouths met. Her hands were on Nell, tearing open her shirt. Nell heard a button pop and felt the shirt slide off her body as she braced herself against the wall.

"Never," Angel insisted, "ever, talk to me that way again." Her tongue circled Nell's navel and she felt herself tremble. Angel glared, eyes blazing, looking aggrieved. "And never betray me again. Do you understand?"

Bloody hell.

"I said do you understand?" Angel's fingers dug into Nell's waist as she circled her navel, then nipped her lower and lower across her belly until she reached her sex. Angel probed her gently with her tongue then took her clitoris between her lips. Nell felt herself swell and groan as the sensation registered in her groin. Angel had her pinned so Nell had to hold onto the file cabinet to keep her balance. Intensely erotic, Angel berated Nell between sucks.

Nell was trembling under her touch. "I'm sorry," she said again between sighs and groans.

Angel looked up, her eyes flashing and Nell saw the blood rise in her face. "You," Angel said, pulling away and letting Nell stand there backed up against the cabinet, her swollen sex glistening between them. "You're pig-headed. It's not all about you. And I know you've suffered losses and I'm sorry about that. But sometimes you have to trust that things will turn out all right even though you don't know. You have to trust enough to love even though it's risky."

Nell could see Angel was shaking, every nerve in her body primed. She went back to sucking Nell and pulled her sex deeper into her mouth. *Oh God.* Angel hadn't finished yet, but came back up for air.

"Do you want this?" she said more gently. "Do you want me to take you like this?" She was asking permission.

"Yes," Nell cried. "Yes." Angel was shagging her mercilessly and she liked it a lot.

"Yes, what?" Angel insisted, swirling her tongue round and round, her fingers probing and gently sliding in and out.

"Yes, please," Nell said, groaning loudly, still pinned against the wall.

"Okay, that's better." Angel sucked and nibbled, then pulled her fingers away, looking again into Nell's face. "I know you're scared," she said, planting feather-light kisses along the length of Nell's inner thigh that threatened to put her over the edge. "But this is about the respect I need from you for who I am and how I want to live my life. What do you say about that?" Angel insisted, flicking her tongue across Nell's clitoris so that she trembled uncontrollably. Angel's fingers held her bum firmly as Nell struggled to speak.

"Come for me," she said. It was another command, Nell realized and she liked it. Her head fell back and her body threatened to explode. Then Angel was on her again, sucking and licking before sliding her fingers deep into Nell's sex. *Oh my God.*

"Whoa..."

"Please say it," Angel repeated as Nell felt herself reaching the edge. Angel's eyes burned hot with emotion.

"I won't ever," Nell cried, clutching Angel's shoulders and moaning into her hair, "I won't ever hurt you again." She cried out her name and three garbled words as her body convulsed in exquisite relief. Nell staggered and then felt her body relax.

"That's more like it," Angel said, tender now and stroking Nell's breasts. "I think you said you loved me, which I appreciate as I love you too." Angel tweaked Nell's nipple and continued. "Except when you're mean to me in which case I won't be happy." Angel smiled and kissed Nell again. "But something tells me you're going to be really nice now, right?"

"Yes ma'am," Nell said, giving her a mock salute and languidly stroking the gorgeous length of her bare thigh. Lightheaded, Nell was moving in slow motion. It was startlingly quiet except for the sound of her own heartbeat thudding in her ears. Nell would remember this and the brazen look in Angel's eyes, for as long as she lived. Breathing heavily, she felt the smoldering desire that sparked between them and this new level of passion in her heart.

"You owe me one," Angel said, rubbing herself against Nell's thigh.

"I do, you're right," Nell said, stilling her breathing and turning to face Angel. "When do you want it?"

"Maybe now," she said, rearranging her breasts into her dress. "Or maybe not."

"Hmm, not sure if you deserve it anyway," Nell said coyly, lifting the heavy mane of hair from Angel's neck and kissing the soft warm skin at the base of her throat. "You're awfully cheeky, especially with not wearing any knickers."

"You're probably right," Angel said. "I am rather cheeky. And that's not just because I worked at the Cheeky Monkey." With that she turned, lifted up her dress to show her bare bum and sashayed out of the office.

Nell was dumbfounded. "Come back," she cried, pulling on her shirt, doing up her jeans and catching up with Angel as she approached her car. "Where're you going?" Nell wasn't sure whether to laugh or cry.

"Home. I'm meeting Maddie. I'll see you tomorrow," Angel said from her car, eyeing Nell speculatively, cool as a cucumber and assertive as all get-out, her breasts falling out of the dress.

Angel drove home carefully, aware of the fact that she was half-naked, smelled of sex and didn't need any embarrassing traffic stops. She considered the evening and questioned her quick exit. It was about control. She was still mad at Nell and wanted to end the evening on top, literally. She knew if they'd had their usual sex with mutual orgasms, she'd be all soft and pliable in Nell's hands. She didn't want that. She wanted Nell aroused and begging for more. She wanted her vulnerable. Angel understood this need to be in control but the insight was still slightly disturbing nonetheless.

When Angel reached the cottage, she changed into sweatpants and a T-shirt, pulled open the blinds and opened the window to let in the evening fragrances of the garden. The darkening sky flushed pink at the edges of the horizon. She poured herself a diet cola and headed outside to her patio to wait for Maddie. She hoped she'd be late as she needed some time alone to come down from the encounter with Nell.

She got her wish. The sun was setting behind the headlands, a huge red dome slipping silently into the sea. She texted Kate to tell her she'd arrived home safely and then pulled a shawl around her shoulders against the chill evening air, contemplating her life. It was true. She was not going to let anyone control her. Ever. As the evening light dimmed, she felt herself relax. It was good to be home.

Home. Looking about she was quietly thrilled to have some climbing roses in bloom that looked pretty against the whitewashed stone walls of the cottage. The magnolia was still hanging on and her kitchen garden was thriving. Angel thought about all that had happened since she first moved in here. It seemed like a lifetime ago.

"Hi love. How's it going?" Maddie jolted Angel from her reverie, coming around the corner with leftovers from the restaurant. "Thought you might be a bit peckish after your trip."

Angel laughed on hearing the English phrase and smiled back at her friend. “I am. I could do with something to replace all the calories I’ve spent sitting on my butt all day.”

“All right then, let’s eat,” said Maddie decidedly, reaching down to embrace Angel on the patio. “Missed you.”

“Mmm, missed you too,” said Angel, hugging her friend and inhaling her familiar perfume.

“Grab a couple of plates, would you love.” Maddie was pulling containers of stir-fry from a plastic bag and arranging them on the patio table. She watched Angel return with plates, forks and another cola. “So what’s new? Other than you and Nell back together again, of course.”

“Not much,” said Angel. “Well actually a lot, I suppose.”

“Do tell. I’m all ears.” Maddie sat down and finished arranging the food. “Okay, let’s eat.”

“Well, where to start.” Angel forked food into her mouth and contemplated her trip. She started by talking about London and all the fun they’d had and went on to explain how Lucas had been invited to the dinner party at Kate’s. When she got to the bit about Lucas telling her he was falling in love with her, Maddie stopped her mid-sentence.

“No, he didn’t?” Maddie’s eyes widened and she had the most mischievous look on her face.

“Why? Are you surprised?”

“Oh my God, that’s so Lucas. Did he say something like ‘I think *que je suis* in love *de toi?*”

Angel sputtered uncontrollably and had a coughing attack as the soda went down the wrong way. “That is so funny.” She was holding her chest, trying to stop coughing, laughing all the while at Maddie’s attempt at French, which included an appalling accent. Maddie caught her eye and started to giggle until both of them were laughing uncontrollably.

“You’re terrible,” squealed Angel. “Completely incorrigible.”

“No really, it’s true. He said that to me too.” Angel exploded with laughter again at the thought. “Isn’t that just like him?” said Maddie. “I should have told you to be prepared for it.”

Angel was still wiping tears from her eyes. Maddie's attempt at translation was really very amusing and Lucas' behavior was so predictable. Eventually their giggles subsided and Angel told Maddie the rest of the story, minus the most recent encounter with Nell. "I'm still pissed with her, though," said Angel, thinking about what just happened. The thought almost made her blush and she didn't blush easily.

"Well she deserved it."

"Right and I don't take that lying down, or standing up, or on top, or bottom." Angel started laughing again and Maddie joined in. Soon they were giggling wildly again.

"Or from behind."

"Maddie!" Angel swatted her with her napkin. "You're too rude."

"Sorry love." Maddie was still grinning broadly. "Oh I've missed you," she said reaching out for Angel's hand. "No one makes me laugh like you do."

"Well I'm glad to be of some use." She pushed her hair behind her ears and started piling the dirty dishes, balancing the tray against her hip as she maneuvered through the door, surrounded by a halo of light from the kitchen. The garden was now shrouded in dusk.

"So how did you leave it with Lucas?" asked Maddie carefully when Angel returned from the kitchen.

"We had lunch at a little place in Covent Garden the day after the party. Funny actually as the waitress was so out of it that she forgot our order, then eventually brought the wrong things." Angel smiled at the memory of how they ended up getting their lunch on the house. "Anyway, it was a good distraction because I was nervous about telling Lucas I wasn't interested. Just a teenage fascination, you know."

"Yes, especially after the 'I think *je suis* in love' stuff."

Angel exploded in laughter again at Maddie's accent. "But actually telling him was far easier than the anticipation of it. He took it well. Absolute gent. Never batted an eyelid and certainly didn't grovel." She realized that Maddie was listening carefully and without specifically noting it, filed it away for future reference.

"Anyway, I hope we'll still be friends," Angel said finally, finishing off a small bowl of peanuts and licking the salty oil from her fingers.

"Oh you will be," said Maddie without hesitation. "He has a big heart even if he's deficient in some other areas."

CHAPTER SIXTEEN

"Let's not talk shop today," said Angel. "Anyone who talks shop gets a demerit and then when you have three demerits you get spanked."

"Promise?" said Nell. "I think I feel a horticultural conversation coming on." Angel punched her playfully. It was their day off and they were sitting out on the brick patio at Nell's deciding what to do. Angel looked gorgeous sitting there drinking sparkling water and munching on grapes.

"You smell divine," Nell said, nuzzling Angel's hair and moving her hand between her thighs. Angel was naked under the silky bathrobe. Nell reached over and slipped the robe down over her shoulders to reveal a long expanse of bare shoulder.

"Here, let's go back to bed." Nell hoisted Angel up on her back, swaying under the weight. Or I could just drop you in the hot tub. That might be fun." She'd been fantasizing for days about getting Angel naked in the hot tub on the deck.

"Stop," said Angel. "Put me down you brute. What if I don't want to get all hot and bothered with you?"

"Really?" Nell hesitated, unsure suddenly.

"Don't be silly," Angel implored. "I'm joking. I want nothing more than to go anywhere with you. Especially if there's fucking involved, 'scuse my French. And sorry I'm such a big-boned gal," she added, laughing into Nell's shoulder.

"The more of you the better," Nell said, tottering and getting no further than the chaise at the edge of the patio. They fell together in a tangle of arms and legs. It was a beautiful day with the sea spread before them. Only the sound of sea birds wheeling overhead and their own voices disturbed the quiet. The side patio was totally private.

"I meant that about the more of you the better," Nell said. "I know you don't believe me, but you have the greatest body." She looked down at Angel spread-eagled, the bathrobe open and her plump naked skin glowing in the warmth of the sun. Nell's head started to pound and she felt the blood rising in her body. It was her fantasy. The recurring fantasy she had about finding a stranger, naked and sunbathing, waiting for her. She wanted that person wet, hot and eager.

"What're you looking like that for?" Angel asked, starting to pull the bathrobe back around her body. "You have a funny look on your face. What are you thinking, you naughty girl?"

"Oh you don't want to know," Nell said, kissing her hard on the mouth and removing the bathrobe so she could see Angel's body again glistening in the sunshine.

"I do," said Angel. "Tell me."

"No, I'm embarrassed," Nell said, reddening and looking away.

"It's okay," said Angel. "I'll play as long as it's fun."

Nell looked at her slyly and started to tell her the fantasy.

"Ah, I think I know this one," Angel said merrily. "Do you want me to pretend I'm asleep and you find me here?"

"Yes," Nell said. "How did you know?"

"I just guessed," she grinned, snuggling back onto the chaise, feigning sleep and spreading her legs so the sun warmed her sex. "Go away and you can find me here. I might have a surprise for you."

Nell laughed low and deep and growled slightly, heading inside. She was so aroused she could barely walk. She threw off her clothes, grabbed a towel and picked up Angel's thong that she'd left on the bedroom floor. When Nell got back Angel had a small smile on her face and her eyes were tightly closed.

"Mmm, who do we have here?" Nell said, stroking her body gently and feeling its warmth from the sun. Angel's skin was incredibly silky. She thought about Angel dancing naked just for her and held the erotic thought in her mind.

"Who are you?" asked Angel, opening her eyes wide and moaning. She reached for Nell and stroked the length of her body as Nell stood above her. "I don't know who you are but I like you a lot," she said, playing the part.

Nell felt herself tremble and crouched by Angel's chaise. "I don't allow naked strangers on my patio," she said. "I've brought you something to wear." Nell held up the thong and gave Angel a dreamy look.

"Oh that," she said. "If you say so." They laughed as Nell tried to put it over her thighs and realized it was on backwards. Angel closed her eyes, trying to get back into the part, so that Nell could pull the thong back on. Nell gasped when she saw that it barely covered Angel's sex. Her body was so soft and full that Nell felt an ache deep in her groin. Angel lay back and let Nell caress her, closing her eyes again as Nell's lips brushed her face. Slowly, achingly slowly, Nell explored Angel's body, pulling the thong aside to touch and taste her. It was so erotic to do this in full daylight: to see her crevices and to kiss her skin in her most tender parts. Nell's tongue circled Angel's clitoris and she felt it harden. *Oh my God, she's so beautiful.*

"Who are you?" Angel moaned. "I've been waiting for you all my life." She was good at this. "I need to be naked," she murmured, pulling off the thong and flinging it on the ground. "I want to be free." She was *really* good at this. As Nell made love to her, she pretended Angel was escaping the night clubs with their randy, slobbering men and had sought her out to love her and keep her safe. Nell kissed Angel again, whispering soft words into her ear as she loved her, every bit of her, a river of kisses between words. She was safe now. Nell let herself see, in broad daylight, the sweet folds of Angel's sex, wet and warm in the morning sunshine.

"I've never had an orgasm," Angel said suddenly, "and I heard this is the place to come, so to speak. She giggled hysterically as Nell kissed her again, stilling her. "Yes," Angel said, composing herself again, "I heard that you could help me have an orgasm."

"I think I can make that happen," said Nell, eyeing her speculatively.

"Good, then I've come to the right place," Angel said, reaching for several grapes from the bowl by the chair and squishing them over her breasts. Nell looked up and watched the pulp slide off Angel's left breast and the juice dribble over a nipple. *Whoa.*

"Oh look what I did? Can you get that off me?" Angel was giggling furiously again. Nell watched the dark liquid oozing over her nipples and moved to cup her breasts, sucking the juice that dripped in her cleavage.

"Mmm," Nell said. "You taste really good."

"Glad you like it," Angel responded, reaching for more grapes and pressing them against her body. Nell traced the juice with her tongue as the heady aroma hit her senses. She followed the sweet trail and tasted the pulp dripping across Angel's skin.

"Mmm," Nell said again. "You like that." She sucked and licked and then hauled herself up to meet Angel's gaze. "I think this might just be your fantasy."

"Might be," said Angel coyly, letting herself fall back so that Nell could kiss her again.

"I think I'm right," said Nell playfully, letting her tongue savor the ecstasy of it all. "Wow, you really, really taste good now."

"I do?" said Angel innocently. "What do I taste like?"

"Like this," she said, rubbing her fingers through Angel's sex and then leaning over to place them between Angel's lips. "See?"

"I see what you mean," Angel said with a dreamy look. "Dry and fruity with a hint of oak, but not too woody."

Nell laughed uproariously and sat back on her heels. "That was very funny. I forgot you used to live in wine country."

"Who, me?" She was laughing again now. "No, I'm just a stranger on a sex mission and I'm learning some new things." She giggled and reached for Nell. "Like this for instance. I wonder what this tastes like." She gave her a slow, sly smile and probed with her tongue between Nell's legs. "Mmm, sort of salty and sweet."

By the time they'd worn each other out, their fantasies satiated, clouds were rolling in. They took showers and now sat companionably in Nell's kitchen nook, deciding what to do with the rest of the day.

Nell knew then that she could handle Angel's past. It just took some creative sex to get over the hump.

Let's go to the beach," Angel said. "I don't care if it rains. We could pretend to be tourists."

"More games?" said Nell, raising an eyebrow. "How about you pretend to be a tourist lost on the beach and I rescue—"

"Stop!" Angel threw her napkin, laughing hysterically. "No more! I'm sore."

"If you insist," Nell said sheepishly, stroking Angel's face. "But seriously, we could go see the lighthouses. That might be fun."

"The lighthouses?" inquired Angel. "Yes, Maddie was talking about that. Very touristy and I haven't done it yet. Let's do that."

"Okay, it's a deal," said Nell. "Go get dressed and I'll pack us a few snacks."

* * *

They drove round a corner and saw their first glimpse of Ransom Head, home of one of the most spectacular lighthouses on the southern coast of England. The sun had disappeared and the air carried a chill as rain started to sprinkle. A few more miles and the massive headland loomed with its lighthouse jutting out against craggy bluffs. Nell heard Angel let out a little sigh of pleasure. Gleaming white, it sat majestically over the churning surf.

They parked and climbed down from the pickup. Angel had pulled a nylon anorak from her bag and was zipping it up to keep out the cool salty air. They stood together against the lighthouse looking up at the looming octagonal tower. It was a great vantage point to feel the immense height of the tower and understand its importance for this craggy coastline. Down below them the sea rolled and churned and Nell was glad they'd decided to leave Gruff at home. A tour guide was gathering a small crowd of visitors and beckoned them to join. Nell looked over at Angel and smiled.

"Eighty-six feet or twenty-six meters," said the guide, describing the octagonal tower. "Made of rubble-stone and mortar in eighteen fifty-eight. The original light was a revolving one, with a fixed red light below the main light, automated in…"

"What year was that?" Nell whispered. She was having problems concentrating on anything other than Angel and her gorgeous body next to hers. Nell's mind was full of their lovemaking, fantasies and all.

"Nineteen thirty-four was when it was automated. I'm going to give you a pop quiz at the end of the talk," Angel whispered, smiling at Nell mischievously.

The guide was going on about how the light flashed every ten seconds, but the red part of the light was only visible if you were in dangerous proximity to the reef. Angel's hand felt soft in hers. She was so close Nell could smell the mint from Angel's gum on her breath and sense the energy from her body. Nell thought suddenly about the dangers in her life and wondered if she ought to be seeing that red warning light right about now. *Loss follows love*. Such negative thoughts were few and far between these days, fortunately, but when they came they still took her breath away. She steadied her breathing and concentrated on staying in the moment.

"Nell, you okay?" inquired Angel, touching her arm as the tour ended. "Want to check out the gift store?" She pulled Nell by the hand in the direction of the shop. "I love this place," she cried as they walked toward the buildings on the other end of the car park that housed the shop and a tiny café. "Winter gales and ship wrecks, stolen brandy and crazy sailors."

"Crazy sailors?"

"Yes, you know, driven to smash their ships on the rocks by the mermaids."

"They weren't mermaids, they were their girlfriends," said Nell, laughing. "Girlfriends drive you to drink and torment."

"Oh they do, do they?" said Angel kissing her hard on the mouth. "Let's get to the gift shop and see how much torment you can handle." She took Nell's hand and dragged her into the shop where a mass of postcards, trinkets and t-shirts were on display.

"Yes, exactly," said Nell, looking around sheepishly. "How about I wait in the truck?"

"Don't you dare," warned Angel. "This is good for you. It builds character." She was already paging through glossy coffee table books about British lighthouses. Nell looked over at her Angel frowning and trying to make out the small print in the low light. Nell loved the way her hair curled around her head and circled her shoulders. She could see Angel's cardigan under the anorak and her eyes dropped to her breasts tight against the buttons up the front. Ten minutes passed and then fifteen.

"Sorry I'm taking so long." As Angel turned to her, eyes huge in the low light of the shop, Nell felt intense longing for her.

"What?" Angel asked as she saw Nell's face. Nell reached for her and kissed the inside of her wrist, bringing it to her mouth. Angel's grey eyes, dark and inquiring, looked into Nell's own. Her mouth was slightly open. Nell heard her sigh softly as she kissed her hard, burying her hands in her hair. It all happened so quickly. The bleached-blond sales assistant with a nose stud and lip ring looked startled and the straight couple by the postcards didn't know where to look. Tough, thought Nell. This is what women in love look like. *Get over it.*

When they left the shop they went the long way back down to the beach, sauntering hand in hand until they came to a small bench at a grassy spot halfway down. "Breathtaking," Angel said quietly, leaning back on the bench and putting her hands behind her head. The sky rose above them, marbled with remnants of clouds now the rain had stopped.

"*You,*" said Nell earnestly. "You're breathtaking." She felt a sudden rush of fondness for Angel, so sudden it made her laugh.

Angel laughed too. Nell felt the laughter as she pressed against Angel and hugged her close. She traced her finger along Angel's nose and around her full lips, loving the way Angel sucked ever so slightly on it as Nell touched her mouth. Their lips met and Nell resisted the urge to kiss deep and strong and instead lightly brushed her lips, lingering with such tenderness that for an awful moment she thought she might be overcome. Those feelings she always kept in check came bubbling up. Squeezing her eyes to control herself, Nell continued to caress and taste without haste or pressure.

Angel gave a soft inviting sigh and slipped her hands inside Nell's shirt, stroking her back. She was kissing her with warm sweet kisses, nibbling Nell's bottom lip. Their tongues touched slowly, softly, in an erotic dance. When Angel tipped her head to the side, loose curls fell across her cheek. Nell removed the clasp that let Angel's long hair tumble about her face.

"Okay," Nell asked, "if I ravish you right here on this cliff top?"

"Be my guest," Angel said, craning her neck as hikers approached on the path. Grinning, they tucked in their clothes and sat up primly side by side on the bench. As two women came into view, panting slightly from the uphill climb, Nell was pointing out the various sea birds wheeling overhead.

"Cormorant," she gestured at a bird diving into the waves, "and guillemot over there. Too bad we can't see any dolphins," she added. "Cornwall's famous for them."

"Lovely view," said one of the women as they passed.

"Wonderful day for birding," said the other.

Nell waited until the women were out of sight and then kissed Angel again, hard and passionate. "You're the only bird I'm interested in," she quipped. "You know that don't you?"

"I'm starting to get the idea," said Angel, laughing as she got up and straightened her clothes. Nell looked at her closely but she glanced away and would not meet her gaze. "There's something you're not saying, I can tell," Nell said, playful at first but with increasing seriousness as she saw Angel look away.

"Well…"

"Come out with it," Nell pleaded. "We promised to be honest with each other and I can tell there's something by the look on your face."

Angel gave Nell a sheepish glance and started to clamber down the path toward the beach. Nell grabbed her from behind and held her firm. "Please tell me." She felt suddenly vulnerable again: exposed and fearful.

"Oh, it's nothing, except I was thinking how much I've been missing dancing lately and how it might be if I did a bit, you know, before I got too old. Or settled down." Nell tried not to be defensive, but the thought of Angel dancing meant her in London or some sleazy club or anywhere except by her side in Cumberland Bay. "I know what you're thinking," insisted Angel. "It won't change things, I promise—"

"But what about the business? Our plans?" Nell tried not to sound critical, but couldn't help feeling the vulnerability of their new life together and how easily it might unravel.

"I'm still committed to the business and wouldn't do anything to jeopardize what we've got," pleaded Angel. "I think maybe there's space for both. I just have to figure out how. Perhaps I can teach?"

"Teach striptease?" It came out gruffer than Nell had intended.

"Nell, don't be ridiculous. I meant dance. Maybe a class in modern dance."

"Or that erotic pole-dancing stuff."

"Well maybe that," said Angel. Nell looked startled. "I'm joking!" insisted Angel, obviously enjoying the look on Nell's face. "Although I think it's actually quite popular in some parts," she added with a sly grin.

"Oh, Mary Mother of God, save us," laughed Nell. "Look I just want you in my life, dancing, gardening, you name it. Just be there, that's all. But speaking of Mary, how about you come to mass with me again tomorrow seeing as how we're spilling our hopes and dreams?"

"Of course," said Angel, "now they have the rainbow banner in the vestry."

"They do?" said Nell innocently. When Angel roared with laughter Nell flicked her anorak gently against Angel's legs. "You stop being so cheeky!"

"What, now you've done it," exclaimed Angel chasing Nell down the path onto the beach. "You're going to get what you asked for." Angel squealed as she caught up to Nell where the sea met the sand.

Nell grabbed her and felt Angel resist. The wind was in her face and droplets of moisture clung to her lashes. Nell felt Angel's hair whip her cheeks and turned to kiss her, holding her upturned face in her hands. Then, suddenly, just as Nell drew her in close, a wave hit them sideward, spraying them with water and sucking the sand out from under their feet. They grabbed each other and together stayed steady.

"You're the one," Nell murmured into her ear. "You're all I need." Nell felt Angel's body relax, her softly solid body yielding against her. Nell remembered the first time they'd made love on the beach and got randy just thinking about it. They'd come so far. They held hands and raced back along the beach, slowing down for the long uphill trek to the car park, in what were now wet clothes.

Eventually they reached the car and Angel had the heater blasting. "Home James," she quipped as they swung out of the car park and headed for the highway. Nell felt her breath catch with anticipation of their evening together. *Hot tub.* At last. She wanted to have Angel in the hot tub.

* * *

"Perfect," crooned Angel, slapping the silky water and slipping into the tub. Steam rose and soaked into their bones as drizzling rain fell steadily.

"You're perfect," Nell said, looking through the steamy haze at Angel with her long black hair piled in a knot, a few wisps escaping, curled in the humidity. Nell looked on, glad of the darkness hiding a blush that still lingered on her cheeks. Her hot tub fantasy of Angel in a wet t-shirt and panties, trounced only by the erotic thought of removing those panties, was about to be realized thanks to Angel's enthusiastic response to that sexy request. The t-shirt was starting to billow around Angel as she submerged herself in the water. Giggling, she tried to manage the air caught inside the shirt.

"Here, let me turn off the jets," Nell said. "Otherwise you might blow out to sea. You've got a regular mainsail going there."

They laughed as the bubbles of air in the T-shirt subsided and stillness descended. Silhouetted against the dark sky, Angel's normally dark skin looked pale and luminous. A glow from two tiny deck lights dazzled silver ripples on the water, illuminating her body in the soft night air. Against the darkening sky she looked to have a halo of light behind her. She smiled at Nell, eyes looming large in her face. Angel laid her shoulders back against the side of the tub and lifted her body, slowly kicking her legs to keep her body afloat. Nell was riveted, unable to keep her eyes off her.

"This is heaven," Angel moaned softly, letting her fingers float and closing her eyes.

"No, this is heaven," Nell replied, covering her face in kisses as Angel held her can of soda above the water.

"You're tickling me. Stop slobbering!"

Nell loved to hear her laugh. She was the most beautiful and amazing woman Nell had ever known. They stood together in the middle of the tub, water rippling around their waists. Nell felt a rising pulse throbbing between them that electrified the air. The t-shirt was molded to her curves like a second skin, showing an edge of green lace at the tops of her thighs. Angel brushed Nell's lips with hers and then bit down gently, slowly teasing her with tantalizing nibbles. Nell ached for her, moaning deep and low into her hair. She was utterly engulfed in her desire.

They stood like this, silhouetted against the night sky, touching and tasting, slowly and gently, where they had left off at the beach all those hours ago. Nell tried to ignore the flashing message on her mobile phone and pulled the erotic visual memory of Angel running in the surf, breasts bouncing, into her mind. Her desire ignited and she felt fire coursing through her veins. It really was an ache, almost a pain, edged with the usual anxiety that always plagued her. *Love turns to loss.* The mantra was starting to fade, thankfully and Nell easily pushed it away. Angel's body was wet and slick, but still solid and real. *Stay in the moment. This perfect moment.*

Now her hands were inside Angel's wet shirt and she could feel Angel's hot breath against her cheek. She leaned into the water and kissed the flesh around Angel's waist. It was incredibly soft and pliable under her hands. Desire shot through her again. Angel was sliding her hands down the slope of Nell's spine, gently caressing the skin around, the top of her shorts.

Light-headed with arousal Nell stroked her back and reached up under the shirt to touch Angel's breasts. They rose and fell as she stroked them, full and firm in her hands. Angel panted slightly, eyes closed, lips parted. Nell kissed her again with a passion that was totally consuming and in one breathless motion lifted the t-shirt over her head. Pleasure danced in her heart. Angel gasped playfully, sliding back into the water and flipping on the switch for the jets.

The water churned again and all that was visible was Angel's head over the steamy foam. Nell moved toward her again and she playfully dodged away, switching to the other side of the tub, eyeing Nell mischievously. Angel kept her eyes locked on Nell's and again dodged her when she tried to grab her. Then, without warning, she went under the water and popped up seconds later by Nell's side, kissing her neck. Angel moved against her, her mouth open and her body soft, but not submissive. Angel pushed Nell against the steps and pulled off her shorts so that they were both naked in the water.

Blood pounded in Nell's ears as tension gathered. Angel circled and teased until Nell could stand it no longer, but she managed to pull away and reach for Angel, catching her hands so they fell back together on the steps. Nell's breathing was ragged as she cradled Angel's body, feeling smooth naked skin as she lifted Angel to the side of the tub and gently spread her legs. Angel's head was thrown back and her legs were spread wide. Slowly Nell's hands glided over Angel's glistening thighs, kneading her flesh. She felt her firm legs and the curve of her hips, caressing the soft spot in the crook of her thigh. As Nell slid a finger inside her and then two, she heard Angel moan.

"Oh Nell, yes," Angel said, crying out as each thrust filled her. When Nell felt Angel swoon against her, she pulled out and turned her around so that her round, firm bum was pressed against Nell's groin. Nell gently pressed her forward and reached around so she could touch Angel's clitoris from behind, circling slowly. Nell heard Angel moan again as she put a hand over Nell's, guiding her in circles round and round.

"I've wanted to take you like this," Nell said, voice ragged. Her own words and the anticipation pushed her to the edge.

"Yes," Angel said, groaning again and pressing her bottom against Nell, then leaning forward and cradling Nell's hands between her thighs.

Gently, biting the back of her neck all the while, Nell gently pushed her forward onto the steps and moved against her, entering her sex from behind with probing fingers. Nell heard Angel gasp as she filled her, fingers deep inside and her thumb gently circling Angel's swollen clitoris.

When Angel had come, several times in succession, she turned sleepily to Nell and returned the favor. "Yes, you now," Angel insisted, gently pushing Nell against the steps and opening her legs. It wasn't long until Nell's world exploded in sweet, delicious release.

CHAPTER SEVENTEEN

Maddie rang the last call bell and flicked the bar light once, twice, to dim and then back up again. A handful of patrons clustered around the bar and drank down their beer, smiling their goodnights at her as they left the inn. A cool night-air breeze swept through the place when the doors opened. It had been a rainy evening and the night had brought little relief. Maddie wiped down the bar one last time, set the till and checked in with her cook who was closing down the kitchen for the night.

"Night love," he said as she headed out the kitchen door to her car. "You drive safely now. It's a horrible night."

"Thanks Fred," said Maddie waving goodbye. "You too." She slipped through the door and fumbled for her car keys in her bag. As the engine came to life she set the windshield wipers and rubbed the inside of her window to clear the glass. She drove automatically, well acquainted with the road, pleased to see her cottage as she came around the last bend. Slowly, she inched up to the curb, turned off the ignition and set the brake.

As she got out of the car, reaching for her bag and some shopping she'd picked up earlier in the day, she saw a car parked over by the side wall. It looked familiar and she found herself suddenly alert, her car keys between her fingers like tiny protruding weapons. As she hesitated, the car's headlights switched on, temporarily blinding her. It was coming straight at her. She jumped aside and the car slowed down, an angry face appearing at the rolled down window. It was Bill.

"Stupid bitch, get out of the way," he slurred, voice thick with drink. "Come to claim my house. Thought you could just get away with it and I wouldn't notice." When he staggered out of the car, Maddie jumped back and tried to run to her front door. Despite his inebriation he managed to grab her arm. "Thought you could get this place *and* the pub did you? Well you've got another thing coming." He grabbed for the keys and yanked them from her hand.

Maddie screamed, recoiled in horror and snatched the keys back from him. Bill yelled, losing his balance. "Fuckin' bitch."

Terrified, Maddie headed for her front door. She cried out, but the other cottages were in darkness—nobody home or their occupants already asleep. As she tried to climb her steps she felt a sudden pounding behind her. Bill was close, panting, his breath hoarse with drink and rage. She felt a sickening thud as he pushed her onto the gravel. Her hands felt on fire as rocks dug into her skin. The keys fell and Bill grabbed them again.

"Ah." He pushed her aside and smacked her across the side of the face before retreating down the path. The sound and pressure of his fist reverberated through her skull. "Leave me alone," she cried, staggering from the blow. Dizzy she reached for the doorframe to steady her fall and thought she might be sick. Excruciating pain from her wrist radiated up her arm. *Thank God Julia is with Mum.*

She watched Bill's car lights recede around the corner and tried to steady her breathing. Her face felt tight and weird where he'd hit her and her wrist was throbbing. She looked up into the night sky and felt the tears fall. *Damn him. Damn him to hell.* It was hard to believe he'd hit her. Her own brother. Sure he was an alcoholic and had always had problems controlling his temper, but still to go this far…He was full of rage because she'd been left the cottage rather than him. Their parents had wanted to see her secure after James had left her widowed with a small child. Overly entitled, Bill believed he could get drunk, act like the jerk that he was and still be awarded a part share in their grandparents' home. She'd heard him bragging in the pub that it was his due. *Stupid arse. Did he seriously think he could steal my keys and the cottage would miraculously be his?*

Holding her sore wrist and gently massaging her cheek, Maddie staggered back into the lane, looking for her handbag. It was strewn on the road, the contents scattered. With her good hand she managed to get everything back in her bag and then heaved the shopping back onto the curb. As she slid into the front seat and closed the car door, she realized she had no keys so couldn't drive anywhere. She also couldn't get into her house without going to see her mother for the spare key. *Definitely not.* Her mother's heart might not survive this. She'd had a pacemaker installed last year, was on all kinds of medication and was quite frail. No, calling her mother was out of the question.

Instead she called Nell. Fortunately the phone had been charging in her car. The phone rang and rang and then went to voice mail. Maddie grimaced and bit on her bottom lip. It had started raining again and she was shivering. She then phoned Angel and got the same result. *Bugger.* They'd said they were going down the coast to see the lighthouses and must have gone out for a late dinner or something.

Maddie got out of the car and walked back slowly toward her cottage. How she wished she'd had a spare key under a plant pot or something like other people did. She tried the doors and various windows but the house was locked up tight. Too embarrassed to try and rouse any of her neighbors, she decided to try Janine. She didn't pick up either. After a while she tried Nell and Angel again, but still nothing. She was just about to call Fred at the inn and deal with the embarrassment that would cause when she suddenly thought of Lucas. She would call Lucas.

"*Bonsoir, ma chérie.* What a surprise."

"I'm sorry, it's late."

"No, darling, it's never too late for you to call." Maddie felt her body relax at the sound of his warm, seductive voice.

"Are you okay? Where are you?" He must be able to sense the urgency in her voice.

"No actually, I'm not," she sobbed. She was shaking now in shock as well as the cold. She told him everything, tears streaming and sobs racking her bruised body.

"Fifteen minutes," he said. "It'll take me fifteen minutes to get to your place. Hold on and I'll be there soon." He hesitated and then asked. "Did you call the police?"

"No I'm a mess. I couldn't."

"Shall I do it?"

"No just come. Please. I don't want anyone seeing me like this right now."

"Okay *chérie*. Hang on and I'll be there soon."

Maddie sat huddled in her car and waited for Lucas, picking bits of gravel out of the cuts in her palm. She felt herself relax and was almost asleep hunched in the front seat when she saw headlights sweep around the corner and a car door slam sharply.

"Oh my love, come here." He tenderly reached for her and wiped the hair out of her eyes. He took in the rapidly spreading bruise across her cheek and the blood on her hands and gasped. A dark look crossed his face and she saw him clench and unclench his fists.

"Stay here a minute and I'll break a window and get inside." She heard a tinkle of glass and then saw a beam of light as the front door opened. Lucas was silhouetted against the light and came bounding down the steps toward her. His arm was around her, supporting her body. She cried out when he touched her wrist and she wondered if it was broken. *Damn Bill.*

Lucas carried her inside and helped her into the bathroom. He ran a bath, made her some tea and then filled a plastic bag with ice and covered it with a dish towel. She took it gratefully, thankful for his kindness. As the hot water seeped into her bones and the ice numbed her face, Maddie could hear Lucas moving about in the kitchen, putting things in the fridge and opening and closing the cabinet drawers. She heard him talking on his phone and heard him say Angel's name. It sounded like he was leaving Angel a message and for that she was grateful too.

The bath had relaxed her to the core and the pain killers were making her feel sleepy. "I'll stay until you fall asleep, he said, "or I'll sleep here on the sofa if you like." The last thing she heard was him rustling in the kitchen washing out the tea cups.

* * *

"I'm going to kill that bugger with my bare hands." Nell was shaking with rage, her face flushed and contorted with anger.

"Nell it's okay." Maddie sat on the edge of her sofa, her legs curled under her and a blanket around her shoulders. Her left cheek was swollen and a formidable purple bruise shaded her eye. Her wrist was sore and her hands all torn up, but other than that felt glad to have survived the ordeal.

"It's not okay. I should have been there for you." Her expression was pained and Maddie knew Nell was seething with guilt because she missed her call last night. They'd said they were in the hot tub and didn't hear the phone.

"Don't be silly."

"Well at least let me go over there and give him a piece of my mind."

"He already got it." Maddie smiled sheepishly and raised her eyebrows.

"I thought you didn't call the police," Nell said, "though God forbid he could have killed someone driving like that."

Maddie swallowed and nodded. She was mortified this morning when she realized such a thing might so easily have happened.

"Did you call the police?" Nell persisted.

"No, it was Lucas."

"Lucas?" It came out as a sneer. "I know he helped you..." Nell took a breath. "I'm glad he could do that."

Maddie smiled and winced as pain shot through her cheek. "Ouch, sorry, that smile cost me."

"Lucas did what?" asked Angel, joining them on the sofa. She'd driven over to Maddie's mother's place with some clothes for Julia and fabricated a story about Maddie slipping on a wet spot at the inn and bumping herself.

"Well," said Maddie. "Are you ready for this?" She took a sip of her tea and massaged her wrist. "He came by and helped me inside. He basically put me to bed." She ignored Nell's look at the mention of bed and continued. "What I didn't know until this morning when he woke me up with a cup of tea is that he drove over to Bill's last night after I fell asleep and found Bill drunk in his living room. He smacked him around by all accounts." Maddie tried to smile again and gave up, holding the side of her face.

"Bill smacked him around?" Angel said, looking horrified.

"No, silly. Lucas took Bill out. Isn't that great? He even managed to get me my keys back." Maddie looked jubilant.

Nell and Angel looked at each other and cracked out laughing. "Well I never," said Nell. "I owe that bloke one." Maddie could see that Lucas might just have earned Nell's respect at last.

"He probably didn't even get his clothes dirty," said Angel, slapping her thigh. "Oh, good for him. I am so impressed."

"I know. I was so worried when he told me because Bill might've really hurt him. Fortunately he was so drunk." Maddie repositioned herself on the sofa and reached for another ice pack. "Anyway, it was very brave," she added with a twinkle in her eye.

* * *

"You're looking really good," declared Angel, eyeing Maddie leaning against the kitchen counter at Tulip Cottage, "not counting your fading bruiser." It was almost a week since the attack. Maddie's glossy hair was pulled into a side ponytail and her slim lanky body looked relaxed inside stretchy faded jeans. Bra-less and wearing a tie-dyed t-shirt, she rubbed the greenish-purple spot along her cheek and raised her eyebrows at her friend.

"Oh no, what're you keeping from me?" exclaimed Angel, looking intently into Maddie's eyes and daring her to disagree. "You didn't."

"Umm, well I did, actually." She looked to make sure Julia was beyond earshot on the lawn and turned to Angel with a smile. "And it was very nice."

"Oh my God, tell me." Angel got up and stood next to Maddie, happy to see her friend's obvious pleasure. Maddie pursed her lips, teasing. "Who? Maddie, you devil. Tell me!"

"If I said 'He is a *trés bon* lover…'"

"Ah!" shrieked Angel, throwing back her head and laughing uproariously. It came out as a snort and that made them both laugh some more. "Was it good?"

"Oh, was it good?" declared Maddie. "Oo la la, if you know what I mean."

Angel snorted again and held onto the kitchen sink to steady herself. "Details please."

"Okay, if you insist. You sure you don't know the routine?"

Angel grimaced. "No, you know there was never—"

"I know, I'm just teasing. Listen, if I had to worry about Lucas' ex-flings I'd be a complete basket case. So many more important things in life." Angel had to agree that was true and felt so much better for hearing it. But it was Maddie's body language, relaxed and smiling, with not a shred of malice or jealousy, which convinced her. Angel felt suddenly inadequate, knowing she could never handle something like this with such grace and good nature. She thought about Maddie losing her husband to cancer and how much strength that must have taken. There was nothing she could say that expressed how she felt, so she drew a breath and listened instead.

"He was so kind after the thing with Bill," Maddie was saying. "I saw a completely new side of him. He's a changed man, believe me. Except in the love department where I'd prefer things never change," she added. A wicked grin now spread across her face.

Angel nodded, intrigued.

"I'm not ready to let Janine know yet," added Maddie, smiling. "Keep it between you and me. You can tell Nell, of course, although I'm not sure how she'll take it. Arch enemies and all."

"So you guys are doing well?" Angel was eager for more details.

"Yes, he's different."

"In what way?"

"He's listening. That's a good start. I was always on him about that." Maddie grabbed some bread and scooped up a huge dollop of hummus, craning to see Julia out in the garden. The little girl had a piece of crumpled paper attached to a string and was whirling it around as the neighbor's cat jumped wildly after it. "Don't forget to bring those in," she said, pointing to Angel's work clothes hanging listlessly on the washing line strung across the lawn. "Looks like it's going to rain again. Where was I?"

"Different. Maddie, focus, I'm all ears."

"Right," she said coyly. "I feel like he's genuinely interested in me rather than thinking about himself and how he's coming across to me. You know what I mean?"

"Yes, I do." Angel looked straight at her friend, eager to confirm this notion. "Sometimes I'd think he was, like, watching himself in a mirror."

"Yes, that's it. You have such a way with words. He's more real now and I'm starting to trust him. And he's helping me figure some things out at the inn. Got a couple of leads."

"Really?" inquired Angel.

"Too soon to tell."

"Humph, what does that mean?"

"Nothing, it means nothing," responded Maddie.

"Well whatever you're doing suits you," said Angel. "You're glowing. Nothing like sex for clearing the skin, or the air for that matter."

"But that's overrated and why I limit myself."

"Limit yourself?"

"Yes," said Maddie seriously. "Sex changes a relationship. I want to get back to knowing Lucas as a friend first, as someone I want to spend time with. I also need to go slowly for Julia's sake," she added wisely. "I used to think he didn't like children."

"Yes, me too. He never seemed particularly fond of kids."

"But he's been very sweet with Julia," insisted Maddie. "I think he just didn't know what to say to them. You know how people who don't know kids get kind of shy around them. Children seem like tiny humans who speak a different language, are unpredictable and might just break if you do or say the wrong thing."

"Yes, that makes sense," mused Angel. "You're one smart woman."

"Yeh, right," said Maddie. "Look who's talking."

"Exactly. I've always been too impulsive with love. Jump first and think later, unfortunately." Angel reached for her spoon and watched the muddy color in her teacup turn lighter as she stirred. "These last few months have helped me see I don't have to worry about being myself. I mean, what's the worst thing that can happen? That you'll get dumped, which probably means you'd never have made it anyway, given that a person dumps you just because you're being yourself." Angel shifted in her seat. "Kate said I fell in love like a ton of bricks."

"Do you think she's right?"

"In the past I would have vehemently denied such a thing," declared Angel, "but now I have to say she's probably right."

"Yes and so what? You're very sensuous, that's all. I don't think there's anything wrong connecting with people as long as no one gets hurt and you know what you're getting into." Maddie dragged the rubber band out of her ponytail before pulling it back again into a tight bun. "Don't you think?"

Angel hesitated before she spoke. "If I'm being really objective I'd have to say I've always fallen in love too hard and too quickly and done what I thought was wanted. Sure, I liked to think of myself as a free spirit who gave willingly and couldn't give a damn, but really that was a cover for feeling fat and inadequate most of the time."

"Don't be silly. You, fat and inadequate?"

"That's sweet of you, but that's how I've felt. Sex made me feel loved and desirable. Stupid…But you and Lucas, that's great," said Angel, changing the subject, sincerely happy for her friend. "Just be careful," she added. "He's a handful."

"I know. Daphne's been out of the picture since he was in London, not to mention the video debacle that didn't earn her any gold stars. Plus he got over you pretty quickly," she added. "No offence of course."

This made them explode into giggles again. "That's our Lucas. Well, be careful," Angel repeated. "Be sure to use a condom on that one time you decide to make wild love."

"Angel!" Maddie laughed and snapped the tea towel at her. At that moment there was a light tap on the door. "Speaking of the love department," said Maddie as Nell appeared in the doorway.

"Love department? Is that what I've been reduced to?" said Nell, going over and kissing Maddie on the top of the head before sitting down by Angel, lifting Angel's hair so she could kiss her at the back of her neck.

"Mmm, like that," cooed Angel, wriggling her body.

"Okay, my cue for an exit," said Maddie. "Plus I've got too many things to do."

"I bet you do," said Angel, cheekily.

"Like what?" asked Nell. "What am I missing?"

"Never you mind," replied Maddie, waving her goodbyes and going to collect Julia.

"What was that all about?" asked Nell, putting her feet up on the chair.

"Maddie and Lucas." A doubtful look spread across Nell's face. "She's a big girl," insisted Angel. "I think she's going to be okay."

"I hope so. She's not as worldly as you. It was awful after James died. Shit, he wasn't even thirty five."

Angel listened to Nell talk about Maddie's devotion and James' brave fight. After a while Angel interrupted, speaking slowly and deliberately so Nell wouldn't misunderstand. "No," she insisted, "I might have traveled more and done crazy thing like being a stripper in Paris, but really, Maddie's not less worldly than me at all—"

Nell started to interrupt, but Angel held up her hand until she quieted and listened again. "If by 'worldly' you mean maturity and competence, she's way ahead of me. I mean she's been tested and must be one of the most emotionally astute people I know. I'm just a babbling idiot next to her."

"You are so full of it," Nell scoffed.

"Absolute truth," insisted Angel. "We were just talking about this before you came in. I was saying that if I was honest with myself I've always liked to think of myself as someone in control of my life, but I've made so many mistakes in wanting to be loved and have done stupid shit because of it."

"Everyone wants to be loved."

"But I'd get consumed by love. I'd lose myself. You know that book, *Women Who Love Too Much*? That was me. Completely insecure."

Nell laughed and squeezed her hand. "I'm glad you love me."

"Me too," she said simply. "You just have to help me from being too much of a marshmallow."

"But that's crazy. No one would *ever* say you're a marshmallow."

"I know. That's how good I am at hiding it." She laughed drily. "And stripping. People look at that and think 'you'd have to have balls,' excuse my French, to do such a thing. And I suppose they're right on some level, but it fit with my wanting to feel desired, to feel wanted. Quite a high to get all those guys slobbering over you. You do the slightest thing, not giving a damn and they get all hot and bothered and seem vulnerable. Yes, that's it. Seeing their vulnerability made me forget my own." Looking out the window she saw the light slumping and clouds, threaded with streams of pink and red, skittering across the sky.

Nell was quiet for a moment and then nodded slowly, taking Angel in her arms until she was sitting in her lap. "It's okay, love," Nell said at last. "Talk to me about it."

"Well," Angel stammered, "it was fun and I felt sexy, attractive, you know. I'd always been such a chubby kid that when I developed and my body changed and people started to notice, I liked that. I've already told you this, but you forget yourself and your problems when you dance and even though I always wanted to be an actress, me and everyone else I knew, of course. Dancing, like acting, allowed me to escape from myself. Be someone different. Be in control."

"I could see that," Nell said. "It must be a real high to have everyone watching you, although, honestly, I would absolutely hate it." Nell seemed to grimace at the thought. "But with the stripper thing, I could see how you could get used to all the adoration."

"Yes, but it's a fake high. You feel powerful for the moment and that's what's so seductive," Angel replied.

"Seductive is a good word," said Nell. "I bet you were awesomely seductive."

"I loved to dance," Angel responded emphatically. "I was good at it. Still am actually." She got up and twirled around the kitchen to make Nell smile.

"How you shake different parts of yourself at the same time is a mystery to me."

"Technique," she said, simulating a belly dance routine. "See?"

"I do see." Nell grabbed Angel around the waist and pulled her back onto her lap. "I see and I like."

Angel snuggled closer, nestling her cheek against Nell's chest. She thought of the first time she'd sat on Nell's lap in this very same kitchen. It seemed a lifetime ago. Nell must have been thinking the same thing. "Remember when you made me dinner?" she said.

"Oh God, not the toasted white bread and cheap jar of pasta sauce. Don't remind me! That was before I knew what an amazing cook you are, or I'd never have had the nerve to invite you in."

"I'm glad you did, although that night is one whole blur for me." Nell pulled her closer. "Damn, I was so scared."

"Of me?"

"Of you and your gorgeous body and me not being able to do anything out of pure fear." Angel stifled a giggle and shook her head. That was not how it had turned out. "No, seriously," Nell continued, "I was a bag of nerves. I knew I'd say the wrong thing, do the wrong thing. If things went well I'd know they wouldn't last and then I'd cock things up so they really would go down the toilet. Prove it to myself. And you were right what you said before. I did judge you. I was so insecure too, that's why."

"Well that's something we have in common," tittered Angel dubiously.

"It's true. They say couples who are more alike have better marriages."

"I'm not sure that works with insecurity, though," she said lightly.

"I don't care if we're completely nuts. I want you in my life Angela Khoury, insecure or not. Even if we do end up with crazy, anxious kids."

Angel bit her lip and met Nell's eyes, piercingly blue as a sunny day. Her mouth smiled down at Angel, full and warm and so kissable that Angel couldn't resist. "No problem. We'll just have to get them a good shrink," she said when she came up for air. Angel heard her murmur "Okay" and she buried her face in Nell's shirt just to feel it against her skin. Nell's body was strong against her own, solidly wrapped around her. Angel felt a rush of peace flow through her that was so intense it was physical.

CHAPTER EIGHTEEN

It sounded like a steam engine. Angel emerged from a deep sleep and registered Nell snoring in her ear. *Ah, life with a woman in your bed.* She reached for the alarm clock and saw they had ten minutes before it would ring. She let herself sink back into the warmth of the bed and closed her eyes. Nell rolled over and caught Angel in her arms, pulling her close.

"Are you thinking what I'm thinking?" she asked, fondling Angel's breasts and starting to slide her hand between Angel's thighs. Her eyes turned a shade darker as she gave Angel a sleepy smile.

"No way!" squealed Angel, squirming and playfully extracting her hands. "We have work to do." It was the day of the party at Audrey's.

"What a slave master." Nell groaned and shaded her eyes from a sunbeam skittering through the gap in the closed curtains. "Let's not go to the party. Let's just stay in bed. Audrey won't care and no one will miss us." She tried to caress Angel's naked bottom.

"Stop," said Angel, disentangling herself from the embrace and padding into the bathroom. "It'll be fun. Everything looks great. We've worked so hard and we're going to enjoy this or else."

"Okay," said Nell sleepily, "if you say so."

"Once we get the flowers and centerpieces, we're done," she insisted. "Come on you can do it. Last leg." It felt good to have this project almost completed. That and the second assignment for *Country Escapes*, which was ready to go a few weeks ahead of schedule.

They ate a light breakfast of delicious cinnamon rolls that Nell had made the day before, served with yoghurt and fresh peaches and then set off for Truro to collect the flowers for the party. Angel had ordered and purchased blooms and worked with a contact in London known for her exquisite flower arranging. The blooms had been shipped overnight and would be ready for pick-up.

Angel sipped on her tea as Nell drove the garden center van, maneuvering along the narrow winding lanes up the ravine and out onto the main road to the city. It was early and hardly anyone was on the roads. They spied a wild pony drinking in a boggy area in the distance and watched as a kestrel swooped from a fence into the grass. Straggly heath with rocks and sparse vegetation littered the horizon.

The drive always reminded Angel of the first time she made this trip in her old Volkswagen, a trip that felt like a hundred years ago now. She reached over and stroked the inside of Nell's arm as she drove. Nell had her shirt sleeves rolled up and was glancing at Angel out of her peripheral vision. The skin at the corner of Nell's eyes crinkled as she smiled and reached over to pat Angel's hand. "Love you," she said.

Several hours later they were driving back with the sun now high in the sky. Hedgerows flew by, vivid splotches of pinky dog-rose, creamy cow parsley and red valerian. Almost home. They had delivered the flowers and just needed to pick up a few orchids from the garden center for Audrey's guest bathroom. Audrey had been insistent about the orchids. This was going to be the party of the century by all accounts. Their guest list was long and included a number of important clients that Audrey's husband, Dave, wanted to woo. Angel breathed deeply and inhaled the lavender mixed with the deep fragrance of roses that lingered in the van.

As they bounced along the narrow roads back toward the village, Angel tried to get herself into the mood for the party. *What to wear?* She had two dresses in mind and still couldn't decide which one would work best. One was safe: a raw silk sheath, cut just below the knee, in a deep apricot color that she knew suited her and looked particularly good against her hair. The dress had a deep scoop neck and looked good with jewelry: either her fake chunky pearls or the pink sparkly rhinestone necklace she'd had forever. Shoes were always a bit of a problem with this outfit. It looked best with heels and the pair that matched was great if you didn't have to walk anywhere.

"What're you thinking?" Nell interrupted her thoughts and patted her knee as he drove.

"Oh nothing, really; just thinking about what to wear..." Angel's voice trailed off as she thought about the second outfit: more daring.

"I vote sexy."

"You would. And here I am going for comfort and practicality. What am I thinking?"

"Exactly, thinking is always a problem." Nell laughed as Angel threw up her hands in mock horror. "Can't go wrong with sexy," Nell added.

Sexy was more in tune with outfit number two. It was a simple silver and fuchsia snakeskin-print dress with an almost-thigh-high slit up the side. The hem hit just above the knee and looked edgy with her black ankle boots: definitely more comfortable than the other shoes. She had a matching fitted jacket to keep out the evening chill. But the dress itself was more revealing and needed some tummy control, especially since Nell's good home cooking. It definitely fit the sexy bill, however.

Angel thought about the various options. She hoped the silk sheath wasn't too creased, although she'd probably have time to steam it if it was. Hair up or down? She pulled at a strand and sniffed. "I think I smell like roses."

"Everything about you smells like roses," laughed Nell. "Or is that coming up roses? Whatever, you're my lucky omen. So don't you dare be leaving me or else."

Angel leaned over and stole a kiss. "I'm not going anywhere," she declared. It felt so good to be loved and to love back. Stretching her legs and letting out a yawn, Angel massaged Nell's neck as she drove. Nell purred her approval. Angel saw her steal a glance at her and watched as Nell's lips turned up in a smile. A sudden thought came to Angel's mind. "Ever had a road head?"

"What?"

"Road head." Angel gave Nell a naughty look. "Sorry, rather a heterosexual euphemism. You know, while you're driving," she added.

Nell laughed and lifted her hips from the seat. "You offering?"

"No, probably not." Angel laughed. "No offense."

"You are such a tease. How could you suggest such a thing and not deliver?"

"Easy. Or you could just think of it as a rain check."

"Okay, if you insist. But I'll take some more of that instead." Nell moved her head toward Angel's hand so that she was massaging her neck again. "This gardening business is exhausting."

"Not to mention throwing huge housewarming parties," said Angel. "It's almost worse than a wedding."

Nell rested her cheek against Angel's hand. "And fortunately we're not the hosts for either. At least not today."

Angel registered the meaning in Nell's words and turned her body toward her so she could see her profile. She loved this woman so much. Keeping her eyes on the road, Nell reached over and grasped Angel's hand tightly. Angel put her other hand on top as if in a pact. They drove the rest of the way in sweet silence, although Angel's mind was full of the surprise she had in mind for Nell. It was her birthday next month. The road rose, then dipped and curved. In another few minutes they were in Borman Lane.

Angel clambered down from the pickup, stooped to get the newspaper and then moved back toward the truck to kiss Nell goodbye through the open window. The sun felt good on her face, but made her squint as she waved goodbye. "See you later." Her party clothes were in her closet in the cottage. She'd agreed to stop by the garden center and pick up the orchids too, so Nell could get home and take care of Gruff.

Sitting in the sunshine eating a makeshift lunch with the cat, whom she'd now named Neighbor, purring on her lap, Angel looked out over the side garden. She had a blue and white theme going with gorgeous lobelia and a scattering of alyssum lining the edges. There were deep blue spikes of salvia or meadow sage alongside agastache with their dense pinky-blue clusters of flowers standing upright against bright green foliage. Masses of different varieties of lavender in varying shades of blues and purples lent a heavenly fragrance to the scene. And here and there she could see the shiny thick cabbage-like leaves of bergenia and small white flowers just starting to appear above the stems.

Across the path daylilies were sending up stems with canary-yellow blossoms, adding a punch of contrast and moving the eye toward her tiny new pond. Framed by a small weeping willow and a smaller Japanese maple on one side and ornamental grasses on the other, the pond looked as if it had always been there. It blended perfectly and gave a soothing backdrop of tinkling water from the small fountain. She'd had a good rebate on her rent for this one.

Angel sighed contentedly. Life was good. She realized with a start that it was ages since she'd wanted a cigarette. Now not even one craving. *Hallelujah!*

Between the rhythmic sound of the water and the mellow feeling of the sun on her body, Angel started to nod off. It was delicious to relax like this. Neighbor got up and kneaded Angel's thighs and then resettled himself in her lap. All was quiet in the garden except for the babble and gurgle of the water and the noise of sparrows twittering in the bushes. As she felt herself drift off into sleep, Angel heard the coo of a collared dove and tried to open her eyes to see if she could spy the pale, pinky-brown grey bird. Through slitted eyes she saw its distinctive plumage with the black neck collar and felt the cat follow her gaze in the direction of the bird. But it was too much to keep her eyes open and soon she was fast asleep, Neighbor settling back down on her lap.

It was the phone that woke her. Bewildered, Angel sat up and quickly realized she'd fallen asleep. Panicked, she grabbed her phone registering that Sylvie had saved her again. Shoot, it was almost one thirty and she still needed to get the orchids. Deciding to let her voice mail pick up the call, Angel flew back inside, grabbed her keys and purse and fired up the old Volkswagen. Neighbor dashed across the path and surveyed Angel from the bushes, looking annoyed that their nap had been so rudely interrupted.

Drumming the steering wheel, Angel navigated the now familiar lanes. She felt the engine shift down in to second gear as it climbed the hill to the garden center. If Angel was lucky Annie would be there holding down the fort and might be able to help her load the orchids.

It was then that she saw it. Her heart almost bounced out of her chest and her breathing came out shallow and harsh. A small Mini Cooper idled in the garden center yard. She watched in horror as the driver stepped out onto the gravel, only ten feet away from her and looked in her direction. The afternoon sun glinted off dark sunglasses that shaded his eyes, but it was him. Her mind flashed back to the Cheeky Monkey all those months ago. Skinny and forty-something, smartly dressed and with an early comb-over. And the car was the same! He dropped his cigarette and stepped on the ember with the heel of his shoe. The gravel crunched. His face now framed her car window.

"Oh," Angel cried, recalling Maddie's assault, complete with a fist through the glass. She quickly locked the doors, heart pounding. Adrenaline coursed through her body. He was saying something through her closed window, but she couldn't hear what. Frantically she rummaged through her purse looking for her phone, trying to avoid his face only inches from her through the glass, so that she could call for help. Fear rose again like bile in her throat as she realized she'd left the phone sitting on the lounge chair after getting the call from Sylvie.

Angel looked up, suddenly aware that the muffled sound of his voice had subsided and noticed a card stuck in the window frame so she could read it from the inside. He'd retreated and was leaning against his car with a look somewhere between amusement and annoyance.

Angel gasped, her face hot and flushed. 'Jonathon Meyers, Assistant to Mr. Gates, Casting Director, Kestrel Productions,' she read and then 'I won't hurt you' hand-scribbled under the address.

Slowly Angel opened the car door and faced him.

"You're tough," he said, eyeing her speculatively. "I already gave up on you too many times, but then got a last-minute lead. Took a bottle of whiskey and a call from the CEO to get that old guy, Reg what's-his-name, to crack."

Dumbfounded, Angel listened as he explained why he had tracked her down. Her eyes widened and her heart beat wildly, this time with excitement rather than fear. Kestrel was working on a romantic comedy, what sounded like a cross-between *Le Moulin Rouge* and *Flashdance* and they needed a stunt double to work the pole and a dance double to do the stripper scenes. *That's* why Jonathon Meyers had been in the Cheeky Monkey and that's why he had said it was a business venture. When Angel didn't respond to their calls, they just went with another dancer. But then filming was delayed and the dancer they hired turned out to be a flake and was fired within the month. Eventually he'd run into Reg again and wrangled Angel's whereabouts out of him. "Once he knew it was legit, he thought you might like it if I found you," said the guy.

Angel was silent, trying to take it all in, remembering the ignored calls she'd thought were from collection agencies. "But at the club you were so," she said at last, trying to figure out how to say it without being rude, "so…"

"Into it?"

"Yes, you could put it that way." Angel's eyebrows shot up and she gave him a sidelong glance. "You were like all the creepy customers I've ever known, but on steroids. No offense."

He laughed out loud, but she could see the embarrassment in his sleepy brown eyes. "What do you expect with an assignment like that?" he said. "I know I was slightly overzealous, I admit. But you were amazing. I wanted to experience it like that, to get a real feel for how you'd be in the film."

"Really?" She looked at him doubtfully, not sure if this was a joke and someone from *Candid Camera* or a reality television show was going to jump out of the bushes. "And how would I be?" she asked instead.

"Bloody amazing," he answered, smiling and apologizing again for scaring her. "Think about it. Can I call you tomorrow?"

She nodded her assent, gave him her cell number and stowed his card in her purse. In a daze, but with a secret smile, she watched him drive away.

"You okay?" asked Annie, coming out the side door. "Persistent buggers those debt collectors. They don't accept no for an answer when money's involved."

"Actually," blurted Angel, he's not with any collection agency…" Her voice tapered off into a bewildered sigh as she kicked idly at the gravel. "I'll tell you later. I'm in shock."

"Good shock?" she asked giving Angel a motherly look that was an invitation to tell all.

"Hope so," replied Angel, rubbing her eyes and avoiding Annie's astonished stare. She had to pull herself together. "Hey," she managed to squeak out, "any chance you can help me with those orchids Nell set aside for the party? I'm super late and still need to get back and change."

"Okay," said Annie, resignedly. "No problem, I was hauling them out as soon as I saw you." She went back inside and returned with one of the orchids with its stunning white clusters fringed in pink along an elegant stem. The plant was in a marble-looking urn that Annie had to hold with both hands.

"Thanks so much," exclaimed Angel, running in and picking up a second plant. Eventually all four orchids were wedged tightly side by side on her back seat.

"Okay, got to dash. Thanks again," Angel yelled, jumping back behind the wheel. Looking in the rearview mirror she saw Annie recede, a quizzical look lingering on her face.

Once home she headed for the shower. She would make it, but only just.

* * *

Angel was in Nell's pickup staring into the vanity mirror and trying to stay calm. She had her makeup bag on a dishtowel across her knees and was carefully applying eyeliner. "Bugger," she said as they veered around a corner and she smeared eyeliner on the side of her nose. "Look what you made me do."

"Sorry love." Nell was looking amused at the process by which Angel was able to transform herself. Angel knew Nell had never been one for makeup and thought it a waste of time, although she seemed to appreciate its effects as far as Angel was concerned. Despite this, Nell had been throwing a variety of witticisms at Angel for the last ten minutes. She pantomimed a poker face as Angel applied her blush and bronzer and attempted to put on lipstick.

"Nice," Nell said quietly as Angel peered at herself again in the mirror. "There ought to be a merit badge for that."

"Maybe I could get my Girl Scout badge for applying makeup under dire conditions," Angel replied, trying for humor in a desperate attempt to stay focused. The elation she had first felt was fading as she looked at Nell. They had a future. She wanted them to have babies together. The timing was all off. How could she possibly spend a few months in London on location? On location! Her heart jumped at the very thought. She'd lose what they had built together. She'd lose Nell. Anxiety rising, she recalled Nell's contempt on seeing the YouTube video of her dancing to "Angel of the Morning." There was no way Nell could cope with her partner being in a movie like this, even if it was set up for her to look like someone else. No, it was impossible. She would have to turn it down.

"Glad you decided on sexy," Nell said, appraising her outfit out of the corner of her eye and stroking her bare thigh with her spare hand. "Good choice."

"I'm hoping I won't live to regret it. Sexy comes with lots of effort. Holding in my tummy, worrying about showing too much thigh and being willing to freeze my ass off."

"Such a martyr," laughed Nell, "but such a good cause." Her fingers traced Angel's cheek and gave her a quick pinch. Angel batted her away, working to blend the blush into her foundation. "Okay, I get the message," Nell said, going back to feeling the long expanse of her bare leg.

Angel reached to pat Nell's hand as she shoved the makeup back in her bag. They had slowed to a crawl, creeping behind a queue of cars following a tractor. Angel chewed her bottom lip nervously and realized she was messing up her lipstick.

"That's the way," said Nell as the tractor made a left turn into a field and the cars sped by. She waved at the farmer and drummed the steering wheel in time to the radio. "Settle down. We're not late. It's okay."

Angel tried to soothe herself by counting sheep as they sped by, but her mind was spinning. A movie, a big-budget romantic comedy dance movie no less, with an amazing cast. She had been selected to double a voluptuous British actress whom she had countless times been told she resembled. It was too exciting for words. And too hopeless. She should tell Nell, but she needed more time to figure out how to handle this. And what would she say? That she was going to do it? She wanted to do it, but she wanted a future with Nell. Could she possibly have both?

Angel tried to bring herself back to the present. Nell looked great. She was wearing black fitted trousers and a dark grey shirt with satiny vertical stripes. She had a hot pink tie knotted loosely and carried her suit jacket over her shoulder. Her tan from working outside was deepening even though she swore by sunscreen and insisted all her employees wear it. The heightened color brought out the violet blue in her eyes and highlighted the crinkles around them as she smiled. Angel loved Nell's golden hair, especially when it got a bit longer. She had really grown fond of the messy, bedhead look. She had, however, insisted Nell get a good cut.

"Gorgeous," Angel sighed, trying to concentrate and gesturing at the spread in front of them as they climbed out of the truck. "Gardens look fabulous. We did good." Hand in hand they walked out of the parking area and toward the house that rose up solemnly, angled toward the ocean.

"My fave friends!" Startled, Angel turned to see Maddie smiling radiantly at them. "Love your dress," she said to Angel. "And Nell you're so handsome."

"Wow, you too!" declared Angel, admiring her friend's outfit. Maddie looked fabulous in a simple but elegant green and black-patterned tank dress that hugged her body and sparkled slightly as she moved. It had a high boat neckline accentuating her strong shoulders and fell mid-calf. It suited her to perfection. Black suede shoes with an outrageously tall stacked heel completed the ensemble. It made her legs look incredibly long.

"Easier for me to survey the crowd," Maddie said, laughing as she pantomimed looking over everyone's heads standing tall and proud.

Suddenly Lucas appeared around the corner, gorgeous too, even if he was a good bit shorter than his date. They made quite a couple. He wore a light grey suit with a green tie almost the same shade as Maddie's dress.

Lucas reached for Angel's hand and kissed her once, twice, on each cheek, as only the French can so elegantly do. Nell and Lucas shook hands cordially, a cautious friendship growing after Lucas' heroic episode with Bill. They were being very civil. She could tell by Nell's body language what she was feeling—if Lucas hurt Maddie, there was no telling what Nell might do. For the moment, however, Lucas seemed to be doting on their friend.

"Look, there's Julia," said Angel as the little girl appeared with her babysitter. Julia wore a long lilac-colored dress with a deep purple sash. Her shoes were patent leather and she had a flowery headband in her long hair. "Your favorite color," said Angel, smoothing Julia's dress. "So pretty."

"Thanks," said Julia, twirling around, getting silly and dizzy. As Maddie tried to settle her daughter, worried she might fall on the steps, Angel had the romantic notion that if things kept going as well as they were, she might be a mother soon. But where did being a stunt double fit in? It was impossible.

The little girl scampered away with the babysitter, a rather harassed-looking teenager who most likely wondered what she had signed up for, and Lucas returned to Maddie's side to help her with her jacket. He put his arm around her shoulders protectively and then let it drop to the small of her back. Angel recognized the intimate gesture and smiled to herself as Nell and Lucas left to get drinks.

"Everything looks magnificent," said Maddie, shading her eyes and looking out across the grounds. "You've planted a ton of wonderful things...What's up? You look a little tense. Everything okay?" Before Angel could figure out how to respond, Nell suddenly appeared. She took each of the women on an arm, steering Maddie and Angel over to a corner table under the marquee where Lucas was already arranging drinks. The DJ was just getting started and a couple was dancing shyly on the tiny dance floor.

"Look at that! Amazing!" Lucas and Nell, now deep in conversation at the table. "We just needed to get those two liquored up," whispered Angel, relieved at the distraction. "And I think," said Angel, her voice barely above a murmur, "that Nell is now prepared to trust Lucas with your heart."

"Ah, well, I trust him too. I don't know when I've been so well-loved," she whispered, "and not just in the biblical sense."

Angel hooted with laughter. "Don't tell Nell," she declared. "It's not exactly her sense of the Bible." She put her arms around Maddie, pulling her out onto the tiny dance floor. "I'm so glad." The two friends twirled together with Angel leading and giggling as Maddie turned the wrong way, stepped on her toes as they ended up in a jumble of arms and legs.

"No seriously. You guys are doing pretty well, I see," said Angel during a gap between songs. "All the juicy details, please."

"We are," replied Maddie, smiling mischievously. "I'm taking it steady though. You know, one day at a time. Just like you said." Angel nodded and Maddie continued. "He's very sweet with Julia and respectful of my time with her. Shoot me if I'm wrong, but he's definitely changed for the good."

"Maybe you've changed too?" Angel was thinking about how the new-and improved Lucas brought out Maddie's soft side.

"Maybe. And you helped, of course..." She paused, looking intently at Angel. "Can you keep a secret?" Angel held Maddie's gaze and nodded. "I think we have an investor for the pub. I might avoid catastrophe after all."

"No! Who?"

Maddie explained how Lucas had a business contact looking to invest in tourism ventures. He had agreed to buy Bill out of his share of the inn so they could pay out the mortgage and refinance at a lower, much more affordable interest rate. Lucas had some ideas for marketing and was encouraging Maddie to get more involved with the Tourist Board. As she finished giving the news she looked closely into Angel's face. "You sure you're okay?" she asked finally.

"Yes, I was just thinking how great that was for you. But," Angel hesitated, not sure how to begin, "there is something I need to talk through. Maybe later if we get some privacy." Although she needed to talk with Maddie, she wanted time to keep the secret to herself so she could work out her own feelings before her friends weighed in.

"Here's my *petite femme*." Lucas announced, sneaking up behind Maddie and kissing the back of her neck. The gesture was slightly awkward given Maddie's height, but sweet nonetheless. Angel was warmed to see her friends' blossoming happiness.

"May I?" Nell gave a stiff little bow and cut in too, ceremoniously inviting Angel to follow her out onto the patio where couples loitered and groups sat at festive tables. They rounded a corner and Angel smiled approvingly at the patio they had both designed, now festooned with flares and tiny blinking lights. She could smell barbecue curling from the grill and newly-baked appetizers now being served.

Nell chose a table in the corner, private and adorned with a single white rose amid sprays of baby's breath. Angel sat down and fingered the soft, velvety petals. She was glad the flower arrangements had turned out so well.

"What? You okay?" she asked, looking into Nell's eyes. Color had risen in Nell's face as she struggled to speak.

"On top of the moon," Nell replied, blushing and ducking under the table, ostensibly to grab a fallen napkin, but reappearing with a small purple box. Her hand shook as she held the box in her palm.

"Marry me. I want to commit to you. Please, Angel, say yes," Nell implored. "And make me the Gardener of the Year," she added impishly.

Angel's heart jumped. She looked into those eyes, dark blue like the evening sky and thought she might die right there. She looked from Nell's face to the box in her hands. *Could it really be true?*

"I love you Angela Khoury. I love you with all my heart." Nell got down on one knee by Angel's side.

"I…I…Oh, Nell," stammered Angel feeling the blood pounding in her ears." Time seemed to stand still. Angel could hear merry laughter from guests at the next table, but it was as if she was watching a movie that included her life. But then the voices dimmed and Angel realized there was a hush in the air. She looked about wildly and realized everyone was looking at them both, Nell with a look of pained embarrassment creeping up to color her face.

"Angel, I…" sputtered Nell, crimson-faced, "please say something."

"I love you Nell. But,"

"But?" repeated Nell with a look of sheer terror in her eyes.

"Something just happened. I mean there's something I need to tell you." Everyone was looking at her, at them. "I just, I mean I was just offered and I need to tell you—"

"What?" Nell was on her feet now and would not meet Angel's eyes.

"Oh Nell," said Angel, her heart going out for this woman she loved. If only everyone would stop looking at them. She shook her head. She wasn't ready to deal with this now. She did the only sensible thing she could think of, which in hindsight wasn't sensible at all. She ran.

* * *

"Angel. Have you seen Angel?"

"She's not with you?" Maddie disentangled herself from small talk and looked at Nell as she spoke. "She must be here somewhere, hardly anywhere to go. She'll show up. Probably yakking away to someone. You know how she is."

"No, I asked her."

"You asked her?" A slight frown as Maddie's eyebrows grew together, then a widening of her eyes as recognition set in. "She, no, she couldn't. She didn't turn you down?"

"Well she didn't exactly say yes. And then she ran."

"No." Maddie was dumbfounded. She had coached Nell on the proposal and never for a moment thought Angel would say no. Disbelief clouded her eyes as she slowly shook her head. "Nell I'm so sorry," she said, her eyes wide with disbelief.

"Something's going on. She said she'd been offered something."

"Offered?" Maddie interrupted. "Yes, she said there was something she wanted to talk with me about too. She didn't say, but I wonder what's going on?" Maddie frowned and sat down at the nearest table, astounded and in disbelief.

"I need to find her," prompted Nell. "See if she's all right."

The thought of Angel in trouble launched Maddie into action. "Okay," she said. "I'm heading for the loo. If she's not there I'll see if she's hiding somewhere else in the house. You go back out to the marquee and then see if maybe she headed out to the car park. Maybe she's in the truck." *Where the hell could she be?*

Maddie tried not to let her panic show. Guests were moving toward the marquee where the buffet dinner was about to be served. Music wafted across the terrace and voices rose and fell, interspersed with cheers laughter. She watched Nell rush across the lawn, her lean athletic body moving quickly through the crowd. Angel had to be somewhere.

It was Maddie who found her. She went to the downstairs loo and saw the locked door. "Someone's been in there for a while," said a server, balancing a tray on her shoulder. "We were just starting to wonder if there was a problem." Heading for the kitchen she sashayed past Maddie.

"Angel. Are you there?" Maddie jiggled the door handle and put her ear against the door. "Angel, it's me. Open up." Maddie thought she heard water running. "Come on, let me in."

The door opened slightly to Angel, her face blotchy, peeping around the door.

"Oh love," said Maddie as she snuck into the loo, sat down on the closed toilet lid and faced Angel. "What's going on?"

"It's all fucked up," said Angel, looking embarrassed.

"You turned Nell down." It was a question, but it came out as a statement.

"No," Angel insisted. "I love her. You already know I was planning on proposing to her on her birthday. It's the timing," Angel stammered and swallowed a sob. "And then everyone was looking at me and I panicked." She shook her head forlornly. "I feel so stupid."

"Timing? Just tell me what's going on." Maddie watched Angel shred up a wadded mound of toilet paper in her hand and proceed to tell her about the casting agent and the opportunity that had within the hour been laid at her feet. Maddie's eyes grew wide. She was speechless. "Really?" was all she could say.

"What do you think?" Angel had an anxious look on her face. Her forehead was drawn into a frown.

A moment passed. "That's incredible," said Maddie at last. It *was* incredible. "This is your dream. You'll be in a movie. You'll be acting and dancing."

"I know. I'm so excited. I mean, it's something I really have always dreamed about," said Angel wistfully. "And then I think about the business, our life together. I really want to do this, but then what?"

"No, you have to do it."

"What if I lose her," insisted Angel. "Sure, she might tell me to do it because she doesn't want me to be disappointed, but eventually she'll feel resentful. I just know it. It would eat away at her to see me half-naked on film, even if it isn't really me in the movie."

"Jesus Angel, it's your dream."

"We're each other's dream. I don't want to be the fallen angel and end up her nightmare instead."

"Well, if you want my opinion, I think you're making a mistake if you think that way. You can't turn this down, not now."

"I'm not sure."

"I'm going to tell her myself if you don't come with me and just lay it all out."

"I'm scared."

"That's ridiculous. You'll definitely lose her if you don't talk about this." Maddie looked into her friend's eyes and saw the anxiety lingering there. "Remember what you said about being yourself. Now is the time to put that into action. I mean, she thinks you don't want to marry her, to commit to her, and she doesn't know why. How much worse could it get?" As Maddie said these words she could see tears welling in Angel's eyes. "Look," she said again, more softly this time, taking Angel's hand, "let's get out of here so no one has to wet themselves in the hallway and go find Nell." She was relieved to see Angel smile at last.

They tottered across the uneven ground on their way back to the marquee, arms tangled. It was still light on this midsummer night's evening, but tiny lights twinkled along the path. The aromas from the buffet hung in the air. They paused in the clearing, facing the tent. The party was in full swing.

Suddenly there was Nell. She was striding toward them, trying not to run. Shadows of anxiety, annoyance and relief crossed her face as she stopped in front of Maddie and Angel. "Where were you?" Nell asked, a shy look on her face. "Look, I'm sorry I rushed you. It's too soon. It's okay."

A blush rose up Nell's throat and Maddie felt so sorry for her she wanted to cry. She felt a tear slide down her face thinking about how far her friend had come. From that insecure person who had internalized fear and loathing had blossomed this trusting person who had not only learned to love again, but also believed she was worthy of love herself.

Maddie left Angel's side and went to embrace Nell. "Angel has something she needs to tell you and you need to listen." She looked from one friend to the other. A moment passed and no one moved.

"Okay, I'm off to find a drink. Well-earned, I might add," Maddie said at last. As she turned Angel threw her arms around Nell's neck, her face buried in Nell's hair. The last thing Maddie saw was them sitting in a corner of the rose garden on a bench, deep in conversation. She resisted the urge to eavesdrop and headed instead in the direction of a lilting French accent she could just make out through the crowd.

Angel took the tiny velvet box and opened it to find a sparkling sapphire, as blue as Nell's eyes, surrounded by dazzling diamonds. It was exquisite. She held it up to the twinkling patio lights, her heart full of joy and smiled as Nell slipped it on her finger. Angel felt tears pricking at the back of her eyes and dabbed at them with her napkin. "Oh Nell yes," she said finally, holding Nell's face in her hands and kissing her closed eyes. "Yes, yes, yes. You'll always be my Gardener of the Year." It looked like both her dreams were about to come true.

Nell had been a champ and surprised Angel by her support. It wouldn't be easy, she'd admitted and she said she'd be a liar if it didn't scare the hell out of her. But if Angel wanted this badly, then Nell said she was committed to move heaven and earth to make it work out.

"I could hardly stand the anticipation," gushed Maddie when they returned to the marquee. "I hoped she'd pop the question this evening, but as for the other stuff, well, never a dull moment around here."

"You knew all along," insisted Angel, "and you didn't let on?"

"Yes, it was terrible keeping it to myself. How do you think the ring fitted so well?" Maddie stopped doing her happy dance and gave Angel a hug. "And then of course there was you," she gestured to Angel, "asking me the same thing. It was a devil keeping your ring sizes straight. I had a terrible fear I'd get them mixed up. I just wasn't sure if Nell would go through with it today or whether you'd do it on Nell's birthday. I was a total basket case."

They laughed and trooped back gaily to a table by the little dance floor. "To my very best friends," toasted Maddie with champagne Lucas had ordered. "To my best old friend and my best new friend. Cheers and you'd better have me as a bridesmaid or else."

"I'm still not a hundred percent sure that Nell's happy with me being in this movie," said Angel quietly when the laughter had died down. Her voice faltered as she looked over at Nell. But when she gazed into those violet eyes there was no resentment or disappointment, just pride and happiness and a little bit of trepidation.

"Of course I'm okay with this," Nell said before Angel could speak again. "You think I wouldn't want to be married to a movie star?"

"I wouldn't exactly be a movie star," insisted Angel sheepishly.

"You'd be in the movie and your name would be in the credits. What more could you ask for?" declared Maddie.

"You should do it," said Lucas. "In fact, you *are* doing it. We all insist. Right?"

"Right," all three said in unison.

"You guys," murmured Angel, fearing she was going to cry. She dabbed at her eyes and then cocked her head. No, surely, it couldn't be.

It was. "Our song," said Nell cheekily at the beginning strains of "Angel of the Morning." "Not quite your version on YouTube, but you get the drift." Angel colored at the memory, but then laughed, letting Nell lead her onto the dance floor. It was the Pat Benatar rendition, but still as beautiful a slow song as was ever written. Nell took Angel into her arms and they alternately took the lead, each moving the other around the floor. Angel looked into Nell's eyes, felt her hands on her waist and shoulder and let the music fill her heart.

They danced like the couple in love they were: arms around each other, nestling close, moving in unison. Although the floor was crowded and people kept bumping into them, Angel experienced the dance from inside an intimate bubble, the two of them moving and twirling inside the perfect oasis. "I love you so much," she whispered into Nell's shoulder. She could tell Nell hadn't heard her above the noise of the music and the crowd, but it didn't matter. Angel pulled her close and buried her face in her collar, kissing the nape of her neck.

As the song died away, Nell put her arms on Angel's shoulders and stepped back so she was gazing straight into Angel's face. "You'll do the movie and any others you want to do," Nell said, "and we'll still have the business. It'll always be there. Annie and I will get it going and you can pick up when you get back." She smiled into Angel's eyes. "And maybe me and the babies can join you on location for other movies, once you get famous," Nell added, a twinkle in her eye.

Angel was so happy she thought her heart would burst from pure joy. She cupped Nell's face in her hands and kissed her deeply before leading her back to their table. "Where's Maddie?" she asked, gesturing at Lucas.

"She went to make you a special drink."

"Did someone say special drink?" exclaimed Maddie, prancing toward the table with a martini glass in her hand. "For you," she said ceremoniously, putting the smoky greenish-looking drink in front of her friend. "I knew being a bartender would come in handy someday."

Angel looked at it and took a sip. She grimaced slightly and then took another. "It's growing on me," she said, laughing. "What is it?"

"A Fallen Angel," declared Maddie ceremoniously. "Perfect eh?" Angel passed the gin cocktail around the table, everyone's eyebrows elevating in turn. When it had made its round and was back in front of Angel, she lifted the glass and made a toast, her heart full of joy. "To all fallen angels everywhere," she declared.

"Amen," they said in unison.

Dear Reader,
If you're craving the drink that Maddie made for Angel, here you go:

Fallen Angel

2 oz. dry gin
1/2 oz. fresh lime juice
1 dash Angostura bitters
2 dashes white crème de menthe
Ice cubes

Tools: shaker, strainer
Glass: cocktail
Garnish: mint sprig

Shake ingredients with ice and strain into a chilled cocktail glass. Garnish and enjoy.

Bella Books, Inc.

Women. Books. Even Better Together.

P.O. Box 10543
Tallahassee, FL 32302

Phone: 800-729-4992
www.bellabooks.com